Jane didn't know what was coming over her.

She stared into Lord Chadwick's eyes that were as warm as a pot of hot chocolate on a cold winter morning. His hand gripped hers urgently, and to her shock, she wished there were not two gloves between her skin and his.

Some part of her knew he must mean to reassure her, but she did not take it thus. He suddenly seemed commanding, very male and not at all what she'd perceived him to be.

"Miss Whittington," he murmured, staring at her mouth, "tell me I do not frighten you."

"I do not fear you," she whispered, realizing she was watching his mouth as well. He had fine lips that looked soft to the touch. Had she ever dwelled on the texture of a man's lips before?

"You don't fear that I might become . . . overpowered by your nearness and your beauty?"

"W-we'll have a chaperone," she said, amazed that she actually stuttered. "Really, Lord Chadwick, I cannot believe such a thing could happen to a civilized man such as yourself."

"Then you don't understand your power over me, my dear." He was leaning closer now. "You make a man feel decidedly uncivilized."

Other **AVON ROMANCES**

GAYLE CALLEN

No Ordinary Groom

AVON BOOKS

An Imprint of HarperCollinsPublishers

This is a work of fiction. Names, characters, places, and incidents are products of the author's imagination or are used fictitiously and are not to be construed as real. Any resemblance to actual events, locales, organizations, or persons, living or dead, is entirely coincidental.

AVON BOOKS
An Imprint of HarperCollins*Publishers*
10 East 53rd Street
New York, New York 10022-5299

Copyright © 2004 by Gayle Callen Kloecker
ISBN: 0-06-054394-9
www.avonromance.com

First Avon Books paperback printing: January 2004

Avon Trademark Reg. U.S. Pat. Off. and in Other Countries, Marca Registrada, Hecho en U.S.A.
HarperCollins® is a registered trademark of HarperCollins Publishers Inc.

Printed in the U.S.A.

10 9 8 7 6 5 4 3 2 1

To my father, Fran Kloecker,
who always believed in my writing,
who, when I was a teenager,
gave up space in his workshop
so I could set up my typewriter.
I love you, Dad.

Chapter 1

London
August 1844

Miss Jane Whittington sat at her dressing table, her chin resting on her hand, and stared at her own reflection. There was a pensiveness about her that put an odd wrinkle between her slim, black eyebrows and turned down the corners of her mouth.

This was now the face of an engaged woman. No wonder she looked miserable.

She groaned and swept to her feet. Her mother was giving a dinner party this evening in celebration of Jane's engagement to a baron, William, Lord Chadwick. Even if Jane had to force a smile, she would do it for her mother's sake, though she still felt hurt by her father's haste and secrecy in arranging the match. She had been waiting for the right time to tell them she didn't wish to marry at all, that she wanted to control her own dowry.

Was it too late?

She picked up her thin gloves from the dressing table and slid them on like armor before a battle. For once she remembered them without having to be reminded. There was nothing left to do but go downstairs, greet their guests, and formulate a miraculous plan of escape from her fate.

When she reached the second-floor landing, she was able to peer over the edge of the wide staircase. She immediately caught the eye of the man glancing up.

Lord Chadwick, her groom. She wanted to look away, but there was something in his gaze she hadn't seen before, an intensity that felt strangely . . . intimate. A hot blush swept over her face. She was behaving like a girl fresh from the schoolroom instead of a sensible woman of twenty-one years. For a moment he didn't smile, and she felt an absurd hesitation, a feeling of something dark and hidden beneath his usually cheerful countenance. Then he gave that irreverent grin that made him seem so . . . shallow, and she dismissed her unusual feeling as nothing but a flight of fancy.

She had become acquainted with Lord Chadwick but a week before, at a dinner party hosted by her sister Charlotte, a widow newly out of mourning. He had been all charm and good manners and decent looks—and rather too talkative, she thought reluctantly.

Giving him a cool nod, she put her hand lightly on the banister and descended the stairs, studying him. He was a man of decent height and nice breadth of shoulders beneath a perfectly cut black evening coat. His face was lean, with a pair of deep dimples scoring his cheeks when he smiled. His teeth were shockingly white and his eyes brown. His dark hair—a nondescript brown to match his eyes, she thought—was slicked back with macassar oil, and his long sideburns had a touch of gray that made his age hard to determine. Her father, Viscount Whittington, hadn't thought to include such personal information in the letter that had told her the unwelcome news about her marriage.

Overall, there was nothing to dislike about Lord Chadwick's countenance—his description could fit a score of her male acquaintances. When he wasn't talking, he could almost be called handsome. Most women would be quite content, but Jane could not understand settling for such a feeling.

When she reached the foot of the stairs, Lord Chadwick bowed over her gloved hand and brought it to his lips for a moment too long.

His eyes, as well as his mouth, smiled up at her. "Good evening, Miss Whittington."

She nodded perfunctorily and removed her hand from his. "Good evening, Lord Chadwick."

As he straightened, she watched his gaze slide down her body. It seemed impersonal, as if he were merely deciding if she was properly dressed for the occasion. She should be offended, but she was only annoyed.

She put her hand on his offered arm and walked beside him into the drawing room. She could see that only a few guests had arrived. They were scattered between overstuffed tasseled chairs and sofas, potted ferns and marble columns. Cluttered on every table and shelf was her mother's odd collection of bric-a-brac, including the unusual gifts from Jane's father.

Just the thought of his many years in exotic countries made Jane sigh with a frustrated longing to travel abroad—something her mother didn't understand. Jane had made plans for her dowry money in anticipation of her parents' acquiescence, mapping out each country she would visit, continuing to learn the appropriate languages. She refused to give up on her dreams so quickly.

Lady Whittington stood arm in arm with Charlotte Sinclair, Jane's sister. The two women were so alike in their petite, rounded beauty; Jane felt like a lanky giraffe next to them. They watched her and the baron with hopeful speculation.

Lord Chadwick led her near a small table,

then turned to face her. "I say, your gown is quite the fashion, my dear."

She began to wonder if he flashed his dimples with deliberation. "Thank you, my lord. You do justice to your garments, as well." Out of the corner of her eye, she saw her mother whiten with shock.

But Lord Chadwick only looked inordinately pleased. "Do you really think so? I must say that since I arrived in London a month ago, I have been frequenting many a tailor to find just the right man for the style I require."

Jane's smile remained frozen on her face. Surely he would not subject her to the details.

"I am quite exacting in my demands about the quality of material and the emphasis on the latest designs."

He suddenly walked about her, and she narrowed her eyes at the spectacle he was making of himself.

"I do have an exacting eye," he continued, "with a little help."

To her surprise, he pulled a monocle out of his breast pocket, and she noticed it was attached to his lapel by a delicate gold chain. He fixed it before his right eye and squinted down at her.

"Is your gown of satin broche?"

"How—"

"And what a lovely shade of peacock blue."

Peacock? What a perfect description of *him*! She was beginning to panic over the thought of

endless evenings listening to such topics, when
he paused and grinned.

"Ah, but you're diverting me from the pe-
rusal of my lovely bride-to-be."

Again she felt his gaze linger below her neckline, and the squint caused by the monocle made
it seem as if he leered at her. She was hardly displaying an immodest amount of skin, and she
was affronted by his rudeness. More and more of
her mother's guests were arriving, and she felt
their curious, amused stares.

"That is an exquisite necklace you're wearing," he murmured.

He had pitched his voice lower, and his eyes
seemed overly warm.

She touched the pearl pendant self-consciously.
"My father sent it to me from India."

"I always knew he had good taste."

She narrowed her eyes as she stared at him.
"And how long have you known my father, my
lord?"

He'd been bending near her, but now he
straightened almost imperceptibly and let the
monocle drop to hang by its chain. "We've done
business for many years, but as you well know,
he's often been abroad. Since he returned to Yorkshire these two months past, we've renewed our
friendship and have begun even closer ties between our families." He grinned. "And naturally
you will be the bridge between us."

A bridge. How romantic. "And what sort of

business do you and my father engage in?"

"Mostly our estates interact—buying produce, wool and other goods."

Her father had based the most important decision affecting her life on someone who bought the estate's farm goods? Although she had not seen her father in well over two years, he could not have changed so much. Why the secrecy about her marriage?

And why had her father traveled directly to Yorkshire instead of London on his return from India? Why had he not visited his wife and daughters? The pain from this almost made tears well in her eyes, but she refused to cry before anybody, especially strangers. And that's all William Chadwick was.

"Excuse me, my lord, I must speak to my mother about the dinner arrangements."

"By all means," he said cordially, bowing again as he blotted his forehead with a handkerchief. "I look forward to sharing a meal with you."

She approached her mother and Charlotte and, after drawing them into the library, closed the doors. A startled servant looked up from refilling a sherry decanter and was promptly waved away by Lady Whittington.

Both women frowned at Jane.

"Why did you leave Lord Chadwick so quickly?" her mother asked. "You wished for an opportunity to get to know him—this is your chance."

"I meant *before* the engagement," Jane answered dryly. "It might have mattered then."

"Jane," Charlotte said with an underlying impatience that was new to her character since she'd become a widow, "you are being very stubborn."

Jane shook her head. " 'Stubborn' would be if I refused to marry at all. But I would never disgrace you that way, Mama." There must be a way out of the engagement without disgracing anybody at all.

"I know you wouldn't, dear heart," her mother murmured, touching her arm. "I just wish that you'd trust your father's choice. He knows you well, after all."

"You don't seem as if *you've* always trusted his choices."

Her mother's face blanched, but Jane would not take back the words. Her parents rarely spoke to each other and usually lived continents apart.

"I trust his love for you, Jane."

Maybe he no longer understood his own daughter, she thought with despair. All those years apart—how could mere letters make him understand her temperament? His correspondence had been full of the wonders of Egyptian pyramids and African tribes. He'd sent her rare, fanciful gifts from all around the world: little statues of wood or stone, fans made from the feathers of birds so exotic she had to look them up in books. Across the continents, her father had been the one she'd confided in, to whom she'd told her deepest wishes to live a different sort of life than her mother's. He had seemed a sympathetic ear, even though he had never encouraged her to openly leave society's restrictions behind. Had he just been humoring her?

She needed to see him, to talk to him face-to-face. Once again she was tempted to abandon all she was, all her mother wanted for her, and strike off on her own to visit her father. The scandal seemed minor next to living with a man she couldn't respect or love.

She turned to her sister, saying aloud what Charlotte had not confided in her. "Surely you understand my concern. You were married to a man you did not love."

Charlotte's open expression instantly shuttered, and Jane despaired of ever understanding her. Charlotte was too much like their mother, so concerned with what society thought.

"Jane," Lady Whittington said quickly, "Charlotte is too recent a widow. Do not hurt her so."

Before Jane could dutifully apologize, Charlotte held up a hand. Her wedding ring glistened in the candlelight, and the three of them hesitated.

Charlotte dropped her hand and sighed. "It has been over a year now, Mama. No longer so recent, I'm afraid. Jane, it is still difficult for me to talk about it, but you must understand that although I didn't love Mr. Sinclair in that girlish way I once thought I would, there was an understanding between us. You tarnish his memory by assuming the worst."

But what else could Jane assume? She had seen how controlling Mr. Sinclair had been, how little Charlotte had participated in decisions that had affected her own life. Nothing had shaken Jane more than realizing the trap that her sister had fallen in. Surely Charlotte was free now—and happier? But such a thing her proper sister would never admit.

"I don't mean to assault your memories," Jane whispered, unusually close to tears. "I just—I don't—oh, forgive me. I know not what has come over me this evening."

Her mother offered a weak smile of relief. "Nerves, dear heart—nothing more. You need to give your young man a chance to prove himself to you. Now go find Lord Chadwick, and before we go into dinner, we'll all offer our congratulations."

Jane nodded and opened wide the doors leading into the drawing room. All seventeen of their guests seemed in attendance now, and as her mother circled to greet the newcomers, Jane wandered the perimeter of the room, looking for Lord Chadwick. With so many people crowded together, it was growing warmer every second, and she felt a trickle of perspiration slide between her breasts.

Soon enough, she saw him standing with three other men beside the columns flanking the tall windows. Lord Chadwick gestured with his monocle in a flamboyant fashion that made her teeth grind together. As she approached, they did not seem to see her, and she found herself staying behind a column, pressing her hands to the cold marble and pausing to listen.

The four men burst into laughter, and she held her breath.

"Chadwick, I've given you my tailor's name," said Sir Albert Dean, a genial friend of Charlotte's late husband. "So now you owe me a game of cards at White's tonight."

"Now come, Sir Albert," Lord Chadwick said with a chuckle still in his voice, "surely one thing does not equate with the other. We all know that I am not a master of card games. I simply can't keep track in my head. Numbers have always bored me."

Sighing, Jane closed her eyes and pressed her forehead to the column. She loved anything to do with knowledge, and she had insisted her tutor train her in advanced mathematics, usually a male realm. But her mother had always told her she didn't need mathematics to be a good wife. It appeared her mother was right.

"Now Chadwick," said another man, who sounded like Mr. Roderick, one of the Yorkshire members of Parliament, "there are more ways to celebrate your loss of freedom than just a dinner party."

More laughter followed this brilliant statement,

and then Jane heard Lord Chadwick's voice.

"But gentlemen, I prefer treating myself to an extravagant suit of clothing rather than gambling. Speaking of my betrothed, she must be back in the drawing room, since I see her mother. Adieu until a later moment."

Jane remained frozen behind the column, hoping Lord Chadwick did not find her eavesdropping. She couldn't help wincing over his mispronunciation of *adieu*. Languages were her great passion.

After a lengthy pause, Mr. Roderick said, "Dean, why ever did you invite Chadwick to join us? The man truly has no idea how to play."

Sir Albert Dean laughed again. "But he managed to take all of your money last time, didn't he? And damned if I know how he did it."

Mr. Roderick grumbled something unintelligible.

"Gentlemen," Sir Albert said, "the queen made a point of introducing him to us. We cannot ignore that."

They were all murmuring their agreement when Jane slipped away, intrigued as to why Queen Victoria had taken special interest in Lord Chadwick.

She had not gone more than a few paces when she saw her betrothed staring at her from across the room.

Chapter 2

William Chadwick met Miss Jane Whittington's startled gaze across the crowded drawing room and for the first time saw naked emotion in her usually cool expression. Something had panicked her, but she quickly submerged the feelings and began to walk toward him.

He gave an inward sigh, then pasted on his usual glib smile. For some reason, tonight it was hard to be "Lord" Chadwick, newly a baron, and a sudden court favorite of the queen. He just wanted to be Will—whoever that was. But Jane Whittington was approaching, and as usual, good old Will didn't have the first idea what to say to her, let alone how to behave in

London society. But "Lord" Chadwick did, and Will slipped him on like a fresh suit of clothing.

Just looking at Jane made speech unnecessary. She had a lithe, slim beauty that was elegance personified: narrow waist leading up to breasts not large and overflowing, but just right for her. He couldn't see her hips beneath her crinoline-supported skirt, but he had a good imagination. She would be perfect there as well.

Her coal-black hair lay smooth and shiny against her head, tucked back in a chignon that made other women's ringlets look girlish by comparison. She had a pale, classical face with a delicately pointed chin and a straight nose saved from severity by the slightest tilt upwards. He supposed there would be men put off by the cool intelligence evident in her startlingly green eyes, but he was not one of them.

He still couldn't believe that Colonel Whittington had so easily offered Jane to him. She was the perfect solution to his plan for a normal life—a woman of society, able to entertain and run a household with equal ease.

Jane stopped before him. "Staring is quite rude," she said.

He took her hands in his. "Staring is the right of all besotted bridegrooms."

She arched an elegant eyebrow. "Besotted? Such strong words, my lord, for a man who has spent mere hours in the presence of his betrothed."

"But I feel like I've known you for a lifetime."

And it was true. Colonel Whittington had spoken often and fondly of his daughters, but there had been a special regard for his youngest. The colonel didn't believe she fit in well with other society women. Will had worriedly expected a hoyden but had been greatly relieved on meeting the classically beautiful Jane, who seemed every inch the demure, perfect wife.

"A lifetime?" she responded, with another one of those polite smiles. "And how would you know me so well?"

"Your father is very proud of you and talks of you often."

Will thought he detected tears in her eyes, gleaming in the candlelight, but just then Lady Whittington rang a tiny bell for her guests' attention.

Will turned to face his future mother-in-law, noticing that Jane disengaged her hand from his. He glanced down at her, but she was looking at her mother with a resigned expression. As Lady Whittington spoke of the joy her daughter's marriage brought the family, he realized the reason for Jane's resignation.

What he'd worried about had come to pass: she didn't want to marry him.

As Lady Whittington continued, he smiled at the correct moments, even offered gracious words of gratitude for being welcomed as a member of the family. Those things came easily to "Lord" Chadwick. But underneath the façade, Will's mind was racing.

Jane had accepted the marriage out of duty and obligation, of course, as any well-raised woman would. But he wanted more than resignation. He wanted a real marriage—one like his parents had, full of love and affection. In his youth, he hadn't understood what a gift his parents had in each other. All Will had wanted was to escape, to live his life in freedom traveling all over the world. He'd craved adventure and excitement—and had received more than he'd ever imagined or needed with a commission in the army of the East India Company.

But he was home now in England, after thirteen long years. His parents were dead, severing his connection to his old life. Jane was his chance to be normal again. Maybe she didn't see it right now, but he would make her the perfect husband. He would make her fall in love with him.

He just wasn't certain . . . how. But it would come to him.

When the toasts and the applause were done, he escorted Jane downstairs to the dining room. The table was set with the usual elegance of flowers and crystal and china, and he had Jane on his right. Using his monocle—an extension of "Lord" Chadwick—he pretended to scan the menu in its silver holder set between them, but he was really looking at her smooth hands, the curve of her breasts, the delicateness of her shoulders. There would be many pleasant ways he could persuade her that marriage to him was not to be dreaded.

When she glanced up at him as the first course was served, he saw the troubled doubts in her eyes. Now that he knew what he was looking for, how had he ever missed it? He had been rated the best agent in the Political department at reading people, at understanding what they were thinking by every twitch of a facial muscle. If necessary, he would use every skill he possessed to win over Jane Whittington. He owed her father too much to turn his back on Jane now. But it would take skill to show her the kind of man he could become, for surely here in England he could never let anyone know what he'd been doing the last five years—least of all his wife. That dangerous life was behind him.

He knew the rules for creating a new disguise, since he'd done it so often before: stick as close to the truth as possible, so as not to get tripped up in lies. He could use his own name, his own childhood. The rest he would have to work on, for what kind of man *was* William Chadwick, baron, knight, ex-spy?

Without realizing at first what he was doing, he used the old "Lord" Chadwick routine of delicately mopping his brow with a handkerchief. Perfectly acceptable on a hot summer night, but the handkerchief also allowed him to take surreptitious glances about the room. He had to stop these old habits. Even though they used to save his life, there was nothing to see in the Whittington household but the silent communication between footmen, the stiff muscles of people forced to talk to people they didn't want to be with—including his own betrothed.

Maybe he was reading too much into her behavior. She wasn't an operative used to concealment—only a young woman who found herself suddenly engaged to a stranger.

As Jane watched Lord Chadwick pat his forehead with a handkerchief, she found herself silently agreeing that the heat was intense. Every layer of petticoat and crinoline lay heavily against her legs. Her corset dug into her ribs until she thought she couldn't breathe enough air. Oh, she knew she was panicking, sitting beside her too-silent groom. Here was a man she thought never stopped talking!

When the footman appeared behind them carrying a large tureen, Lord Chadwick politely spooned a helping of cold pheasant pie onto her plate and then his own. The servant bowed and stepped back, and Jane found herself looking into her betrothed's eyes.

"Your mother has prepared a wonderful evening, Miss Whittington."

"Thank you, my lord."

He waved at the table with his monocle. "The flower arrangements have quite the touch of elegance, especially the use of the Michaelmas daisies with the white roses. Did you do them yourself?"

"No, my lord," she answered, never having met a man who cared about table decorations. "I leave that to my sister. She and my mother claim that I can't tell weeds from flowers."

He laughed as if she were joking. "Your sense of humor is refreshing, Miss Whittington. I have greatly regretted that business has kept me from your side this last week. Might I remedy that situation? Would you perhaps care to ride with me tomorrow in Hyde Park?"

"My lord, you know that I cannot go riding alone with you."

"Of course not. I assumed you would bring a groom from your stables. But since there is a certain . . . awkwardness between us, I thought if we spend time together, to understand each other's passions—"

She let out an involuntary gasp, and Lord Chadwick actually reddened.

He mopped his brow again. "Heavens, that is not what I meant—not how it sounds, Miss Whittington. Oh dear me, do not think me so crass as all that. Please accept my sincere apologies if I offended you."

"Of course, my lord."

"I meant that there are things we don't know about each other, our favorite pastimes, for instance. I thought tomorrow we could have a lively discussion about horsemanship."

Horsemanship.

"You do ride, do you not?" he asked doubtfully.

"Of course, my lord. Do put your fears to rest."

"And what manner of horses does your family own?"

She answered his questions patiently. Then his conversation switched to dogs, and his eyes almost sparkled in the candlelight.

"I would enjoy introducing you to my pet, Miss Whittington. You two will get along superbly, I am sure."

It would be too impolite to tell him that dogs drooled and shed and ruined carpets. Many a man had tried—and failed—to impress her with a dog.

"And what is your dog's name?" she asked.

"Killer."

Killer.

"But it is a humorous name, to be sure," he continued. "A friend suggested it as a jest, but I quite took a fancy to it."

Smiling painfully, she glanced down the table and found her mother watching her with an encouraging gaze. Jane sighed.

When dinner was over and the men had rejoined the ladies in the drawing room, Jane realized that the men must have continued drinking their port when they'd been alone. There was much merriment, although she noticed that Lord Chadwick did not seem to be in step with every joke. Perhaps that was simply because he had not overindulged in liquor, something she could at least feel relieved about.

Gradually the guests began to depart, until after another half hour, only Lord Chadwick, Sir Albert and Mr. Roderick remained with the three Whittington ladies. Jane and her sister sat on a sofa, while their mother stood by helplessly, watching the antics of the men. Mr. Roderick had imbibed far too deeply, and beneath his twitching mustache, his red face glistened with perspiration. Though Sir Albert tried to restrain him with an arm wrapped around his chest, Mr. Roderick was leaning unsteadily toward Lord Chadwick, shaking a finger in his face.

"Chadwick, I insist you come to White's with us. Don't give me this nonsense about hating cards. Gad, you played willingly enough the other night."

Lord Chadwick smiled tolerantly and studied the other man through his monocle. "You're embarrassing yourself before the ladies, old chap."

Jane's eyes widened as Mr. Roderick struggled to break free. Her mother was wringing her hands and glancing repeatedly at their butler. Shaw, an elderly man who'd been serving their family since her father's youth, waited nervously for his mistress's command.

"Chadwick, ye took all my money. Now I need the chance to win it back!"

Mr. Roderick broke free, and a collective gasp rose from the women as he lunged forward, one fist cocked and aimed at Lord Chadwick. Surprisingly, Lord Chadwick stepped forward as if to meet the punch, then at the last second stumbled and fell heavily to his knees just as Mr. Roderick launched his assault. His flying fist missed its target and smashed into the marble column with a solid thud. The man howled and fell backward, hitting his head on the elbow of Lord Chadwick, who was just rising.

Mr. Roderick landed hard on the floor and lay still. In the momentary silence, Jane quickly glanced at Lady Whittington's horrified face. Jane knew instantly that her mother feared the scandal of brawling in her own house—and God forbid Mr. Roderick be seriously hurt.

Lord Chadwick put his hands on his hips and loomed over his opponent. "I say, that didn't seem quite fair, did it?"

Sir Albert laughed and shook his head. "Well, he got what he deserved."

"Is he . . . well?" Lady Whittington asked, a hand to her throat.

Sir Albert nodded. "Worry not, madam. He'll have a bump on his head and perhaps a broken hand, but nothing worse."

"Come, man," Lord Chadwick said, taking one of Mr. Roderick's arms. "Let's be of service and escort the poor chap home. I always was a clumsy fool—didn't mean to hurt him."

"Of course not, my lord," Jane replied, standing up to take her mother's trembling arm.

"Sir Albert and I will make certain no one knows of this," Lord Chadwick added, "and I doubt Roderick will even remember what happened."

Between the two men, they lifted Mr. Roderick up and slung his arms across both their shoulders. He slumped between them, legs dangling.

"Oh, do be careful of his hand!" Lady Whittington called.

Lord Chadwick glanced at Sir Albert with a wicked gleam in his eye that caught Jane's attention. "What shall we tell him about his injuries?"

The other man laughed. "That he made a fool of himself over some doxy—ah, forgive me, ladies, I mean—I meant—"

"We understand," Jane said, trying to hide her smile. "Thank you for your kindness—and your discretion, gentlemen."

Lord Chadwick grinned and hefted Mr. Roderick further onto his shoulders. "Not the way I would have chosen to end the evening with you, Miss Whittington. I shall see you on the morrow."

She only nodded and found, as he turned away, that she was quite amazed at how easily he held the awkward weight of a grown man.

Perhaps he was stronger than he looked. Oh, but he'd simply tell her that gardening gave him strength, or some other such nonsense.

The butler hurried to follow the men to the front door, then opened it and held it for them, passing out top hats to both men, and a walking stick to Sir Albert. With a last wave, they went out into the night. When the door slammed behind them, the three women were silent, standing still in the hallway as Shaw bowed his head and retreated from the room.

"Mama," Jane began, but her mother burst into noisy tears and fled up the stairs. She turned to her sister. "Charlotte—"

"We'll talk later. I must go to her."

Then she too was gone, leaving Jane to follow at a slower pace. She returned to her bedroom to find her maid, Molly, fast asleep in an upholstered chair before the bare hearth, a single lit candle on a table at her side. Feeling melancholy and on the verge of a change she didn't want, Jane wandered the room as if she were a ghost who no longer belonged there. She lit the candles on her bed tables, and on the writing table at the foot of the bed. The heavy draperies had already been closed, so as she began to undress, she looked about her at the ornate wardrobe and the dressing table with its heart-shaped glass. Her father had bought that for her when she was young, and though it was girlish, she could not bear to part with it.

Eventually she had to awaken Molly for help with the fastenings at the back of her gown. The plump, curly-haired girl was the daughter of the chef, and she took great joy in hearing about the parties her father prepared food for. Jane answered a few of her questions, but Molly must have sensed her mood.

"I'll let ye sleep in peace, miss," Molly said, taking up a candleholder and walking to the door. "Ye seem tired."

Jane belted her dressing gown over her night-dress and smiled. "Thank you for understanding, Molly. I'll be happy to tell you everything in the morning. Sleep well."

Jane splashed her face at the marble wash-stand, then began to slowly braid her hair. At last she took a seat at her writing table and opened up her journal to record the day's events. She had always kept a journal so that whenever she wrote her father a letter, she could remember everything she wanted to tell him. He always said she had a vivid way of telling a story.

But what to write about Lord Chadwick? She didn't know what to make of him. She hadn't enjoyed speaking to her betrothed, and part of that had been her own fault for not bringing up her own favorite topics. She supposed she'd been testing him, discovering what he would say to her. At least he'd been polite enough not to fight in her home even when provoked. She had to admit that he'd been very good-natured about it all and had seemed to take little offense, which she appreciated. There was nothing worse than a man who thought too highly of himself.

But why had she never heard of him? Oh, her father was convinced she had, but even the rest of society had seemed oblivious of him until two months before. A baron, who did not come to London for the Season?

There was a soft knock at her door, and after Jane called out a welcome, Charlotte leaned her head inside.

"Mama asked to talk to you."

"How is she feeling?" Jane said as she rose to her feet and walked swiftly to the door.

"Better. But don't upset her, please."

Jane frowned irritably. "What do you think I would do—cry because two men got into a disagreement at my betrothal party?"

"Mama already is, so please don't make her feel badly about her female weakness."

As if Jane wasn't a true female if she didn't cry as often as her mother and Charlotte? She gritted her teeth and made no reply as she lifted up a candleholder and followed her sister into the hall. Charlotte murmured, "Good night" and slipped into her old chamber, which she still used when she spent the night. Jane continued on down the stairs.

The master suite occupied the entire second

floor of the town house, with two dressing rooms and a large bedchamber in between. Her mother slept alone here, and had for years. Much as she loved her father, Jane had always been determined not to live like this, using dinners and balls to substitute for a man who came home so seldom. She wanted to be her own person and depend on no one.

She found her mother curled up in a window seat looking out over the dark courtyard behind their town house. She looked pale, and with her black hair let down, it was easier to see the gray threaded through it.

"Charlotte said you wanted to see me, Mama," Jane said and sat down beside her.

To her surprise, her mother pulled her into her arms, something she hadn't done in years. It was a brief embrace, then her mother plumped the pillows at her side and motioned Jane to sit back. Side by side, they looked out over the courtyard in silence.

Finally, Lady Whittington said, "I had wanted to make this the perfect evening for you."

"Oh, Mama—"

"No, allow me to finish. I know you're not happy with this engagement, and I had hoped to give you a pleasant, relaxed evening to see the kind of man Lord Chadwick is."

"It was pleasant, Mama. Don't allow the last moments to mar your memories."

"I knew you'd say that, because you're such a

good girl, Jane. So what did Lord Chadwick
mean when he said he'd see you tomorrow?"

"He invited me to ride with him in the park."

"He is a kind man. Did you notice how he attempted to lighten my concern regarding Mr.
Roderick?"

"Yes," Jane replied, holding back a sigh.
"Mama, may I ask you a question about Lord
Chadwick?"

"Of course, dear heart."

"I really know little about him. Has the title
been in his family long?"

To her amazement, Lady Whittington did not
meet her eyes. "I didn't think it would bother
you, but no, he was recently granted the title
from Queen Victoria. He was knighted too, but I
don't know why."

"Of course it doesn't bother me, Mama," Jane
said, but it did. Why had she never heard of this
man until he was made a baron? Could her own
father really be using her only to create ties to
another family rising in power? But the pain of
thinking that was too great, so she turned her
curiosity back to Lord Chadwick. "Do you
know why the title was given to him?"

"Your father didn't mention it in his letters."

Jane's mind worked feverishly over this new
piece of news. Titles did not matter to her as
they did to her mother. But the queen had
knighted Lord Chadwick, granted him a barony,
and then proceeded to introduce him into soci-

ety like a long-lost relation. What was going on?
Why all this for a man with a simple Yorkshire
estate?

Her mother sighed and slid her hand into
Jane's. "Do not think worse of me when I say
that I too worried about this engagement until I
met Lord Chadwick. But he seems to be a good
man, and I must say, you will have beautiful babies with him."

"Mama!" Jane cried, surprised at hearing
such a personal thing from her mother.

"I promise we'll soon have a talk about babies
and husbands—and wedding nights." With a
laugh, her mother covered her red face. "I guess
you can tell how I long for grandchildren. Go
on, dear heart, go to bed, and leave me to my
dreams."

After kissing her mother's cheek, she left the
room and climbed the stairs in a much more
somber mood than before. Her mother's words
reminded her that she would have to share . . .
intimacies with Lord Chadwick, something she
foolishly hadn't considered. And she didn't
even enjoy being in the same room with him.

Chapter 3

When Will left Roderick's town house, he didn't bother hiring a cab, for he only lived a few streets away, and the night was warm. There were plenty of gaslights dotting the streets, piercing the pale yellow fog. Carriages rolled past, and at one point, someone called out his name and waved. It was amazing how recognition from the queen could make a fellow popular.

As he took long strides, whistling softly to himself, he felt a vague sensation, a prickle of awareness from his spine up the back of his neck. His senses came alert, and for a moment he was back in Afghanistan, feeling alone and hunted.

But this was London, and he had given up the life of a spy. Yet why was he suddenly uneasy?

As he turned a corner, he used the opportunity to glance behind him, still whistling. He saw no one but two men in formal eveningwear walking in the opposite direction, arguing loudly with slurred voices.

Out of habit, he walked a circuitous route home, moving quickly but silently through the alley behind his courtyard. At the high wall hiding his garden, he felt along the bricks for the small depressions that he'd carved himself one dark night: toe and finger holds. After one last searching glance of the alley, he scaled the wall and dropped down into the garden.

He felt a little foolish as he let himself in the kitchen door, because anyone could discover where he lived if they wanted to. And thieves would have simply jumped him in the first well-shadowed area.

He almost would have liked that. Inflicting a good pummeling would have vented a few frustrations that he couldn't take out on Roderick. Damn the man for provoking a confrontation in Jane's home. He'd seen how it had bothered Lady Whittington, and it could hardly do him in good stead with Jane. "Lord" Chadwick was obviously not a fighter, so he couldn't have shown otherwise. Maneuvering to bring about that blow to Roderick's skull had been most satisfying.

But how had it all looked to Jane? Surely restraint proved his good sense.

He knew he wouldn't be able to sleep for a

while yet, especially now that he was on edge from his walk home. He picked up the lamp that his housekeeper had left lit for him and went to his study. During the day, the room was bright with sunlight from the large open windows. At night, the edges of lamplight showed only the three walls of bookshelves in the shadows. Sitting down at his desk, he pulled out the listing his lawyer had compiled for him of estates available for sale in the countryside. He sorted through the sheets until they were in order by their proximity to London.

Of course he already owned an estate near the town of York. It had belonged to his parents, but he'd never felt that it was *his*. A very old feeling of guilt made his stomach twinge with uneasiness. There were too many memories in that place of broken promises and dashed dreams.

No, he would start over where the only memories were the ones he would make with his new family.

At dawn, Will was just sitting down to a large breakfast when Barlow limped into the room. The butler had only newly come to the position. He'd been a soldier in India in the Bengal army, where Will had completed his last political mission. Barlow had lost part of his foot on a mission Will had ordered. Though the man was at least fifteen years Will's senior, Barlow was still one of the best soldiers Will had ever worked with. Will couldn't stand to see him pensioned off into poverty, so he'd invited Barlow to work for him.

Will sat back in his chair and reluctantly pushed aside his poached eggs and toast. "Yes, Barlow?"

"A messenger delivered this letter just moments ago, my lord," the butler said, setting an envelope beside Will.

With his usual disapproval and doubt, Barlow eyed Killer, snoring beneath the dining room table. The two never did get along, even though Killer had saved Barlow's life. At least there was respect between them. With a stiff bow, the butler retreated from the dining room and closed the door.

Will smiled as he recognized the wax seal of Colonel Whittington. He removed several sheets of paper, then took another bite of eggs and began to read. But the letter's contents made him choke, and he quickly swallowed a mouthful of tea.

That same morning, Jane paced the library, an opened book abandoned next to her favorite comfortable chair. She was home alone but for the servants, since her mother had decided to return calls. Lady Whittington thought she was making Jane nervous—which was foolish, of course, but Jane *was* doing an inordinate amount of worrying, probably giving her an air of distraction. She was going to be practically alone with Lord Chadwick today. If it went on longer than an hour, she would manage to suffer a debilitating headache.

When there was a soft knock on the door, she literally jumped. A good curse would have helped, but instead she pressed her lips together for control, then called, "Come in."

Shaw opened the door and stepped inside with a nod. "Miss Whittington, Lord Chadwick is here to see you."

"Show him into the—"

She was about to say "drawing room" when she saw that Lord Chadwick already stood at Shaw's back, looking over his shoulder into the library.

"—the library," she finished.

Lord Chadwick's eyes lightened, and he stepped around the servant and entered, drawing the butler's obvious disapproval. As Shaw left, he deliberately kept the door open.

"This is a lovely room, my dear," Lord Chadwick said, bending forward to take her hand and raise it to his lips.

He kissed her gloved knuckles.

"Thank you, my lord."

She took a step back as he straightened. He was wearing a vivid green frock coat and thinly striped green-and-fawn trousers so fashionably snug as to make her uncomfortable. His neckcloth was patterned to match his coat and trousers.

"I imagine you spend much time here," he said.

"Why would you say that?"

He nodded toward the chair she had vacated. "I've disturbed your reading."

"Of course not, my lord. I knew you'd soon be arriving and was simply passing the time."

He wore an almost secretive smile, as if he thought there was more than she was saying. Smugness always irritated her.

"And what are you reading?" he asked.

She should have put the book away. "Nothing that would interest you, my lord. It is a history of India."

His glance at her was sudden and assessing, but that dimpled smile seemed calculated to hide it. Would he begrudge a woman knowledge? He took out that annoying monocle and peered at her through it.

"And why would you be interested in such a cruel and distant land, my dear?"

"My father spent many years there, and I wished to understand its fascination for him."

"He was a soldier. Surely he was ordered there?"

"At first. Eventually he could have transferred closer to home, but he didn't. Something must have kept him away from his family."

"Duty to his country, perhaps," Lord Chadwick said quietly, although he waved his eyepiece almost as an afterthought. "But perhaps he wishes to make up for his absence."

"What do you mean?"

"I received a letter from him this morning. He enclosed one for you as well."

She put a hand to her throat as a feeling of unease raced through her. Suddenly she remembered her mother making the exact movement the previous evening. Jane dropped her hand quickly. "Why would he give you a letter he meant for me?"

"He wished me to speak with you first. Sit down, Miss Whittington, and I'll explain everything to you."

It seemed he wouldn't speak until she complied, so she seated herself on the edge of the sofa before the set of three windows and clasped her hands together in her lap. He leaned back against her father's massive mahogany desk, not quite sitting, and crossed his arms over his chest as he regarded her.

She was shocked to see that he looked . . . broad-chested in that pose, quite impressive instead of the sort of silly man she imagined. A man did not become so . . . physically imposing by just dancing with ladies at balls and lifting an opera glass to his eyes. But surely she was seeing what wasn't there, because when he smiled that shockingly irreverent grin at such a time, he only made her think poorly of him.

"Miss Whittington, your father has asked that I accompany you to visit him at Ellerton House."

Jane knew she gaped at Lord Chadwick, but how else could she react? She hadn't seen her father in so long, and instead of visiting the entire family in London, he wanted her to travel to Yorkshire, to their family estate?

With Lord Chadwick?

He shook his head in obvious amusement. "I can see that this has come as quite a shock to you, my dear."

Absently, she said, "Please do not call me that. It is quite improper."

His grin widened, but he nodded his head.

"Lord Chadwick, you must understand how improper it would be for you and me to travel together."

"We would be chaperoned at all times. And we *are* practically married."

She felt her face pale. "We have not even set a wedding date, my lord. And be that as it may—"

He held up a hand. "Before you protest further, I have a question. How would you have me answer your father? That you don't wish to see him?"

She opened her mouth to speak, but nothing came out. Hadn't she wished for just that thing these past two years? But they had no close male relatives to accompany her, and her mother was frightened of traveling "alone," regardless of the number of servants in attendance.

"Of course I wish to see him," she finally said, looking down at her skirts and smoothing them across her knees. "I have—I have dreamed about such a thing. But there is my involvement in the charities to think about—the British Ladies' Female Emigrant Society, of which I am secretary, and the General Domestic Servants Benevolent Institution—"

She broke off, knowing she was rambling. When she glanced back up, he was looking at her with kindness.

"What is the harm in getting away from London, in finding someone else to take on your duties? Do you care so much about what people think?"

She inhaled swiftly, angrily, and knew her face betrayed her as she glared at him. "My behavior is at all times proper, my lord. I do not *have* to care about the opinion of others."

"But you care what your father thinks."

Her anger faltered, then fled, and she realized that once again—so many times in how many days?—she was near to tears. She blinked fiercely. "You have no need to question my love for my father. I will go with you. And certainly this invitation includes Charlotte."

She thought he stiffened, but then he lowered his arms and rested his hands on the desk. "Of course, my—Miss Whittington. I can have my carriage ready whenever you are."

Carriage? She swallowed her disappointment.

She had never ridden a train before. Surely she could convince him to travel by railway.

"It will take us several days to prepare and make our good-byes among my friends," she said. "We will be accompanied by my maid, and arrangements must be made for her."

He only nodded.

"As for the carriage," Jane continued, "surely it would be quicker—and safer—to take the train."

He shook his head. "I have business I need to attend to along the way. And we'll be safe in the carriage—we'll have Killer."

"Killer?" She didn't even try to hide her dismay. "You wish to bring a dog on the trip with us?"

"Killer is not just any dog, Miss Whittington," he said as he straightened and began to walk toward her. "Killer is a fierce guard dog with unswerving loyalty to myself. When I was last attacked by brigands while on the road, I was lucky to have Killer with me."

"What happened?" she asked, telling herself that her curiosity was only for politeness' sake.

"Killer quite frightened the thieves with his vicious growl and overpowering manner."

Suddenly Lord Chadwick sat down beside her, closer than was proper, until their knees just brushed. She felt a shock to her system that made her limbs shiver.

"Miss Whittington," he murmured, again taking her hand, "will you not feel safe with me?"

Chapter 4

Jane didn't know what was coming over her. She stared into Lord Chadwick's eyes, which were as warm as a pot of hot chocolate on a cold winter morning. His hand gripped hers urgently, and to her shock, she wished there were not two gloves between her skin and his.

Some part of her knew he must mean to reassure her, but she did not take it thus. He suddenly seemed—overpowering, very male and not at all what she'd perceived him to be.

"Miss Whittington," he murmured, staring at her mouth, "tell me I do not frighten you."

Even his voice seemed different, lower, with a harsh edge that caused a feeling of danger to sweep through her. It wasn't ... unpleasant, which was frightening in and of itself. She should force him away, call for Shaw—but she didn't.

"I do not fear you," she whispered, realizing she was watching his mouth as well. He had fine lips that looked soft to the touch. Had she ever dwelled on the texture of a man's lips before? "As you are a friend of my father's, I trust that you will prepare adequately for the possibility of thieves."

He shook his head, and again his gaze strayed to her mouth, then lower, causing her stomach to tighten. He rubbed her knuckles with his thumb in little round circles that made her want to . . . squirm. What was wrong with her, she wondered, feeling a panicked wave of heat move through her body.

"But you don't fear me? That I might become . . . overpowered by your nearness and your beauty?"

"W-we'll have a chaperone," she said, amazed that she actually stuttered. "And Killer, of course. Really, Lord Chadwick, I cannot believe such a thing could happen to a civilized man such as yourself."

"Then you don't understand your power over me, my dear. You make a man feel decidedly uncivilized."

He was leaning closer now, and she told herself to get up, to slap him—anything. But moving was beyond her abilities.

"Miss Whittington," he said in a whisper, "might I have your permission to kiss you?"

A kiss? With Lord Chadwick, a man who couldn't even count in his head, who cared about only the most shallow of subjects? The absurdity of that thankfully washed every other disturbing feeling out of her head.

She shot to her feet, giving him her most withering glare. "My lord, your conduct is offensive."

Will felt as shocked as Jane obviously did. He had come here with no physical intentions, had only wanted to begin this journey together, to eventually persuade her that all would be well when they married.

She looked affronted and haughty—and incredible. He sat on the little sofa and stared up at her, where she faced him down like Venus chastising a mere mortal.

He still wanted to remove every layer of clothing and expose the real woman—and he must have looked it, for her face flushed even redder.

He didn't remember the last time he had felt so out of control. And it was that thought that finally made him regroup.

"My dear Miss Whittington," he said, rising to his feet. "I—can you ever forgive me? I am just a man, overcome by your loveliness and the thought of marriage to you."

"You cannot possibly make me believe that just thinking a woman is lovely would make you behave so improperly, my lord," she said with disapproval.

"It is a weakness that perhaps other men have conquered, Miss Whittington. I am sorry that my display of affection makes you think less of me."

She seemed to be taking a moment to think on that, and he found himself looking at her sedate, deep blue riding dress, so formal and acceptable, with its neckline clear up to her throat, and its tight sleeves outlining the litheness of her arms. Beside her on a little table he saw the book on Indian history that she'd been reading. It made him uneasy to imagine what she concealed beneath the outward perfection of a young miss of society.

He wondered sardonically why he thought he was the only one with secrets to hide.

Earlier, she had as much as admitted that she cared little what people thought. This worked out well for their journey, but not so well for his plan for the perfect family. Maybe her father did not understand her as well as he thought.

"I don't think less of you for your ardor, my lord," she finally said, looking the picture of serenity again. "It is your inability to control it that disturbs me."

"I will do my best not to disappoint you again, Miss Whittington." Would she refuse to travel with him? Would he have to find another means to persuade her?

"Will this dog you are so fond of protect me from you?"

He allowed himself a relieved smile. "He can be quite jealous of my attentions to others at times. I imagine you'll have Killer on your side in the battle to keep us apart."

Her demeanor cooled. "It will not be a battle."

"Of course, Miss Whittington."

"If you have nothing else to say to me, my lord, then I must begin my preparations. If it is convenient for you, shall we leave in say . . . three days?"

"That is perfectly acceptable." He gave her a short bow. "Does this mean we will not be riding today?"

As she walked toward the door, she glanced over her shoulder at him, wearing a small smile. "I am sorry to disappoint you."

"Ah well, I do have to meet with my tailor and rush my autumn wardrobe. We shall have plenty of time to get to know one another later."

Her smile disappeared, and she fixed him with another of her penetrating stares. "I hope you mean by discussion only, Lord Chadwick."

"Naturally, Miss Whittington."

In the drawing room, Jane called for her butler, who promptly appeared. Efficiently, she had Chadwick's horse brought around. She then said her farewells from the drawing room, closing the door behind Chadwick and leaving the final escort outside to her butler.

As Will stood out on the street and breathed deeply of the hot, muggy air, he gathered together the tattered edges of his plan. While a groom held his horse's head, he mounted, then rode away from the Whittington town house.

He couldn't believe he'd forgotten all about Charlotte—and didn't understand why the colonel had not included her as well. It seemed suspicious for one daughter to be forgotten, but since it played into Will's plans, he would ponder it later. He didn't want Charlotte accompanying them to Yorkshire. Without her presence, he would have more success persuading Jane how happy their marriage could be.

He'd have to arrange for Charlotte to be invited somewhere important enough for her to remain in London. He had more than a few connections left over from his time with the army of the East India Company. Even the queen herself might help in a pinch. Her Majesty enjoyed the stories Will told her about his service— stories he could never tell anyone else, of course.

He urged his horse into a trot and reflected on the day's triumphs. More and more he realized his almost-kiss with Jane must have been a subconscious inspiration on his part. There was a tenuous thread of desire between them, and he would make sure it consumed them by the time they reached Yorkshire.

After Jane sedately closed the drawing room doors, she turned around and sagged back against them. Lord Chadwick had almost kissed her—and she had almost allowed it!

She told herself not to think about it—after all, she had never been kissed by a man. Didn't every young girl aspire to such things when growing up?

But Jane had long ago given up the idea that there was a perfect man for her somewhere, a man whose kisses would make her swoon. And yet—just brushing against Lord Chadwick's *knee* had made her feel light-headed!

She had to stop thinking about it. Lord Chadwick now understood that he was not to do such a thing again. Her sister—and even a dog, she thought with distaste—would be with them on the journey.

She suddenly remembered her father's letter and felt chagrined that it had flown her mind when Lord Chadwick had asked to kiss her. She found it on the floor, shook her head in dismay at her neglect, then opened the seal.

My dearest Jane,

I hope you do not mind that, with this journey, I have forced William into your life yet again.

*He is a good man, and can be trusted to bring
you safely to me.*

*I am counting the hours until I see you
again, Jane.*

> *Yours affectionately,*
> *Papa*

She was going to see her father in mere
weeks! And of course, Papa must want Charlotte to come too. He'd probably been in such a
hurry to send the letter that he'd forgotten to
add her name.

She laughed aloud and hugged herself until a
sudden inspiration made her sober. Could she
convince her father to let her break this betrothal? Surely he would understand her reasons for not marrying—especially a man like
Lord Chadwick. She decided she would take ex-
tra care with her journal every night, recording
all her objections, all the things that were wrong
with her betrothed. Her father would see that although Lord Chadwick was adequate as his
friend, he was wrong for his daughter.

For more proof, she would insist Lord Chadwick show her his town house before they left
London. And she wouldn't warn him before-
hand, either. She would see how he lived—how
he expected *her* to live.

Later that afternoon, Jane was not surprised
to find her mother more than pleased with the

traveling arrangements. Any concerns about scandal were overridden by her relief that Jane seemed to be accepting Lord Chadwick.

Charlotte, who'd been staying at their town house for the last several days, agreed to come on the journey and said she was glad at the thought of visiting their father. But she also seemed distracted about something, and Jane believed that getting away from London and its memories would be good for Charlotte.

Two days later, Jane and her maid were in her bedroom surrounded by several trunks and portmanteaus, trying to decide what to bring. When someone knocked on the door, Jane absently called for the visitor to enter.

She glanced up to see Charlotte, who was looking at the trunks with an almost guilty expression.

Jane set down her list and approached her sister. "Is everything all right?"

Charlotte wrung her hands just like their mother did. "I can't go to Ellerton House with you."

Stunned, Jane signaled Molly to leave, then waited while the girl closed the door. "But Charlotte—"

Her sister whirled toward the window and leaned her hand against the frame. "I know you're disappointed in me—as I am in myself," she said over her shoulder. "I want to see Papa as much as you do. But today we received an invitation to a ball that's being held at Lord Arbury's home. Have you ever driven by it? It is a magnificent estate, not just a town house. Even Queen Victoria and Prince Albert shall be attending. I have no idea how we were fortunate enough to be included. It is my first chance to attend such an event since—since my husband died."

Jane put her hand on her sister's shoulder. Though she had never understood what motivated her mother and sister where society was concerned, she knew that it was time for Charlotte to begin living again. "You don't have to say anything else, dear sister. Molly will accompany me."

She heard Charlotte sniff, and she thought her sister even wiped away a tear before turning to face her.

"Thank you for not making this difficult, Jane. I felt quite distraught over this decision."

"That wasn't necessary. Papa will understand, and he loves you just as you are. I'm sure he'll be coming to town soon."

Charlotte smiled more naturally. "Thank you for understanding. Now let me return the favor by helping you pack."

Jane's spirits sank. "But I'm almost done."

Charlotte glanced about at the garments draped across every available surface, then eyed

Jane skeptically. "You don't look ready. You know you need at least two gowns for each day, preferably three."

Jane sighed. "Charlotte, Ellerton House is not nearly so formal as London. I never wear that many clothes."

"But you're traveling with your betrothed, and you'll want him to see you at your best. And Papa might be entertaining guests, since he's been gone so long."

Jane held her tongue. All she wanted to do was curl up at her father's feet and listen to his stories, not share him with the neighbors.

Charlotte put her hands on her hips. "You'll need another trunk."

On the day of their departure, at midmorning, the Whittington town house was in an uproar. Molly had finally found Jane's cloak. Two trunks and two portmanteaus were scattered around the hall as Jane moved among the servants, saying good-bye. Shaw announced the arrival of Lord Chadwick, and she turned to find his lordship surveying the chaos with amusement.

"And I worried that my single trunk was a bit much," he said. "It is good that you're a woman after my own heart where a basic wardrobe is concerned."

For some reason that irritated Jane, but all she said was, "Our footmen will bring the trunks to your carriage, my lord. I can take care of the portmanteaus."

Molly slipped out of her tearful father's embrace. "I can carry me own, miss."

"Nonsense," Lord Chadwick said. "I'll have my coachman do it. Barlow!" he called out the front doors.

Jane turned away and rolled her eyes at his chivalry—only to be seen by her mother. Lady Whittington frowned and took Jane's elbow to walk to the other side of the hall.

"Jane, do be polite."

"I am, Mama. 'Impolite' would have been rolling my eyes where he could see me."

Her mother turned to face her, taking her by the shoulders. "Promise me you'll give him a chance."

"I have already promised you this."

But that was a lie, and guilt tasted like ashes in her mouth. She felt even worse about not telling her mother she intended to visit Lord Chadwick's town house first—but she didn't feel bad enough to back off from her plan.

When all her good-byes had been said, Jane allowed Lord Chadwick to lead her out to his carriage, followed by Molly. It was certainly an impressive vehicle—tall and black, with glittering lanterns hung front and back, and a coat of arms secured to the door. The sturdy horses were a perfectly matched black foursome. A groom stood at the head of each of the leaders.

The coachman was a white-haired, older man in a wide-skirted greatcoat with shiny brass buttons. He wore a wide-brimmed, low crowned hat, which he dipped toward her. As he came forward to assist them, she saw that he had a slight limp that didn't detract from his quick pace.

"This is Barlow," Lord Chadwick said, "my coachman on long journeys, and my butler while in London."

She was taken aback by the unusual delegation of duties to one man, but before she could speak, Lord Chadwick waved his monocle at her.

"I'll explain later. We'll have plenty of time to talk."

She wanted to shudder. He would have no problem finding topics of conversation, she knew. She had brought several books, hoping his carriage was well sprung enough to read— and hoping to drive across her point that they could have peaceful silence on occasion.

But as she neared the carriage, the low sound of growling reached her ears. Perhaps peaceful silence was too much to wish for.

She turned curious eyes up to Lord Chadwick, but he only took her arm and beamed with the pride of a proud papa.

"I imagine you've been anxious to meet

Killer," he said, wearing an indulgent smile.

"I am not certain that is the correct word for my feelings, my lord."

But she found herself watching his hand reach for the door handle. It seemed to take an inordinately long time, and the growling got louder and louder.

When he opened the door wide, Molly screamed.

Chapter 5

Jane stiffened, prepared to find a hideously large dog leaping out at them. But the growling turned into a surprisingly high-pitched repetitive barking, and she gaped at Killer.

Leaning out of the carriage was a little terrier who couldn't possibly have reached her knees. He had peppery colored fur on his long body and shaggy white hair on his stomach, both of which almost touched the ground. A white beard surrounded his mouth, and a white tuft of hair on his head made him look utterly silly.

Jane laughed aloud, while Molly seemed embarrassed by her scream.

The dog launched himself out of the carriage and was neatly caught by Lord Chadwick. The man watched Jane speculatively, although his dimpled smile was evident.

"Oh, forgive me for laughing, my lord," she said, covering her mouth with her gloved hand. "But—Killer?"

He shrugged and petted the furry head of his dog. The animal stared fixedly at Jane, his growls softer but nonetheless present.

"He was fierce from the moment of birth, Miss Whittington. I thought it a prophetic name."

"And has he killed someone?"

"Almost—once or twice. But those are tales for another time."

She noticed that Mr. Barlow was grimacing as he regarded the dog. When he saw her studying him, he reddened and went to lower the step to the carriage.

Mr. Barlow helped Jane and Molly into the rear seat, and then Lord Chadwick climbed up and sat across from them. He slid the glass window down, and Jane leaned forward to wave to her family. Soon they were rolling down the Mayfair street between hackney coaches, horse-drawn wagons, and omnibuses carrying passengers.

Jane folded her hands in her lap and took a deep breath. "Lord Chadwick, I would like to make a stop before we leave London."

His eyes twinkled. "Ah, perhaps you need something to keep you occupied on the journey." He knocked on the roof, and Mr. Barlow began to steer toward the side of the street.

"No, I'm prepared for that. But I would like to see your town house."

She hoped he would redden or stutter or try to talk her out of it—some indication that her plan would succeed—but all he did was smile, and those dimples suddenly looked wicked.

But no, she could not imagine such a thing in silly Lord Chadwick.

"Curious about where we will live?" he asked.

The thought of living with him made her uneasy, but it was this she hoped to avoid. "In fact, I am. Do you mind?"

"Not at all."

While he leaned out to tell Mr. Barlow their change of plans, she told herself not to be disappointed. He might be very good at keeping his feelings to himself. She sat back on the padded leather bench and looked at her betrothed and his dog, realizing with dismay, when his knees bumped hers, how very long his legs were.

Will felt thoroughly scrutinized, and he returned the favor, admiring Jane's rose-colored carriage dress and the way it emphasized her delicate figure. Her petticoats were obviously few in number, to keep the interior of the carriage roomier for all of them. She wore a small bonnet tied with ribbon beneath her chin and pressed her knees to one side, as if she didn't

want to touch him. Properly ladylike, he reminded himself.

But not too ladylike to visit a gentleman's
home.

This was an intriguing side to her he hadn't
expected. Her father had described a very
proper young lady, the perfect society wife, the
kind Will wanted. But now he wondered what
was going on in that lively brain of hers.

Killer growled, and Will restrained him.
"Easy, my boy. You don't like her much, do you?
That will come with time."

"Then perhaps we shouldn't marry," she said
lightly.

He frowned at her. "That was not very amusing, Miss Whittington. Worry not—I shan't need
to choose between you and my dog. You two
will be the best of friends by the time we reach
Yorkshire."

She gave this silent consideration. "How do
you bear the shedding?"

He knew he was being teased. "I brush out
my clothes."

"Heavens, that reminds me—where is your
valet? Surely you don't brush out your *own*
clothes?"

He arched a brow. She was showing a different sort of spirit, and it worried him. Society
women didn't show so much . . . sarcasm . . .
did they?

"It was difficult, but I forsook the services of my valet for this trip." He made himself sound serious, as "Lord" Chadwick would, and kept his eyes from sparkling at her.

Her amused expression faded to one of puzzlement, as if she saw something in his face. He was affronted by the very notion. No one, be it man or woman, had ever been able to read what he wanted to keep hidden. He was a master at deception. But he studied Jane and wondered if perhaps his skill had faded with time.

He couldn't imagine such a thing.

After a few minutes, the carriage turned off the main road.

"This is my street. We're not very far from your home."

She eyed him coolly. "I am quite good with maps and though I am but a *female*, I do know where we are."

He put a hand to his chest. "I do not mean to imply otherwise. I am quite impressed with your directional abilities."

Now she was glaring, and he hurried to prove he was not teasing her.

"Myself, I cannot easily keep maps in my head, so I trust Barlow implicitly."

Although she turned aside, he could have sworn she said, "What *can* you keep in your head?"

"Pardon me, Miss Whittington?"

"It was nothing, my lord."

Molly choked on something, then gave a few halfhearted coughs.

Jane told herself to be patient, that this errand might yet prove fruitful. He was staring at her, petting that ridiculous dog—which was also staring at her, but in a less than friendly fashion.

Lord Chadwick's Georgian town house had fewer levels than hers, but she imagined it was fine—for a bachelor. Mr. Barlow helped her out of the carriage, then limped up the stairs ahead of them to open the front door.

Lord Chadwick put down his dog in the front hall, and Killer promptly trotted over to Molly.

She reached down, then hesitated. "Milord, might I pet your dog?"

"Of course, Molly. In fact, you can keep him company while your mistress and I tour the house and have luncheon. When you're hungry, Barlow will show you to the kitchen."

Jane felt the first flutter of panic as she realized that she would be alone with him.

With a breathless "My thanks!" Molly went down on her knees and leaned over. Killer put his front paws on her thighs and began to lick her chin. As Lord Chadwick led Jane away, she could still hear the girl's giggles.

"Killer has a new friend," he said.

Ignoring the talk of his dog, Jane said, "Luncheon, my lord? I did not mean to intrude upon your hospitality. I thought we would tour the house and be on our way."

"Patience, Miss Whittington," he said.

He took her hand before she realized what he was about and tucked it into his elbow.

"Another hour will only save us from the poor quality of food we'll find on our journey."

"But your cook will—"

"Be delighted. It will probably be a cold luncheon, of course, if you don't mind."

How could she mind without sounding churlish?

She endured the rambling monologue about the details of the architecture and allowed herself to be grudgingly impressed with his town house. The previous owners had obviously decorated and furnished it. She could find nothing out of place, and his servants seemed very well trained. She'd come here for nothing.

In the drawing room, he halted next to a grand piano.

"Do you play, Miss Whittington?"

"Yes, my lord, though not with the passion it takes to be a true talent."

He released her arm and sat down on the bench, running his hand across the top. "I find myself wishing I had learned to play."

She stepped closer and looked down at him. "Why did you not conceive of such a wish when you were younger?"

He shook his head, and his rueful grin made him look . . . engaging, and even sad. "Too concerned with other things, I imagine."

For a moment, she thought he was going to say more, and she found herself leaning forward in anticipation, her elbows on the piano.

When he stood up, she was too near him, and he caught her chin deftly between his fingers.

"Perhaps you'll be displaying your talents before our guests in this very room, Miss Whittington," he said softly.

His fingers felt warm and intimate, and his eyes stared down into hers. After a shocked moment, she pulled away.

"Perhaps we should have our meal, my lord."

His mouth quirked up in one corner. "We haven't seen the bedchambers yet."

She drew in a quick breath and found herself dropping her gaze. This was such a mistake. "Certainly inappropriate, don't you think?"

Before he could respond, she walked ahead of him, back down the stairs to the dining room. For a woman who prided herself on being different from her fellow females, she knew she was displaying a surprisingly missish retreat. She didn't understand how he could be so irreverent and foolish one minute, then talk about his past with a melancholy air that made her curious and concerned all at once.

In the dining room, Mr. Barlow was awaiting them. Though he had not changed back into a butler's uniform, he'd removed his greatcoat and hat. He rang a bell when he saw them, and from the serving room two footmen carried in a large silver tureen and several covered platters, which they placed on the rosewood sideboard before leaving. With a bow, Mr. Barlow left as well, closing the door behind him.

Jane looked at Lord Chadwick in confusion.

"Please be seated," he said, pulling out her chair for her.

After she had done so, he guided her chair closer to the table for her. His place was at the head, she at his right. China plates and crystal goblets and silver service were spread out before her on a fine linen tablecloth. Instead of sitting down, Lord Chadwick filled her goblet with wine.

She was so confused. Where were the footmen? Who was going to serve them? She took a sip of wine and realized her hand was shaking.

"I'm sorry I didn't give you enough warning so you could arrange flowers for the table." She tried to sound sarcastic, but it came across in a teasing manner that sounded like she was . . . flirting.

He laughed. "I'm sorry to disappoint you."

"Are you not going to be seated, my lord?" she asked, hoping to hurry along their meal.

"Not yet."

Out of the corner of her eye, she watched him return to the sideboard and remove the lid before bringing a round tureen to the table. Stunned, she watched as he ladled soup into her bowl and his own.

Lord Chadwick was serving her?

He sat down next to her and grinned. "Not everything's cold after all. I always say, to keep and train good servants, one must know in advance their every duty."

" 'Practicing' their duties is an . . . interesting concept."

"But effective—especially when it allows me to be alone with my betrothed."

He said the words as if she were his newest piece of property—which marriage would make her. But she put aside her displeasure because the turtle soup was delicious, and Lord Chadwick's merry eyes watched her. She almost wished he were wearing that silly monocle. It put a distance between them that she preferred.

When he served her slices of cold roast beef and duck, he leaned very near her, and she wondered if he was arrogant enough to think he could muddle a woman's head that way.

But oh, something was wrong with her, because when he went down on his knees beside her chair and asked simply, "Might I have your permission to kiss you, Miss Whittington?" she found herself staring at his mouth. He wasn't smiling now, and those deep dimples were shallow creases in his skin. For the first time, she imagined what it would be like to kiss him.

When she realized her own frozen indecision, she blinked and turned back to her plate.

"I think not, Lord Chadwick," she said in a voice that didn't sound like her own. "I can show my gratitude by merely saying thank you."

He shook his head and smiled as he rose to his feet. "Ah, someday I shall convince you that a kiss is a far better way to express yourself—and even reward your intended husband."

"Perhaps between married persons," she said disapprovingly. "Although I do not believe affection should be withheld as a reward."

He rested his hand on the table at her side, leaning over her. She looked up at him and found that she could not seem to draw a deep enough breath.

"That is very true," he murmured. "Kisses only satisfy when freely granted."

She stilled as his warm, bare hand cupped her face, then she softly gasped as his thumb trailed along her lower lip. The sensation was hot and pleasurable, and she trembled.

When he straightened and went back to his own seat, she almost felt . . . bereft.

Chapter 6

The beginning of their journey out of London was slow and overheated, but Will enjoyed spending time with Jane, and he was hoping to make her see that they were well matched. Coaches and wagons crowded the streets, and vendors wove among them all, shouting their wares.

It would be good to get away from London with his betrothed, away from the feeling of being followed. He had never found anyone in the shadows, never proven anything, and it was frustrating.

Killer stood on his hind legs in Molly's lap and looked out the window, taking everything in with his usual intensity. When Molly wasn't petting him, she held a handkerchief to her red nose, which, as the day wore on, began to drip. She sneezed repetitively and mumbled an apology each time.

Jane was staring out the other window, jostled regularly by the movement of the coach. She and Killer gave each other wide berth, which Will found amusing. He enjoyed "accidentally" bumping her legs. He'd done it so often in the first few hours that now she kept her knees pressed to the wall of the carriage.

He was getting closer and closer to victory in his quest to kiss her. He had barely restrained himself from sweeping her into his arms all during luncheon.

He talked to Jane about subjects that she might find interesting: the Royal Italian Opera, and the fete that the Duke of Devonshire had given in honor of the Tsar of Russia earlier in the summer. Although she didn't respond with enthusiasm, she listened politely and had an occasional comment. He found it troubling that a proper society woman wouldn't converse on these subjects. She never offered anything about herself or her amusements.

As the crowded streets of London finally gave way to the Middlesex countryside, where open farm fields were separated by hedgerows, Jane actually turned to look at him.

"Lord Chadwick, I have a question to ask."

"Of course, Miss Whittington."

Molly sneezed miserably, they both said, "Bless you," and the maid apologized again, her eyes streaming tears. He saw Jane watching her with concern.

"My lord," Jane said, "you earlier mentioned that you wanted to travel by carriage because you had business to attend to. Might I ask what business it is, and how much it will lengthen our journey?"

She was a little too forthright, but it would hardly be polite of him to chastise her. Besides, she would have found out his agenda eventually.

He nodded his head toward the window. "What do you think of the countryside here?"

She frowned. "It is lovely, of course."

"It is good that you think so. There's an estate nearby that's for sale."

"An estate? You wish to purchase property?"

"I wish to find a home."

Her eyes widened and she blushed in that lovely way she had. "But don't you already have a home—besides the London town house? You're our neighbor in Yorkshire."

"That was my parents' home, and although I will never sell it, I wish to start anew somewhere else."

"Why?"

He looked away. How could he say he felt like a fool over how he'd behaved in his youth? "It's so . . . provincial. We need somewhere more suitable for entertaining."

Jane studied him in a way that made him feel naked—and not in a sensual way. He'd said the wrong thing, of course.

Molly sneezed. Killer harrumphed and lay down in her lap, glaring at Jane as if everything were her fault.

Jane walked in the orchard of the Hertford-shire estate while Lord Chadwick spoke with the housekeeper. The owners were in London, and the housekeeper had just given them a tour, her pride in the house very evident. He had wanted Jane to be as excited as he obviously was, but she just couldn't. It felt like she was playing dolls with someone else's life—not her own. The house was lovely, though a bit too small for "entertaining," she thought morosely. Now she knew that her future husband found Yorkshire "provincial." If they married, he probably wouldn't take her to see her father much.

The wind shook the trees gently, sheep bleated in the distance, but there was another sound, something not quite right. She stilled, listening.

Someone was crying. And whining?

She walked soundlessly until she reached a low stone wall marking the end of the orchard. The sobbing was louder now, and she could see just a touch of curly brown hair draped over the wall.

"Molly?"

There was a gasp, then the hair disappeared.

"Molly, you don't need to hide from me. You

can't be afraid—I've known you your whole life."

Jane put her hands on the rough stone and leaned over the wall to find Molly huddled pitifully, her eyes swollen and red. She sneezed and cried at the same time. Killer rested in her lap, whining and halfheartedly wagging his tail.

"Oh Miss Jane, I didn't want ye to see me like this!"

She ran her sleeve across her nose, and Jane handed her another handkerchief.

"I can't stop sneezin' and me eyes are itchin' so bad they're makin' me cry."

With a playful bark, Killer licked at her chin. Molly sneezed twice as hard.

And then Jane knew. "Oh, Molly, it's Killer's fault."

The maid only looked confused.

"You were fine until the first time he crawled into your lap. You started sneezing almost immediately."

"But I don't understand, miss. How can a little dog make me sick?"

"Some people can't be near certain animals. Cats made my late aunt Edith sneeze."

Molly brightened, as if relieved. Then the dog licked her chin and she frowned—then sneezed again. "But Miss Jane, we're all in a carriage together. What will I do?"

"Leave that to me," Jane said. "For now, let's find someplace private to wipe the dog hair off your face and hands and brush off your uniform."

They went around the main house, keeping as far away from Lord Chadwick as possible. Jane tried to shoo away the dog, but he continued to follow, with that silly mop of hair on top flopping with each step.

In the kitchen, they asked a maid to bring water and linens up to a guest bedroom. While Molly washed herself, wearing just her smock, Jane brushed the dog hair out of her clothes. All of this embarrassed Molly, who insisted it wasn't Jane's place to help her.

Jane ignored all her concerns until Molly said, "Miss, where's Killer?"

Jane absently looked about on the floor. "He's here somewhere. Probably under the bed."

"No, miss, I would have heard 'im. But I know he came in the house with us."

How well-trained was that dog? Could he be making mischief—expensive mischief? From somewhere below, a crash echoed through the house, and she groaned.

"Miss Jane—"

"I know." She tossed the dress to Molly. "Put this on and then come help me look for the dog—but don't hold him! Keep him away from your face."

Jane raced down the curved marble staircase that took up the western end of the hall. Light streamed in a set of long windows above her head and illuminated the graceful furnishings. It *was* a lovely house.

There was another crash, and then a shriek. Jane followed the sound through a drawing room, then a billiards room, and into a library. A low bookshelf had been overturned, and a maid was trying to pull a book away—from Killer. The little animal had his teeth sunk in, and he pulled with all his might.

"Killer!" Jane shouted.

The maid glanced up frantically. "Mistress, can ye not do something? He already over-turned a bucket of milk in the kitchen!"

But the dog ignored Jane until she reached for him. Then he dropped the book and, with a cheerful bark, ran from the room.

It was her own fault, she thought, picking up her skirts and running. She hadn't even real-ized Killer had followed them into the house. Wherever was he going? She ran after him from room to room, and he sniffed as if he were look-ing for something. Soon another maid was giv-ing chase behind, and a footman joined in the pursuit.

She followed the sounds of barking into a nar-row passage leading into the servants' wing. At the end of the corridor, just before it took a sharp left turn, there was an open door. Killer was standing on the threshold, barking furiously at something within.

The maid skidded to a stop just behind her, then gasped. Jane turned to face her curiously, but the maid was looking beyond her, into the room.

"Tommy!" she said suspiciously. "What are ye doin' here?"

A young man was eating a freshly baked pie off a counter. At his feet, a satchel overflowed with jars and packages.

He hurriedly swallowed and wiped the back of his hand across his mouth. "Anne, I was just fetchin' supplies!"

"It's been you all along, 'asn't it?" she demanded, pushing past Jane and stepping into the pantry. "You're the thief we been lookin' for!"

Killer sat down on his haunches, tongue hanging out, watching the scene as if he understood every word of it. Jane reached down to grab him, but with a yip he darted past her, back down the hall toward the main house. She ran after him as fast as she could, turning down several corridors. Finally, she thought to be cautious, and as she peered around the next corner, she saw Killer skid to a halt in front of his master.

Lord Chadwick made some sort of sound that Jane couldn't understand, and immediately the dog dropped onto his belly, head down.

Jane backed away, not wanting him to catch her chasing his dog all over the estate. She walked quickly down another hall, beginning to wonder if she was lost. Turning a corner, she tripped over the foot of a statue. Someone caught her from behind before she could fall, and strong arms hauled her back and turned her around.

She found herself face-to-face with Lord Chadwick.

Her hands clutched his shoulders for support; his arms were wrapped around her waist. She was breathing hard, and every movement made her breasts brush his chest, which strangely made her feel hot and restless. His face was so close to hers that they could have shared a kiss. If she put her arms out, they could have been dancing—but standing against him, alone in a deserted corridor, didn't feel like dancing. It felt . . . wicked and daring.

He smiled at her, flashing his deep dimples. He gently tucked back a loose strand of her hair, and his fingers trailing along her skin and up over her ear made her shiver.

"In a hurry to get back to me?" he whispered.

"I beg your pardon!" she said in the coolest voice she could muster. But instead of dignified, she sounded breathless.

At their feet, Killer whined and tried to thread himself between them. From somewhere behind Lord Chadwick, the housekeeper called his name.

When he didn't release Jane but just smiled lazily into her eyes, she gave him a little push. "My lord!"

"I like the sound of that from you."

When they heard footsteps, he finally released her and she whirled away, tucking her hair back with shaking fingers and trying to calm her breathing. What had just happened to her?

"Lord Chadwick?" the housekeeper said again.

Jane turned to see the woman reach down and pat Killer's head. Jane only wanted to glare at the animal.

With his hands in his pockets, Lord Chadwick faced the housekeeper. "Yes, Mrs. Lambert?"

"Your cute little dog solved a dilemma that has been frustrating me for many weeks, my lord."

Jane wanted to roll her eyes.

"There's been a thief raiding our kitchens, and your dog—Killer?—discovered him."

"I am delighted he could help," Lord Chadwick said in a smooth voice.

"It was one of the stable grooms all along—can you imagine?"

Jane cleared her throat and ignored Killer's answering growl. "But my lord, Killer did do some damage to other areas of the house."

He frowned.

The housekeeper only laughed. "Chewed on a book, knocked over some milk—nothing much compared to the service he's done us."

Jane sighed.

"We want to bring him a special meal, my lord. Surely you don't mind?"

"Of course not." He picked up Killer, and the dog settled in the crook of his elbow. "But let us celebrate outside, so Killer is not tempted to do worse. Then if you could tell us where the nearest inn is—"

"Gracious, no!" she said, leading them through the great hall and out the front door. "You'll have your dinner here."

"That is very kind of you, Mrs. Lambert," Lord Chadwick said, "but—"

"And you'll spend the night with us," the old woman added, blushing clear up to her lace cap. "The master would insist, after all the money you've saved him."

Jane watched her betrothed drip with charm and graciousness. The way this had all worked out, she almost thought he'd planned it.

After Molly joined the servants and Killer was put upstairs in a bedroom, Will and Jane were left alone in a private family parlor, awaiting the announcement for dinner. The heavy velvet drapes were drawn against the setting sun, while candles and lamps glowed about the room. The soft lighting framed Jane, haloed her. Will knew he watched her too much, upsetting her, but he couldn't help it. "Lord" Chadwick's little inanities had deserted him. He only wanted to remember holding her in his arms.

It had been a long time since he'd held a woman. Even that last year in India, he had only once or twice eased himself with a partner. Even then he hadn't felt safe, and his pleasure had been furtive and quick.

Looking at Jane made him think of long, warm nights spent learning to know her body and her pleasures. Here in England, he didn't have to fear discovery or a deadly assassin. The only discoveries to be made were things about each other.

But right now she looked anything but comfortable. She held a book in her lap and kept her gaze on it. The long strands of her hair he'd so recently touched were once again falling from behind her ear. He wanted to kneel at her side and free the rest of it, feel it brush his body as he held her.

"I say, Miss Whittington," he said, dropping his monocle into his breast pocket, "do tell me what book you're reading. The one I have is dreadfully boring."

He wanted to groan at his own stupidity. But he couldn't say what he was really thinking: *Come up to bed with me, Jane.*

Slowly, she lifted her head. From the way she blushed, Will realized she must be remembering the afternoon, too.

"It's a book about a Frenchman's journey through France," she said in a soft, hesitant voice, as her face grew redder.

Didn't she know she sounded like a woman newly awakened? He cleared his throat. "Would I like it?"

"I don't know. It's written in French."

"Lord" Chadwick didn't know any languages. "Why shouldn't a book in England be written in the Queen's English so we all can enjoy it?"

Her smile was strained. "Perhaps because the owners brought it from France."

"I daresay that means you're fluent in French."

"And several other languages."

His smile died. Languages were his specialty, how he blended into a culture no matter where he went.

Then he caught a glimpse of the title, *La Peau de la Belle Femme*, The Skin of a Beautiful Woman. Now he knew why she was having a hard time meeting his eyes. She'd probably thought the book was about beauty secrets.

But he knew better, because he'd read another of the "Beautiful Woman" books. They were about a merry widow's naughty romp through Paris. He could only imagine what was making her lovely eyes widen. But she didn't put the book down. As he imagined what she was reading, a sultry feeling of arousal swept through his veins. His cravat was surely choking him.

"Read me something," he said in a low voice.

Her breathing quickened, and he watched her breasts rise and fall.

"In French? Even if you can't understand it?"

She spoke quite evenly, and he admired that.

"I enjoy listening to you."

She met his gaze once more, and he saw that

his challenge—or the book's real contents—had
fired her spirit.

She began to read in French, going very
slowly as she made up a description about the
wine country in Normandy. Will closed his eyes,
disappointed but not surprised. He'd hoped
that she would read the actual text, since she
thought he couldn't understand the words. But
her boldness only went so far.

As she continued on, he found himself trying
not to wince. Whoever had taught her languages
had never left the schoolroom, for her pronunci-
ations were stilted and, in some places, incorrect.

She stopped, took a deep breath, and glanced
up at him. "That was about the province of
Normandy."

"Ah," he said, nodding. "Are you well educated, Miss Whittington?"

"Enough," she replied vaguely.

Good, he didn't think a woman should be
overly educated. The perfect wife should have
some knowledge about several subjects, of
course. He tried not to smile as he wondered if
the risqué French book would give her knowledge useful on their wedding night.

He lapsed back into silence, watching her. She
returned his stare for a moment, then looked
back down at her book, which trembled slightly
in her hands.

When the bell rang for dinner, she shot up so
quickly that he almost laughed aloud.

Chapter 7

On the way out to the carriage the next morning, Jane felt her stomach flutter. Looking all too handsome in the bright sunlight, Lord Chadwick was waiting beside the open carriage door, holding Killer. When the little dog caught sight of Molly, his tail started wagging and he tried to break free.

"Now, Killer," he said, holding the squirming body, "you'll be with her soon enough."

He smiled at Jane, and she thought he looked rather tired.

"A good morning to you, Miss Whittington." He bowed from the waist.

She nodded and tried to step into the carriage unassisted. He smoothly caught her elbow and helped her up. When he helped Molly too, the girl giggled—and sneezed. The dog soon followed them in and lightly jumped onto Molly's lap. As Lord Chadwick sat down, she started sneezing and wiping her eyes and nose.

He frowned at her with concern. "Molly? Are you well?"

"She is obviously not well," Jane said. "I have come to the realization that it is your dog causing her problems."

His eyebrows rose. "Are you certain?"

Killer started licking Molly's face, and the sneezing became so unbearable that Lord Chadwick pulled his dog away.

"I'm so sorry, milord." Molly's voice was muffled from beneath her handkerchief.

"My lord," Jane said smoothly, "the poor girl is suffering. I fear we'll have to send Killer back to London."

"No!" It was Molly who protested first, to Jane's astonishment. "Oh, no, miss, Killer would be so miserable. He wouldn't understand, and he'd think he was bein' punished." She blew her nose. "It's me that's got to go."

"No!" It was Jane's turn to protest. Angrily, she noticed that Lord Chadwick was barely attempting to hide his smile. "Molly, you'll feel better once the dog is gone."

"No, miss, I'm feelin' pretty bad. It'll be awhile before I recover. And there's me papa, who'll be very worried if I'm sick. Frankly, I'm missin' him terrible."

Her last sentence faded, and Jane knew that there were real tears being mopped up by her handkerchief.

Lord Chadwick opened up the door and swung out. "I'll return shortly. I heard Mrs. Lambert say that she was driving into London to shop. I'm certain she can see you home, Molly."

After the door was shut, Molly sniffed loudly. "I'm sorry, Miss Jane."

"Don't be, Molly. I had no idea you were so miserable."

"Killer helped me feel better—he did, miss. But now that I can't even hold him . . ."

"I understand." And Jane did. And though she knew the wise choice on her part would be to return to London with Molly, her father was expecting her.

She would travel unchaperoned with Lord Chadwick, which would not have seemed so dangerous if she hadn't read some of that scandalous book last night. Even now she felt her cheeks heating with a guilty blush. Why hadn't she put it back immediately when she'd realized what it was? And then Lord Chadwick had asked her to *read* from it. She'd made up something awkward, while in print were words about a man kissing the heroine's breasts!

She bit her lip and looked out the window,

trying to forget that in her dreams last night, Lord Chadwick had done the same to her. And she'd liked it.

Jane and Molly descended from the carriage when Lord Chadwick returned. Silently, she watched Mr. Barlow untie Molly's portmanteau from the roof.

"Stay with me, Jane."

She froze, feeling Lord Chadwick standing at her back, his breath soft in her ear. The use of her Christian name made her shiver.

"Do you really want to go back to London, to sit there in that house where you've spent most of your life?"

"I don't just sit there," she hissed at him, keeping her face turned away from the curious stares of Molly and Mrs. Lambert. "You don't have any idea what I do with my time."

"Why won't you tell me? You say not one word about yourself, Jane. Are you afraid of me?"

She whirled to face him and pointed a finger into his chest. "I have not given you permission to call me by my Christian name. And I am not afraid of you! I had already decided to finish this journey to my father."

He grinned, and it was wicked and knowing and arrogant, as if he thought he was the one who'd persuaded her.

Wearing a tight smile, Jane told Molly she'd see her in a few weeks, waved good-bye, and allowed Lord Chadwick to take her arm. She would have dearly loved to yank away, but she could not bring herself to cause a scene.

The carriage tilted as he climbed in and sat across from her, that infernal dog in his lap. Jane could swear it was glaring at her more than normal, as if it was all her fault that Molly wasn't coming.

Jane crossed her arms over her chest and looked out the window. She would not give Lord Chadwick the satisfaction of looking at him.

Barely a quarter hour had passed when suddenly he lifted himself off the front seat and dropped Killer where he'd just been sitting. With a squeak of surprise, Jane pressed herself against the wall of the carriage to avoid being sat upon. With a sigh, Lord Chadwick leaned back at her side, stretching out his long legs. His whole arm brushed against hers.

"What do you think you're doing?" she demanded, wishing desperately that she dared to thrust her elbow into his side.

He looked down at her, his face far too close.

"My legs were cramped. And besides, I get quite sick facing backwards."

"You did not mention that yesterday."

"And what was I supposed to do, displace Molly from protecting you?"

"Protecting me! I don't need protection."

"That's not what it seemed like. You were trying to keep a sick girl at your side so you wouldn't have to be alone with me."

"She was not truly sick!" Jane insisted. "If your dog"—she pointed at the animal, and he growled at her—"would have been removed, she'd have been fine."

"Wishful thinking." He leaned into his corner of the carriage and watched her. "I'll repeat: you just don't want to be alone with me."

"And what do you mean by that?" she demanded.

"You're afraid that I'll ask to kiss you again, and you won't be able to refuse."

"That is ridiculous." She crossed her arms over her chest and stared out the window. But his words had made a flush of heat start in her belly and rise through her. Beneath her corset, her breasts ached, and she cursed that book for giving her a glimpse of what she was missing.

Will liked baiting Jane; there was something about her that made him lose control. Battling with her was actually . . . arousing. He looked forward to what she'd say when he told her about the plans he'd made for their wedding and honeymoon.

But it was obvious she was in no mood to talk now, so he turned his head and looked out the window. A mist of rain and fog was rolling in, and he hoped Barlow was well wrapped.

The carriage had been following a curve in the road, and out of habit, Will glanced back. He frowned when he saw a horse and rider in the distance. It was a gray gelding with black trappings, just like one he'd seen yesterday. The man wore a top hat and rode with an easy grace that struck him as familiar, even though Will couldn't see his features.

Was he being followed again? He told himself that the rider probably lived nearby and just happened to be out and about both days. But Will was only alive because he'd long ago learned to heed his suspicions. When the carriage stopped for luncheon, he would speak with Barlow.

"Is something wrong?" Jane asked.

He relaxed his muscles as he turned to face her. "Nothing at all. Why do you ask?"

"You seem . . . tense, and you keep staring behind us out the window. Don't you like to travel?"

What to say to that? That he knew nothing else? "I miss the comforts of home," he said, finding himself impatient with "Lord" Chadwick.

"You could hardly call last night uncomfortable."

"It was an adequate house," he said neutrally, not wanting to tell her he hadn't even slept in the bed. "But a bit—"

"Too small," she interrupted.

Will grinned at her. "You thought so too?"

"No, but I knew you would."

"Know me so well already, do you?" he asked with amusement.

"A few things." She folded her hands in her lap and looked back out her window.

Will studied her delicate hands and wondered what she'd do if he tried to hold one. A demure young lady might blush and allow him the privilege, since they were to be married. But he was beginning to know Jane, and thought she might pull away from him.

Jane kept her eyes on the passing countryside and thought to herself that she didn't know Lord Chadwick at all. Just . . . surface things, his amusements.

"So where have you traveled?" she asked.

When she glanced at him he was gazing at her, leaning his head into the corner, his eyes half-closed—but watchful. *That* was something she knew about him. He seemed very aware of everything going on around him.

"I've traveled . . . about."

She frowned. "Be more specific, please."

"It all blends together. I have no great love for journeys for their own sake."

"Have you been to the Continent?" she asked, her teeth clenched as she fought for patience.

"Yes."

"But you don't understand any of the languages, so that must have made things difficult."

"Not really. So many of the gentler people of society speak English. And an opera is the same no matter where you go, is it not?"

Jane studied his face and thought, *He's hiding*

something. She didn't know or understand why she had such a feeling, but it was a certainty inside her. There were things he didn't want her to know. Surely this should give her father reason enough to let her escape this marriage. Her father would not countenance a man lying to his daughter.

But instead of feeling relieved, she felt more and more curious by the minute. Lord Chadwick was an enigma, a puzzle she had to solve.

That night, they stopped at an inn in Huntingdon, after spending the day jarred by uneven roads. Will could tell that Jane was in a poor mood. She'd asked to stop and explore the ruins of a castle that had been on the Great Northern Road since Roman times, but he'd had to say no. He'd made up an excuse about reaching the inn before twilight, and although she'd accepted his decision calmly, he could tell she was upset.

He couldn't allow her to wander the countryside, not until he knew if he was still being followed. He would find out tonight, long after she was asleep, even if it meant he had to search the county, leaving Barlow to watch over her.

The inn he'd chosen overlooked the Ouse River and an ancient stone bridge spanning it. Since the coming of the railroads, inns had lost many customers, and they treated graciously the few they did get. While he rented two rooms and made sure Jane would have the assistance of a lady's maid this evening and the next morning, he watched her out of the corner of his eye. She was standing in the doorway to the public dining room, obviously trying not to stare with too much fascination at the wide variety of customers. Perhaps she had an unrealistic interest in travel because she'd done so little of it.

When he tried to suggest eating in her room, or at least in the private dining room, she refused, saying that she liked to sit and listen to people talk.

Before he knew it, she was asking the innkeeper if there was anyone present who knew the local history. Was she lining up the sites she wanted to see the next day?

She actually left his table to talk to someone sitting by the massive hearth. The man had one foot propped up, a cane against his side, and a shabby cloak draped over the chair. He wore a workingman's cotton shirt and trousers held up by suspenders. When he tilted his head to talk to Jane, the light caught and glittered in his eyes.

Will froze. He was no mere farmer. As if he sensed Will's stare, the man glanced at him and tipped his head with subtle amusement.

He was Nicholas Wright, a fellow agent with the Political department. Whereas Will had left the spy business, Nick was still very active— and had obviously come looking for him.

Chapter 8

Will sat alone in his room for another hour after Jane had retired to hers. He wanted her to be long asleep before he went back down to the taproom. Barlow had brought Killer up earlier, and the dog was now snoring on his bed.

Although Will was tired, he wasn't worried about accidentally dozing off. In Afghanistan, where he'd been in constant danger, he had snatched brief but refreshing hours of sleep. In England, where nothing threatened him, he spent his nights frustratingly awake, only dozing for a few hours before dawn.

He finally slipped on his coat, locked the room behind him and went downstairs.

The taproom still had at least a dozen men sitting at various tables and at the bar. Nick was settled before the hearth on a wooden-backed settle, his "injured" leg stretched out on the bench. The atmosphere was smoky and loud, but Will still wouldn't risk talking business here. For business was what it had to be, especially since Nick had taken the trouble to track him down and appear in disguise.

Will drank a beer sitting at the bar, talking to the innkeeper about nearby estates available for sale. Occasionally he dropped his hand down to his side and made a gesture that he and Nick had long used for "meet outside in the back." Once he was certain Nick couldn't possibly have missed the message, Will strolled out the front door.

The night was cool, and the damp smell of the Ouse River settled about him. He took the alley back toward the stables. When a woman's sultry voice called to him from the shadows, he only shook his head and kept going. The carriage was parked near the stable, and he knocked softly so as not to startle Barlow. The man immediately sat up, and Will knew there would be a pistol in his hand.

"It's me," Will whispered. "Nick Wright's inside. He'll be back here in a moment."

When Barlow nodded blearily, Will continued, "Here's the key to my room, the last one down the hall on the left. Go up there and keep watch on Miss Whittington. She's next door."

"What about Killer?" Barlow asked.

"Don't bite him and he won't bite you."

After the coachman had left, Nick walked out of the shadows, the dark cloak swirling around his cane as he limped. He was a broad, tall man, with an air of mystery that usually kept people away from him.

"Is the wound real?" Will asked.

"No," he said in a low, gravelly voice. "Nice to see you too."

Will shrugged. "I'm not sure I'll be able to say the same. The disguise doesn't reassure me."

"It shouldn't. There's trouble. I never would have bothered you otherwise. But let's not talk here. I have a room above a tavern nearby. Follow me."

The alley deteriorated the farther they went. With each building they passed, the smells of stale smoke, slatternly women, and cheap beer blasted out at them.

Finally Nick held up a hand. "This is the place. I'll go in first. Take the steps in the back, right corner. I'm the first door on the right at the top."

Will slouched against the wall as he waited, pretending to swig from an empty bottle he'd found in the street. When enough time had passed, he plowed through the front door, then deliberately staggered sideways and caught himself on a loaded table. The patrons angrily pushed him away. He gave them a bleary smile, tipped his hat in apology, and headed for the stairs.

He found the correct door and knocked softly. Nick let him in. The room had been built into the eaves of the roof, so the ceiling slanted over the bed. Nick was almost too tall to stand straight. There was a crude table and chair, an oil lamp for light, and not much else. Peat smoldered on the iron grate in the fireplace to give the room warmth. Nick's cane and cloak had been carelessly tossed on the bed.

Nick grimaced as he examined Will. "I should have given you the cloak. You stand out around here."

Will looked down at his own expensive clothing. "They thought I was drunk, so I fit in well enough. Now what do you want?"

With a sigh, Nick nodded toward the chair. "Sit down."

Will did as he was asked, then waited as the other man sat on the bed.

When Nick turned up the lamp, his unshaven face looked shadowed and grim. He was a dark man anyway, black hair and eyes, perfect for a life in the shadows. That's what he and Nick had done together, roamed the Afghanistan mountains, blended into tribes, sent their information back to the Honorable East India Company—who acted on it or passed it on to the Queen's army.

When Nick didn't immediately start talking, Will said, "That wasn't you following me the last few days."

"No. I sent Sam."

Samuel Sherryngton was the third member of their trio of agents. "He's here, too? I never thought he'd leave Afghanistan."

Nick shrugged. "He's not in Huntingdon. He's following someone else tonight."

"Are you going to tell me who?" These games were tiresome after all the years he'd played them.

"Eventually." Nick smiled, which was never really a cheerful sight. "So who's the woman? She looks of quality, yet she's traveling with you."

Will snorted. "*I* am of quality now, old man, thanks to our good queen. But her name will tell you who she is—Jane Whittington."

"As in 'Colonel' Whittington?"

Will thought Nick looked almost resigned. "She's his daughter. I'm bringing her north to see him."

"And she doesn't mind traveling alone with you?"

"We're engaged." He deliberately displayed proud satisfaction, hiding his own uncertainty.

Nick leaned back on his hands and whistled. "Well, look at you—a nobleman, a dandy, and soon a married man. Hard to believe."

Will braced his elbows on his knees, knowing he would make all of it work out. "Miracles happen. Now why did you feel the need to find me?"

Nick sobered. "Do you remember General Reed? He had a sister named Julia."

"I remember. He was with the Bengal army."

"Yes. Do you remember how his sister came with all the other army families into Kabul? She was always foolishly brave, even more so than her brother, I think."

The last was said so bitterly that Will tilted his head and said, "You knew her?"

Nick's lips twisted. "Intimately. We both agreed it was only for a short while because I wasn't going to be in Kabul long. Sam had introduced us. He grew up in the same parish as the Reeds."

"So what does this have to do with me?"

Nick looked away into the fire. "She was sending British troop information to the Russians."

Will straightened, and for a moment, he was again in the mountains of Afghanistan, wrapped in a huge sheepskin cloak to fight the bitter winds, knowing that beneath his beard and turban he could be exposed as an Englishman at any time. But Will had banished those feelings of isolation and ruthless purpose. He wouldn't be that man any more. "How can you accuse a woman of treason, let alone be certain she actually did it?"

"The Reeds didn't have much money. They were from an old family whose investments had long ago gone bad. I knew then that she wanted more than someone like me, a mere cousin to nobility, could give her. She took matters into her own hands."

Will stood up to pace, knowing that such a charge of treason could sentence a man—or woman—to death. "All right, you've given me motive, but not any proof. I assume you know for certain this happened?"

"Originally, the word 'treason' was whispered by one of my Afghani informants. I knew he was playing both the Russians and us, but he could be useful. I think he was shocked when he realized that a British woman was involved. She sent the information in a coded letter, and he saw her deliver it."

"And you know it was Julia?"

"He described her perfectly—how many women can there be in Kabul with hair so blond as to be almost white? One who would roam the bazaars dressed as a boy?"

Will couldn't take just an informant's word as proof of treason. "Maybe she spurned his advances, and he's decided to punish her."

Nick shook his head. "She left a necklace I had given her with a certain Russian officer. I saw it myself."

"Nick, you might be only one of many she bedded. How do you know she wasn't simply involved with this Russian?"

Nick's eyes were black and brittle in the lantern light. "Because I traced her accomplice back to England. He's here now, ready to testify against her. He gave me one of the letters, and he has the matching code letter. They look innocent—except for little blobs of ink, certain letters filled in, as if someone just randomly scribbled on them. She would send two letters, by two different routes, and you could not read the code until both letters were side by side. The accomplice will give me the matching code letter when I reach Leeds and get him to safety. He's afraid she's going to have him killed for what he knows."

Will leaned back into his chair, understanding Nick's desperation. Nick's guilt was driving him, and finally he had enough proof for any English court. With the feeling of a trap closing about him, Will was beginning to sense what was coming next. "But why now? This all happened over a year ago."

"It's taken me a long time to track this man down. But the main impetus is that my lovely Julia has made a good match for herself. She's supposed to marry the Duke of Kelthorpe."

Now it was Will's turn to whistle as the complexity of the situation multiplied. Julia's perseverance was about to be rewarded.

Nick scowled. "I can't let a traitor to England marry into one of the highest families in the land—hell, the groom is a distant cousin to the queen!"

Between them, the silence lengthened. They

could hear the sound of glass breaking down below, and a merry group of drunks singing.

Will understood how important the monarchy was, but he reminded himself firmly of his new life. Jane would need all his attention. "I understand your position, Nick, but I've left the Political department—and the army. I can't do anything for you."

"But you can. I don't need much from you."

"No."

"I'm not calling you back into service, Will. Sam found out that Julia left London today. Maybe she discovered that we know about her accomplice and the letters. It will be the final jewel in our crown of evidence if we can follow her right to this man and then intervene. But if she reaches him before we do—"

"Is she honestly a murderer?" Will interrupted.

"Her information helped murder sixteen thousand British troops and their families in the Khyber Pass," Nick said, sitting forward on the bed. "They were cut down by the Afghani tribes from the hillsides."

Will remembered too well those treacherous, rocky peaks, and the ravines where their enemy could hide and fire at will. Over and over in his dreams he changed the past, somehow making General Elphinstone listen to his warnings rather than underestimate the Afghanis.

"The tribes wouldn't have had the courage to do it if the Russians hadn't goaded them," Nick continued. "Why should Julia stop at killing one more man?" He scowled and slammed his fist into the bed. "I wish I would have smothered her when she slept at my side."

Will put a hand on Nick's shoulder, feeling the twin traps of duty and regret tighten about his neck. "You couldn't have known what she was capable of."

Nick sighed. "I know. So tomorrow I need you to get yourself invited to the house party Kelthorpe is holding. If Julia is to marry this man, then surely she can't afford to miss the event, even for those letters."

Will almost laughed at the audacity required for Nick's plan. "You want me to just walk up there and ask to spend the weekend?"

"Aren't you looking at estates? You could start with that."

"Thorough, aren't you?" Will asked sourly.

"I know your persuasive powers—you could get yourself invited to live there permanently if you wanted to. You *are* a baron now, right?"

How clever of Nick to imply that only Will could accomplish this one crucial task. Will ran his hand through his hair and slumped back in dawning defeat. He had one more card to play. "I have Jane with me. I can't put her in danger."

"You're only to keep an eye on Julia and see who she talks to. I can't imagine the duke is involved in betraying the queen, but see what you think. I'll be tracking Julia and her henchman beyond the estate. Frankly, Jane will make the perfect cover."

Will glanced up at Nick sharply, surprised at his own rising anger where his betrothed was concerned. "I don't want her to be my 'cover.' I won't use her."

"But England needs you," Nick said softly.

Will slammed to his feet. "I gave England thirteen years of my life! Yes, I did important work! But it cost me, Nick, and you know it. There are others to carry on for me."

"But not men I trust, and certainly no one nearby. I'd go myself, but Julia knows me. By the time I call in anyone else, it might very well be too late. What happens if she marries into the royal family? How will that look to every British citizen when her treachery comes to light? Already people don't like Prince Albert. This would be a blow the monarchy couldn't withstand." Nick sighed. "Will, I need you."

Will had never heard those words from Nick, a man who believed he could do everything himself. But now Nick was relying on Sam— and Will, too. Will let go of his anger, let go of all emotion where the mission was concerned.

"All right, I'll do it," he said with a nod, and as the decision was made, he put his regrets behind him. There was no point dwelling on what could have happened. He studied Nick's weary expression and decided to lighten the tension. "I've heard that Julia is pretty," he said casually. "If you need me to, I'll seduce her. But then I'm finished."

A smile curved Nick's hard mouth. "Not necessary," he said dryly. "Besides, your attributes are surely inadequate—remember, she's had me."

Will rolled his eyes. "How will we contact each other?"

"Sam will be moving between us, relaying information."

"Will he keep to one disguise?"

Nick shrugged. "He'll do whatever he wants to—you know that. I'll need to know immediately once you have something for me."

"Very well. Where is the duke's estate?"

"Langley Manor is in Rutlandshire, near Stamford."

"I'll leave you then. I don't want Jane to be alone more than necessary."

Nick suddenly grinned. "She spends the night with you already?"

The thought of Jane naked and warm in his bed tempted him, a prize he hadn't won yet. "Hardly. But her maid became sick—"

"She became sick," Nick echoed with amusement.

"Yes. So Jane is alone but for Barlow and myself. She wants to see her father more than she *doesn't* want to be with me. Just imagine when I insist on staying at Langley Manor."

"Sorry."

"Don't worry—I can convince her there's nothing like a good house party, Nick old boy." Will whipped out his monocle and peered through it. "The excitement, the intrigue, the fashion challenges."

"You've been playing a dandy for too long, Will."

"Perhaps, but it makes things easier." He slid the monocle back into his pocket. He tried not to dwell uneasily on the fact that he didn't know how else to behave.

"Hmm." Nick eyed him. "You probably won't want to hear this, and I wasn't sure you even needed to know—"

"Just tell me."

"I have Jane's sister with me."

Will's mouth fell open. *"Charlotte?"*

Chapter 9

Nick grinned and shook his head. "I didn't mean to bring Charlotte with me—frankly, she won't tell me why she was at Lord Arbury's party—"

"You were there?" Will said, wincing. "It's my fault *she* was there. I didn't want her traveling with Jane and me, so I had Arbury send her an invitation. Of course she couldn't refuse."

"You had to send her to *Arbury's*?" Nick said with obvious exasperation.

"Who else did I know so highly placed? Hell, Queen Victoria was going to be there. Charlotte was beside herself with anticipation for her first ball since coming out of mourning." How could he explain to his old compatriot about his all-consuming need to be alone with Jane?

Nick's face went still. "Mourning? For who?"

"Her husband. Didn't you know?"

"She's not exactly speaking to me."

"Why not?"

"Because I've gagged her."

For a moment, Will could only blink at him in shock. "Why the hell would you need to gag a gently bred woman—the colonel's daughter?"

"Because she thinks I'm a traitor," Nick said and started to laugh. "I think she fancies herself a spy like her father. But she overheard things and now thinks I'm threatening all of England. I had to bring her, so she wouldn't ruin all our work."

"*Bring* her?"

"A more accurate term might be *kidnap*."

Will sank back in his chair and wiped his hand across his face. "How the hell will I explain this to Jane?" he wondered aloud, as visions of her anger and retribution swirled through his brain. Nick had complicated everything.

"You can't tell her, of course. We can't risk Julia escaping justice should Jane have a loose mouth. Charlotte is safe. When I'm not with her, Sam or Cox is. Soon she'll understand that I'm a friend to her father, not a traitor."

"Make it soon," Will said, getting to his feet and finding his hat.

Nick grinned and stood up. "Maybe I'll just hand her over to you. After all, her sister would be anxious to comfort her."

"I think not. When Charlotte finally understands the importance of your mission, send her
back to London. I'm sure she won't want to miss
the end of the Season." Will put his hand on the
door handle and looked back over his shoulder.
"Take care, Nick, and best of luck."

"To you too. Shall I guide you back to the inn?
I wouldn't want you to get lost."

Will shut the door in his smirking face.

Jane sat on the edge of her bed and tried to
control her irritation. Lord Chadwick was not in
his room. Oh, she hadn't actually knocked, but
earlier in the evening, she'd peered out her door
and seen him leave, and a few minutes later Mr.
Barlow had come up and taken his place.
There'd been silence ever since.

She was curious and frustrated at the same
time. What could Lord Chadwick be doing?
Was he sitting down in the taproom talking to
common laborers, men he hadn't thought good
enough to speak to her? Of course he *had* been a
gentleman farmer until a few short months ago.

Suddenly she heard low voices in the hall,
and she hurried to press her ear to the door. She
thought it was Lord Chadwick, but she couldn't
quite be certain. Very carefully, she opened the
door a slight crack. With his back to her, Mr. Barlow was heading down the stairs.

"Jane?"

It was Lord Chadwick, and so close he could

have been talking in her ear. She held her breath, not answering, hoping he would think her asleep and go away. She was afraid to close the door for fear he'd hear it.

He said her name again, this time with more urgency. Suddenly the door pushed open, and she tumbled onto her backside, bracing herself with her hands. With the door now wide, her betrothed loomed over her.

"Are you all right?" he demanded, glancing quickly about the room before focusing intently on her. "Is someone—"

Then his voice choked to a halt, and she realized why. Her legs were bare all the way to midthigh, exposed to his wide-eyed gaze. With a gasp, she frantically tugged the material down as far as she could, but some of it was caught under her, leaving her feet and ankles vulnerable. He continued to stare.

"Are you going to help me up?" she demanded, striving unsuccessfully for a cool voice.

"There's not an intruder?" he asked.

She noticed he didn't even bother looking around again. He just stared at her legs.

"No!"

He reached for her hand and lifted her so swiftly to her feet that she stumbled against him, her other hand flattening against his chest. They stood that way, breathing into the silence. She told herself to keep her gaze away from his face, but her hand felt hot in his, bare flesh against bare flesh. His thigh almost nestled between hers. Her heart was pounding so loudly that she thought there must be something wrong with her.

Unable to stop herself, she looked up—and wished she hadn't. His narrowed gaze was piercing, hard, and full of an awareness that made something shudder inside her. He was staring at her mouth, and she felt so dry that she licked her lips. He swiftly inhaled, and with the expansion his chest touched her breasts. The pressure on her nipples through the thin night-dress made her breasts ache in a way she'd never felt before.

As if from a great distance, she heard the door close, then his free hand slid up her back, pulling her tighter to him. The ache spread even further.

What was happening to her? These strange sensations were foreign to her—but wildly exhilarating.

She felt the pressure of his thigh increase, and she caught her lip between her teeth to stop a moan as the strange ache centered between her thighs. She was shocked to realize she wanted to push harder against him.

Wildly, she broke their shared gaze and found herself staring at his mouth. If he asked permission to kiss her, she didn't know if she could deny him.

But he didn't ask. With no warning, he covered her mouth with his, freeing her hand as he pulled her hard into his embrace. He had none of the tentative nature of a gentleman, as she once might have suspected. He pressed swift kisses to her lips with a knowledgeable passion teetering on the edge of control.

Jane felt like a new, different person, as if there was something inside her that needed freedom. So this was what it felt like to kiss a man. When she burrowed against him and kissed him back, she felt the vibrations of a groan rumble through his chest. His mouth slanted across hers, and as she gasped with pleasure, his tongue traced the fullness of her lower lip. Her moan was muffled as he deepened the kiss, opening her mouth wide to accept the stroking of his tongue. She had never imagined doing such a thing, but it felt incredible. She could taste him now, the faintest essence of beer and man.

She wanted—needed—to be closer to him. There was an impatience deep in her blood, in her very skin, to touch him. He wasn't wearing a coat, so she slid her hands up his linen shirt. She could feel the rise and fall of hard muscle through his arms and up his neck.

When Will felt her soft, cool hands slide up into his hair, the last of his control shattered. She tasted like an angel and had the long legs of a temptress. After her first tentative exploration with her tongue, she kissed him now like a woman who knew what she wanted. She clung to him. Her round breasts teased his chest; her thighs trembled against his, where he could feel the moist heat of her.

With a sigh, she dropped her head back, her black hair glistening in long waves in the candlelight. He burrowed his face in the warmth of her neck. She smelled like sweet jasmine, an exotic, exciting scent that hinted at mysteries unrevealed. Marriage to such a passionate woman seemed like a glimpse of heaven.

He licked a path up behind her ear, then back down to her collarbone. As he suckled the skin there, tasting its softness, he allowed his hand to slide down her lower back and capture one round cheek.

When Jane stiffened, he took her mouth again in deep kisses to relax her. With both hands, he pulled her hips tighter against his, but she turned away from his lips.

"Lord Chadwick—"

"It's William," he murmured, kissing her cheek, then nibbling on her earlobe.

"Lord Chadwick, you must stop!"

She put both hands on his chest, pushing away until only their hips still pressed together, her buttocks cupped in both his palms. He rubbed his thigh higher against her, and she gave a sweet little gasp, her face full of passion and curiosity and indecision.

"You don't want me to stop," he said in a

husky voice, leaning forward to kiss her again.

But she held herself away. "I do—you must!"

"Jane, we're to be married soon. The pleasure could begin now."

She pushed hard, and he let her go. She stumbled back and put her hand against a small table to steady herself. He helplessly watched the rise and fall of her breasts.

"And so would the guilt," she said, her voice growing stronger with each word. "This is not right, Lord Chadwick. And please do not use my Christian name. I have not given you permission."

He grinned and leaned back against the door, folding his arms across his chest. He tried to pretend that he was not so overwhelmed with desire for her, that he was not gazing with slavering fascination at her nipples pointing against the thin nightdress. "After that heated exchange, I'm to go back to using 'Miss Whittington'?"

"It will remind us of the proper decorum."

To his great regret, she picked up her dressing gown and turned her back to don it. Will bit back a protest, knowing it was useless.

"You can have no doubts about our marriage now," he said softly.

She turned to face him, cool inquiry on her elegant face. "Then we think differently, my lord. I have even more."

"People with no feeling for one another don't kiss like that—Miss Whittington."

"I wouldn't know, because no man has been rude enough to force a kiss upon me."

"Force?" he repeated, amused.

"*Force*. You did not even ask my permission."

His smile died, and he gave her a heated stare full of the desire that still simmered in him. "You gave permission with your body, my dear. No words were necessary."

She averted her gaze, and he knew she was well aware of the truth.

"It was a mistake," she said flatly. "It will not happen again."

In frustration he took a step toward her, but when she only lifted her chin in haughty challenge, he stopped.

"It *will* happen again," he replied firmly. "You are to be my wife."

"But I'm not yet. If such . . . intimacies happen again, I shall board the nearest train north, regardless of my father's request that I travel with you. And perhaps I'll even tell him what happened."

Will grinned. "Resorting to threats, are we? You forget, my dearest Miss Whittington, that I know your father well. When I tell him that I found your door open—"

"It was not open!"

"I noticed it was unlatched, and I was worried for your safety."

"And because of you and your dog, I was alone and defenseless."

"Ah yes, the intimidating Molly was not at your side to frighten off ruffians."

She hesitated, and he knew he'd won the point.

"And where were you, my lord?" she demanded. "Why were you not in the next room for my protection?"

He hid his wariness. "Barlow was there. You were not alone."

"But where were *you*?"

"I was down in the taproom, Miss Whittington. Could you not taste the beer I'd consumed?"

That shocked her into silence, and her green eyes grew shadowed with memory. "That was crude, my lord."

"But true, Miss Whittington. If you must know the details, I was inquiring after available estates for sale in the shire. Go ahead and ask the innkeeper if you don't believe me."

She said nothing, and he smiled without smugness, for the lies he had to tell her were never far from his mind.

"Very well," she finally said. "It has been a trying day. Have a pleasant sleep, my lord."

She said it with sarcasm, but he answered in a low, sincere voice. "Sleep will be difficult, sweet Jane, for through the night I'll be thinking of you and what we could be doing together."

For a moment she looked confused, vulnerable, a woman who guessed what she might be missing. To keep from making an even bigger fool of himself, he turned and left the room.

Jane's knees buckled, and she almost fell into the chair beside the table. She wiped a shaking hand across her mouth, but there was no way to erase the feel of his lips on hers. He had tasted . . . wonderful. She hadn't imagined a man could make her lose her thoughts and forget her every goal.

Now confusion wormed into her mind. She could still almost feel his hot palms sliding down her back. Her buttocks were imprinted with his hands.

He had known everything she was feeling, as if he'd experienced it all before—many times. A painful emotion flared through her, and with dismay she recognized it as jealousy.

Jealousy!

Why should she care that he had practiced those kisses on other women before her? It was obvious men were weaker creatures where the flesh was concerned.

But maybe she was weak, too, because as he'd pointed out, she *had* gladly given him permission to do as he pleased to her. She even wanted to call him back. She felt . . . incomplete, restless. She didn't know much about the sex act itself, but she knew there was more than kissing.

And with a dark hunger, she wanted to know it all. She prided herself on her knowledge, on her exploration of mysterious subjects, and Lord

Chadwick—William—was her newest mystery.

She could not reconcile the man who talked of fashions and opera with the man who could seduce her senses. Tonight he was a forceful, enigmatic stranger, one she could imagine being granted a peerage for some specific reason. She would insist that he explain his rise in status—and keep him talking as much as possible. Otherwise she would spend the endless hours in the carriage trying not to think about what they'd done together.

There was something dark and dangerous buried in him; if she understood it, surely it wouldn't call to her as it did now.

She realized with despair that he had made it even more difficult for her to refuse the marriage. How could she lie to her father and say Lord Chadwick did not affect her, that there was nothing between them?

Chapter 10

The next morning, Jane decided to abandon her corset and cheerfully stuffed it into the depths of her trunk. Now that Molly was gone, it seemed ridiculous to need a stranger's help getting dressed. She would ask for a chambermaid's assistance at night ironing out the next day's garments, but that would be all.

The freedom to breathe was wonderful. As she went down to the public dining room of the inn, she concentrated on that rather than her impending reunion with Lord Chadwick.

She'd had a difficult time falling asleep the night before, knowing he was nearby. Every time she closed her eyes, she relived the touch of his hands, the erotic invasion of his mouth.

But she was determined to spend her day discovering his secrets—and distracting herself from his nearness.

Lord Chadwick stood up as she entered the dining room. He was dressed as if he were making calls in London today instead of traveling by carriage. His black cravat was knotted intricately, and he wore a blue-and-black striped frock coat over black trousers. He was so perfectly turned out that she had to wonder if his valet wasn't secretly following them.

Jane had worried how she would react when he looked at her, and for good reason. His warm gaze took her in from the top of her smartly tilted hat to the tips of her half boots peeking out from beneath her dark green carriage dress. The places where his hands had touched her body seemed to throb.

She was ready for a comment alluding to their kiss, but all he said was, "The dress quite becomes you, my dear. It is made of merino, is it not?"

She found herself staring at him almost dumbfounded. Again, he seemed like a different man. He didn't want to talk about the kiss—but about her clothing? Perhaps if she'd been wearing more last night, he would have been distracted enough to discuss fashion rather than attempt to seduce her.

As she took a seat, allowing him to push her

chair in, she thought she saw just a hint of amusement in his eyes when he walked around the table, though it was gone before he sat.

She didn't understand his game, but if he was using clothing to divert her, it wouldn't work.

They ate a healthy meal of fried trout and eggs, discussing only the weather and their travel plans. He reluctantly agreed to allow her to visit the ruins of a castle at midday as long as it wasn't a lengthy delay, and he thoughtfully asked the innkeeper to pack them a picnic luncheon.

When Mr. Barlow brought the carriage around, the innkeeper helped Jane carry her portmanteau out into the courtyard. Once she'd been assisted into the carriage, she slid as far to the left as she could, staring out the window while Lord Chadwick stepped in and deposited Killer on the opposite bench. The carriage rocked gently with his weight, and she felt the brush of his elbow as he was seated. He knocked on the roof and the carriage jerked into motion.

The silence gnawed at Jane for several minutes as they drove away from the Ouse River and up through the town itself. Not only did Killer glare at her but he also gave an occasional low growl, until her betrothed admonished him. Could Killer actually tell her relationship with his master had altered?

When only scattered farmhouses dotted the ripe fields, she turned to look at Lord Chadwick.

He was watching her, one arm behind his head as he leaned into the corner. He smiled, his dimples so deep that she wanted to trace them with her finger. The muscles low in her stomach suddenly tightened with that same forlorn ache she'd first experienced in his arms last night. Although she felt a blush sweeping over her face, she didn't look away.

"How long will it be before we arrive at the castle?" she asked.

"Soon, I imagine," he drawled. "Shall we play cards to pass the time? Unless you'd like to wait excitedly on the edge of your seat for your first view of the castle."

This time she rolled her eyes. "I have a question I'd like you to answer instead."

"So you want to speak to me again?" He raised one eyebrow in mock amazement.

"I have never stopped speaking to you, my lord," she chided.

"Perhaps I should be more specific: you've been speaking about nothing but the weather since we greeted one another this morning."

"And *your* topic of conversation was the material of my clothing."

He grinned. "Touché."

She winced when he pronounced it as "toochay." She corrected his pronunciation, and he thanked her so seriously that she almost gave a reluctant laugh.

"I hope you are not offended by the personal question I'll be asking you."

"You're my intended. You are allowed to know personal things about me."

She chose to ignore the gleam in his eye. "My mother told me you only recently received your title."

He continued to smile, obviously unoffended. "That is true."

"It is seldom the queen grants a new title. Why did you receive it?"

"Because I helped her over a puddle."

She eyed him with disappointment. So much for telling her anything.

"It is true, Jane. Without me, Her Majesty would have been quite up to her knees in mud. I risked damage to my own garments for her."

"Did she knight you for that, too? And you are to call me Miss Whittington."

"After that kiss—"

"We are not to discuss your reprehensible behavior."

"Reprehensible? I don't think you'll say that after our wedding night—if we can even wait that long."

He reached out to finger her skirt, and she slapped his hand away.

"Lord Chadwick! Please let us keep our discussion to the topic I brought up."

"Very well. You wish to know why I was made a baron."

Will watched the determined look on her face, her skepticism over how truthful his words would be. And after last night's intimacy and the knowledge that he would be deceiving her because of Nick, he realized he didn't have the heart to tell her another lie.

"My family has been in Yorkshire for many generations, and over the years we've been the nearest thing to peers in our parish. The estate is vast, and the holdings numerous. Perhaps the queen wanted me in the House of Lords. Those are things that certainly fit into the equation. There is one other thing about which I'm not permitted to speak, a favor I did the queen, shall we say."

She looked thoughtful, and he allowed himself to relax. He looked at her hands, folded loosely in her lap, well covered in gloves, and remembered the tentativeness with which they'd touched him.

"You spoke of things fitting an equation," Jane said. "My lord, certainly you know that that is a mathematical reference. Don't numbers bore you?"

"And who told you that?" he asked, relieved to find that she was teasing him, though she might not recognize it herself.

"I accidentally overheard you."

When she looked away, he saw the blush staining her cheeks. He found himself leaning nearer, tantalizing himself with her scent.

Close to her ear, he whispered, "Things aren't always as they seem."

Even as the words escaped him, he knew they were a mistake.

She turned to face him and was so near that he was able to read the triumph in her eyes, quickly replaced by alarm.

"My lord, please keep to your own side of the carriage."

"Shall I draw a line down the center?"

But he sat back as he said it, and her shoulders relaxed.

"I've asked before—do you fear me, Jane?"

"It is not you I fear," she admitted reluctantly.

"Then you fear yourself."

She actually groaned. "This is not a topic of discussion, William."

"Aha!" he said with triumph, even as she amended his name to, "Lord Chadwick."

She fixed him with her cool eyes, so green and challenging. "My lord, are you saying that *you* are not as you appear?"

"I most certainly am not. But you cannot take seriously what I might say to other gentlemen in order to escape a boring game of cards."

"They said you won."

"Handily. I always do. That's what makes it boring. Don't you feel that way at times?"

She parted her lips, hesitated, then nodded.

"And you are so clever, Jane, that I imagine many things bore you. So you study languages."

"And other things."

"Mathematics?"

She didn't answer.

"I find intelligence in a woman fascinating," he murmured, reaching for her hand and kissing her fingertips before she could pull away. "As long as she can be a proper wife."

By her expression, he'd made another mistake, and he felt uneasy at her reluctance to discuss their marriage—especially her part in it. Hadn't their encounter last night proved to her that they belonged together?

Jane regarded him thoughtfully. "And what do you consider the characteristics of a proper wife?"

"Intelligence, of course," he said, smiling at her, using every bit of charm he could muster.

She did not smile back.

"The ability to keep a well-run home, and to raise happy children. The ability to discuss anything with your husband. To entertain as befits a baroness."

"I was wondering when you'd get to that," she said frostily.

"I expect the same things of myself, sweet Jane. I anticipate endless hours by your side with our children."

When she said nothing, he leaned closer, and she froze. "And of course, conceiving them is the most pleasurable of all."

With admirable boldness she faced him, and he looked at her lips, so plump and inviting.

"I would not know," she said stiffly. "But of course, such ignorance is also what you require of a wife."

"Only ignorance of other men, my sweet." He was so close that he thought he could see her tremble. "I would show you anything you asked right now."

She faintly smiled. "Then I wish to view the castle, my lord."

She gave him a little push and he sat back, not wanting to frighten her away. Killer issued a sharp, jealous bark.

The roof of the castle was long gone, and the remains of the walls rose in jagged peaks to the sky. The eeriness of the scene called to Jane, and she touched the old stones reverently, wondering how many hundreds of years ago it had been built. After following her about for a while, Lord Chadwick seemed restless, and when he excused himself to go sit outside, she was glad for the respite. She could barely look at him without trying to imagine the exact way one conceived a baby.

Why did such ancient places call to her, she wondered, trailing her hand across the stones of a broken parapet. With this view, she could see across the vast plains of England. In her imagination, the countryside could not have been so very different five centuries ago, but men and women had been. Surely women had had even less freedom.

But something about a knight protecting his people, his castle—his woman—called to her. He was a king unto himself, and a wife ruled at his side, in charge whenever he was away. A woman had to understand every facet of a medieval estate, not just the household and its servants.

Would a knight have treated his wife as an equal? After all, she would have been so much more to him than a pretty decoration in his household and on his arm.

When she felt she could delay no longer, Jane strolled back outside, where a grassy meadow stretched down the hillside. At its base nestled a little stone village on the banks of a brook.

She watched in stunned surprise as Lord Chadwick played a game of cricket with a group of local children. Killer pranced among them, barking and yipping and darting away from curious hands. Jane sat on the blanket he'd spread and for the first time felt a lump of emotion in her throat at the thought of children—her own children running about her.

Watching Lord Chadwick at play drew her almost as much as his passionate kisses. He had not lied when he'd said he wanted to share in the task of raising children.

Once, he laughingly ran toward her, and she caught her breath at how handsome he looked. What would she do if he tried to touch her? But all he did was throw his coat and cravat onto the blanket and run off again with his shirtsleeves exposed. She tried to imagine another proper man of her acquaintance doing such a thing, but she couldn't. She watched his wavy hair blowing in the breeze and realized that since they'd left London, he'd given up slicking it back with macassar oil, as was the fashion. She just didn't understand him.

Mortified by her own scandalous thoughts, she walked back the short distance to the carriage to retrieve a book. She found Mr. Barlow napping inside, although he did wake long enough to nod at her before his head drooped again. When she closed the carriage door, she saw Lord Chadwick standing still, watching her. Then, as if satisfied, he went back to the children.

What did he think she'd do—leave?

When she returned to the blanket, she found Killer curled up in the exact place she'd been sitting, looking triumphant even with his floppy hair hanging in his eyes. Though the blanket was big enough for both of them, Jane had had enough.

"Please move, Killer."

The dog's ears twitched, but that was all.

"I said move." This time she pointed to another part of the blanket. "Go on."

He dropped his chin on his paws, still watching her. She reached for him, and he darted away rather than allow himself to be touched by his enemy. Jane triumphantly sat down in her original spot. With a grumbled growl, Killer curled up on a corner of the blanket as far away from her as possible.

Then Jane suddenly saw herself as if she was looking from a great distance. What was she doing—proving her superiority over a dog? Sitting here like a good little girl as if all of society were still watching her? She didn't need to prove anything to anyone.

She threw the book down and stood up. She unpinned her hat, tossed it onto the blanket, then strode off down the hillside toward the cricket game. She knew how to play, though it had been years since her girlhood exploits in Yorkshire. She almost hoped Lord Chadwick would try to stop her.

He stood openmouthed as she joined the opposite team, but she simply lifted her chin and dared him to say something. He didn't, although he no longer looked so comfortable.

Jane spent an hour running and laughing. She didn't get too many hits with the bat, but she was decent at throwing the ball. When she was finally hot and sweaty and breathless, she bowed out of the game. She had to walk by Lord Chadwick to get to the blanket, and he watched her with a strange look on his face. He pushed his damp hair back and wiped his forearm across his forehead, never taking his eyes off her the closer she came. She swung her arms and strode briskly rather than sedately. He gave her a crooked grin as his gaze wandered down her body. She was disheveled and dusty, but she knew he wasn't thinking of the state of her garments. They were both remembering the heat of their kiss.

Uneasy, she sat down on the blanket and distracted herself reading and studying until a shadow fell across her book. Using her hat to shield her eyes, she looked up to find Lord Chadwick standing over her, his fists on his hips.

"You're blocking my light," she said, trying to hide how strange it felt to have him standing above her, his thighs too near. Surely his trousers didn't have to be so tight that she could see his leg muscles.

She was suddenly overheated by where she was staring and wished she could splash cold water on her face.

"So sorry," he said. "The game was more enjoyable when you were playing."

And then he made her feel even stranger when he stretched out at her side, unfolding his long body, propping his head on his hand. Killer gave an angry yip as he found himself pushed off the blanket. He curled up behind Lord Chadwick's knees.

"What are you reading?" he asked. "You're moving your lips."

"I'm studying Italian," she said coolly.

"Such a romantic language."

"And how would you know that?"

"I overheard two sailors unloading their ship."

"Two sailors—how romantic."

He opened his mouth, but nothing came out. To her surprise, he reddened.

"Why Jane Whittington, you're teasing me."

"I am not. I'm stating a simple opinion that you thought two sailors talking Italian were romantic."

"No," he said rather more forcefully than she thought necessary. "I said the *language* was romantic. Oh, never mind." He reached behind him to pet his dog.

"And now you're sulking."

"Little boys sulk. Grown men just get moody. At least that's what my mother used to say."

She closed her book and stared at him. "Really? Why would she say that about you?"

"It wasn't about me, but my father. And she laughed when she said it." He was wearing a smile now, and his eyes seemed to be seeing something in a distant memory.

"And was your father angry?"

"He laughed too. And then he chased her up the stairs until I couldn't see them anymore."

"Oh." Jane thought she'd blushed more in the last few days than she had in her whole life.

"They were like that. And I was a boy, so I didn't understand and thought they were just silly."

"It sounds wonderful," she said softly, thinking of the arguments she'd overheard the rare times her parents had been in the same house. "You must have been very happy."

"Sadly, I didn't know it at the time. I only wanted to escape."

"Little boys think like that."

"Not little girls?" he asked, watching her too closely.

"Little girls are more practical."

"I can see that by the Italian you're studying," he said doubtfully.

"I like to educate myself. Surely that is practical."

"Say something in Italian."

He rolled onto his back, forcing Killer to snuggle against his waist. Folding his arms beneath his head, he just watched her.

In Italian, she said, "You are impossible."

"What did you say?"

"The sky is blue."

He sat up, and it took all her effort not to move away from him.

"Is that really what you said? Now don't lie."

"I'm not."

But her voice was trembling—*she* was trembling. His gaze was no longer on her face but had lazily drifted lower.

Softly, he said, "I noticed you're not wearing a corset today."

She barely resisted the urge to cover her chest, as if he could see beneath her dress and chemise.

Before she could manage speech, he continued, "I noticed immediately, of course. You simply move more freely—especially when you run. When you lean over, the blood doesn't rush into your face."

"If my face is red," she said in a low voice, "it is out of embarrassment at your appallingly bad manners."

He put his hand on her waist. "This even feels much better."

"Remove your hand at once! There are children watching us."

"The children are from the nearby village and come from families who don't think less of almost-married people for showing affection."

He slid his hand up her back and pulled her a little closer. She couldn't even gasp her affront, because she was barely breathing as it was. In her mind she was seeing flashes of his kiss in the candlelit darkness of her room, and the image was no less erotic under the bright sunshine.

His lips touched hers gently, differently than the previous night. Soft, moist kisses on her mouth, the corner of her lips, her cheek. He smelled like heat and summer, and she found her eyes closing as she savored the gentle assault.

And then they heard childish giggles. Lord Chadwick glanced up at his new friends, then with a quick kiss to her nose, he took off running again, leaving Jane baffled and disappointed and full of a new, frightening longing for him, this man she didn't want to marry.

Chapter 11

With his eyes half-closed, Will watched Jane as she stared out the carriage window. The roads they traveled through the flat countryside toward Langley Manor were rougher today, making her lovely breasts bounce. That was the first thing he'd noticed about her that morning, and he'd spent the day wishing he could cup a handful of each. Of course he wouldn't be able to stop there.

But since he'd kissed her that afternoon near the castle ruins, there was a fragility to her that unsettled him. It was her fault that she'd put temptation in his path. He hadn't wanted to explore a castle and had only allowed it because he now knew that Sam was the one following them. Between the two ex-soldiers, they should be able to keep Jane safe.

And then she'd forced him to talk about his parents, and for once the guilt hadn't overwhelmed him. How could she make him say things he hadn't wanted to?

She was intelligent, his future wife. He couldn't help but admire a woman who studied subjects a wife didn't need. He actually enjoyed talking to her. He hadn't wanted such things from a wife, but he was determined to overcome the worries her restlessness caused him. She was a spirited woman, and that was all.

"I have a surprise for you," he said.

Jane gave a little jump at the sound of his voice, then eyed him with obvious hesitation.

"We're going to catch our own dinner tonight."

"Catch?" Her nose wrinkled with distaste.

"I have fishing equipment stowed beneath the bench you're sitting on."

"Oh." Her frown smoothed a bit. "But won't the delay—"

"Surely your father would want us to eat several times a day. And I am an expert with a fishing rod, so you will be eating within an hour. And of course, you'll want to study and learn a new skill."

When she only gazed at him, eyes narrowed, he gave a sharp rap on the roof of the carriage to get Barlow's attention. After a quick conference with the coachman and another half-hour's drive, they reached a suitable stream, with a small copse of trees nearby for firewood.

As Jane allowed William to assist her from the carriage, she tried to picture him with a smelly, wriggly fish in his hand. Contrary to his smug assumption, she had indeed fished as a girl at Ellerton House in Yorkshire, and she understood what was involved.

But did he? As he brought forth the fishing equipment, she glanced at his fashionable garments, wondering what they'd be reduced to in another hour. But when he discarded his coat and waistcoat, her curiosity was at its peak. Would she ever understand him?

While the men dug for worms, they shared a quiet camaraderie that intrigued her. She took a deep breath of the pleasant, honeysuckle breeze, listened to the swaying of the trees, and tried to feel at peace. When William knelt on the bank and washed his hands in the stream, she put the worm on her hook and rather enjoyed his astonishment when he turned around. No, "enjoyed" was the wrong word: she was merely satisfied with his expression.

He studied her as he baited his own pole. "I'll admit, the breadth of your studies is quite impressive, Miss Whittington."

"No studies involved here, my lord. I spent much of my childhood in Yorkshire and enjoyed the companionship of local children."

"Your mother let you play with the villagers?" he asked doubtfully. "Is that where you learned cricket?"

She couldn't quite hide a smile. "I see you've formed the correct opinion of her already. But you're right—she would not have allowed it. I often managed to . . . escape her notice."

"Don't let me hear of such things."

He spoke with a severity that cooled her amusement.

"Because you'll find that I quite admire resourcefulness in a girl."

She waited for the inevitable "but not in a wife" or "not in a grown woman."

But he smiled at her in that lazy, wicked way she found so fascinating and said in a voice meant only for her ears, "I find it rather arousing."

Blushing, she held her silence as they stood fishing side by side on the bank of the small river. Killer stood with his paws in the shallow edge, his long belly hair trailing in the water. Amazingly, he never disturbed the fish by barking or jumping in.

When William's line caught in the branches of a dead tree that had fallen across the stream, she expected him to send Mr. Barlow out to fix it. Instead, he jumped up on the tree trunk, his arms stretched out for balance, and began to walk out across the water.

She glanced at Mr. Barlow, who had limped

over to stand at her side. He crossed his arms over his chest and shook his head. She thought he mumbled, "Bloomin' fool," but surely he would not speak so about his employer.

"Should you . . . help him?" she asked.

She held her breath as William's arms began to whirl in wider and wider circles. He fell back into the water with a giant splash.

"And get dragged in myself, miss?" Mr. Barlow said innocently.

Killer jumped and barked, running back and forth furiously along the bank of the stream. When the waves settled, William was sitting waist deep in water and—laughing! She covered her smiling mouth. He struggled to his feet, only to slide and fall face-first this time. Her shoulders ached from repressing her laughter. It caught in her throat and faded when he finally gained his footing and she was able to see how his white shirt plastered to him. By the time he trudged ashore, still carrying his fishing pole, she was suitably composed enough to only raise her eyebrows.

"I daresay, my lord, your tailor would not like to see you now."

He hesitated, watching her with such speculative amusement that she almost thought he would lunge and hold her along his wet body. To her dismay, it was not an unpleasant thought.

He seemed to think better of his original intentions, whatever they were. "Miss Whitting-

ton, my tailor would be thrilled, for it would
mean I'd be buying another set of clothing from
him. He is a practical businessman, you know.
I'll go change in the carriage. No peeking."

She rolled her eyes.

"And you can continue catching our dinner.
Up to the challenge?"

"No challenge is necessary, my lord, although
I will have to move upstream a bit. You've surely
scared away all the fish, and I'm in too much of a
hurry to wait for their return. A quickly caught
dinner means a quicker departure."

He sighed. "How practical of you, Miss
Whittington."

"Thank you, Lord Chadwick," she answered,
turning back to her fishing.

She glanced over her shoulder once to watch
Mr. Barlow throw a portmanteau down to
William, who then easily swung up inside the
carriage. Mr. Barlow paused as he saw her, but
she turned away before he could make too
much of her curiosity.

By the time William came back out, his damp
hair beginning to show a hint of curl, his clean
clothes slightly wrinkled, she and Mr. Barlow
had each caught a fish, and Mr. Barlow was reeling in another. The two men went off to start a
fire, leaving her mercifully in peace.

Will left five fish frying in a pan under Barlow's watchful gaze and went to sit down in the
grass at Jane's side. She'd been watching him

rather closely throughout the afternoon, and he wondered if he'd revealed too much to her.

"We have one more stop on our schedule today," he said, leaning back to rest his weight on his hands.

He saw her flash of irritation. "There's not much daylight left, my lord. Shouldn't we be searching for an inn?"

"But Langley Manor is nearby."

"Isn't that the seat of the Duke of Kelthorpe?"

"Very good, Jane. I can see your studying has its worth."

Her green eyes flashed for a moment before she calmed herself. "I do not study such things, my lord. But one cannot live in London without knowing who Kelthorpe is. Have you ever met him?"

"No."

"Neither have I. Then why are we going?"

With a sigh, he finally accepted the fact that Jane would never be the kind of wife who would meekly accept his decisions. "Because I have heard of the magnificence of the estate, and I wish to see it. Pretend it's a ruined castle just waiting for your exploration."

To his surprise, she said, "Very well, my lord." She gave a subdued nod, but her eyes were watchful, as if she didn't trust him.

He hated lying to her because it wasn't a good start to their marriage, he thought, watching Barlow as he served them each a helping of hot fish on a linen napkin. The three of them picked at the fish and blew on their fingers and managed to eat enough to satisfy their appetites. Jane never complained once about the lack of tableware—or even a table, for that matter.

She had good reason not to trust him now. Her safety in the coming days weighed heavily on his mind. How would he protect her in a house full of people, when they wouldn't even be sleeping in the same wing?

"Lord" Chadwick liked parties—it was expected of him. But Will found the thought of trying to converse politely with strangers a trying exercise. The only things he knew about the *ton* he'd gleaned from newspapers. Though he was a quick study, facing enemy soldiers seemed preferable.

Jane must enjoy these sorts of things—surely she was only reluctant because they had not been invited.

As late afternoon settled over the land and a soft rainfall began to pelt the roof, the carriage rounded a bend and the magnificent expanse of Langley Manor came into view. The mansion was of mellow brick and seemed to rise out of the hillside like a monument to nobility. Every window on all three levels reflected the setting sun as it sent a last few beams beneath the gray clouds.

Jane thought she heard William sigh, but

when she looked at him, he only smiled. Something just felt wrong to her—besides the delay in their journey. Short of stomping her feet and throwing a childish tantrum, she couldn't see how she could get out of this.

William had allowed her a visit to a castle; she must allow him this. But as they turned into the drive, a carriage pulled away from the front portico, leaving several women and men to walk up the marble stairs to the waiting servants.

Jane smiled, trying to cover her relief and triumph. "The family must be at home, Lord Chadwick. Surely we cannot interrupt."

"But we don't know that for certain. We'll ask the butler."

She sat back stiffly and tried not to groan. When the carriage stopped, she thought she might wait inside, but William took her hand firmly and helped her out, opening an umbrella over her head as they walked between the carriage and the manor. They found the butler waiting just inside the open front door.

"Good day, my lord," the man said in a stentorian voice. He sketched a stiff bow.

"A good day to you," William replied as he handed the butler his card.

The man glanced at it. "I'm afraid I do not have your name on the guest list, my lord."

Jane felt herself redden, even though she knew they could now leave.

"Guest list?" William responded. "Dear me, I

had no idea that His Grace was in residence. I had merely hoped I could show my betrothed, Miss Jane Whittington, the grounds of the estate. When I last spoke to our good queen, she told me stories of its beauty and thought my betrothed would appreciate it. We'll be on our way then."

The butler glanced at the card again. "Do wait, my lord. His Grace would not want me to turn you away. Please step inside, and I'll tell the duke of your visit."

"How kind of you!" William said.

Jane wished the floor would swallow her.

When they stepped inside the great hall, she looked up to see the ceiling painted in fresco two stories over her head. All the accents were in white and gold, with gold velvet curtains bracketing two-story windows. A massive staircase rose from the center and curved as it flowed up to the first floor.

The butler led them to the left. "If you would wait in the drawing room, please."

They were shown into a long room that ran the length of one wing of the house, scattered with sofas and chairs and ornate tables, and hung with landscapes and portraits so close together they almost overlapped. With a bow, the butler withdrew.

Jane stared about herself, and then directly at William. "Lord Chadwick, you have embarrassed me greatly."

"I have done no such thing. I merely proclaimed myself a tourist, graciously insisted I didn't want to intrude, then allowed the good butler to insist otherwise. Now isn't this house splendid?"

"You had to use the queen's name to get what you wanted. Deception does not become you." She strode away from him toward the window, staring unseeingly out at the countryside shrouded with a misty rain. He followed, but she didn't realize how closely until he spoke.

"I assure you I am not lying, Jane," he murmured, his breath fanning warmly across her skin.

She stiffened when she felt his lips on the nape of her neck, just below the edge of her bonnet. The soft, moist pressure sent an unwelcome shiver through her. He was trying to distract her. "Lord Chadwick—"

The opening of the doors interrupted her lecture. They turned to find an imposing man striding toward them. He was well into his forties, not tall, but broad through the torso. He had the regal face of a born peer, with a slightly crooked nose, as if he'd been more physical in his youth.

"Lord Chadwick?" he said, his smile guarded, yet interested.

William bowed.

"I am Kelthorpe. Welcome to Langley Manor."

"Your Grace, allow me to present my betrothed, Miss Jane Whittington, daughter of Viscount Whittington."

As the duke took her hand, she sank into a deep curtsy, murmured, "Your Grace," and was relieved to see he was still smiling when she arose.

"It is a pleasure to meet you both. Higgins told me of your wish to view the grounds."

Jane spoke before William could. "We did not realize you were in residence, Your Grace. Please forgive us for intruding."

"It is no intrusion. In fact, I've heard much about you recently in London, Chadwick, and I see this as a good opportunity to know you better. Do you have plans for the next few days?"

Only through great effort did Jane keep her eyes from widening further with each word from the duke. He'd heard about William, a man made into a baron for some mysterious reason by the queen? The duke and Queen Victoria were cousins, she was given to understand. And now he wanted them to stay for what was obviously a house party?

"Your Grace," William said affably, "we have no wish to impose upon you."

"But I wish it. I have plenty of room, and I'm certain you'll know several of the guests." He turned his bright blue eyes on Jane. "Miss Whittington, will you stay?"

She could have groaned aloud at the delay, but all she said was, "You are so kind, Your

Grace. Thank you for the invitation, and I accept it with a glad heart."

Almost immediately, a maid was leading her away, and she heard the butler call to Mr. Barlow about driving the carriage around to the back. She was shown to a spacious bedroom that overlooked a sloping lawn leading down to a maze of trimmed hedges. Her trunks arrived quickly, and when she admitted that her own maid had taken ill, a lady's maid was sent up to assist her in preparing for dinner that evening.

The last of her anger with William faded away as she lay soaking in a sunken tub in the bathing chamber connected to her room. Ah, such luxury, to have individual bathing chambers for guests!

At seven o'clock, a maid came to guide Jane through the intricate corridors to the drawing room. At the entrance off the great hall, the maid left her with a smile, and Jane found her breathing shaky. She had never had reason to feel inferior to anyone, and she refused to start now, she chided herself. Her green silk gown brought out the color of her eyes, and although it was plainer than several of the gowns she would likely see tonight, it was not out of fashion. For once, her sister Charlotte had been right about the gowns she should bring.

When she stepped into the room, about two dozen people stood and sat in various clusters talking. She saw William speaking with the duke before the windows. As she debated whether to join them, a woman of her own age approached. She was the typical English beauty of golden hair and creamy skin, but her smile was generous as she took Jane's hand.

"You must be Miss Whittington. I am Lady Harriet Irving, acting as hostess for my brother. I regret that I wasn't here to greet you this afternoon."

Jane curtsied. "It is a pleasure to meet you, my lady. I hope our arrival is not an inconvenience for you."

"Nonsense. There are plenty of bedchambers in this old house. And I can deny my brother nothing, as he is practically a father to me. Do you know His Grace?"

"We have never met before today."

"But he knows of your betrothed. I am glad they had the chance to meet. Come, I will introduce you to the rest of our guests."

Jane spent the next half hour strolling from group to group with Lady Harriet. In general, people were kind, and only a few felt themselves superior enough to look down upon her in an obvious manner. She was relieved to realize she knew several of the guests.

As she conversed, she could not help glancing occasionally at William, elegantly garbed in formal black eveningwear. He spent a long time talking to the duke, and then His Grace introduced William to another group of men. She found herself tensing, waiting for their amusement over whatever foolish things William spouted in company. But when they eventually left one by one, they said nothing that might offend their host.

When William was finally alone, Jane excused herself and approached him. He gave her a smile so wicked that it heated her blood, even as she hoped no one else saw it.

"Lord Chadwick," she murmured, bowing her head briefly.

"Jane," he answered back.

She narrowed her eyes at him in cool disapproval.

"How can I go back to calling you Miss Whittington, when I've kissed that pouting mouth?"

"I beg your pardon!" she said angrily—softly.

He reached for her gloved hand and brought it to his lips. "Now Jane," he murmured against the cloth, "people are watching."

She understood that, but she was appalled to realize she was more concerned with the heat from his mouth, which spread through her glove to her skin, than their audience. "Then perhaps you should not so obviously display your affection for me."

As he straightened, she removed her hand from his.

"We are engaged, Jane; some leeway is granted us for this alone. Now if we really wanted to seem like everyone else, we would work out a special signal to alert me when to come to your bed."

"Lord Chadwick!" she said reprovingly, while wearing the sweetest smile. Her blood rushed into her face, and it took all her effort not to glance around to see who was close enough to listen. "Please do not insult me, or the duke's guests."

"It was meant as no insult, my dear, except to make you understand that a large number of the guests here will be clandestinely meeting people other than their spouses this night. Watch the way their eyes meet, or the way one person is quick to hand another his candelabra for the night. It is all rather a given at a house party, and something not usually discussed."

"Then don't discuss it." But it would be difficult not to *think* about it when all the guests began to depart for their beds. She gritted her teeth and changed the subject. "You did this deliberately."

"And what did I do now?"

"You were hoping for an invitation to stay at Langley Manor, and you maneuvered until you received one."

He laughed. "Of course I was hoping, after what I'd heard from Queen Victoria. But I had no way of knowing if Kelthorpe would be amenable. To my distinct pleasure, he was."

"But—"

"Jane, can you not share in my excitement? This is surely not something you would ever have dared on your own."

"Of course not," she said slowly, beginning to understand his intent. Did he know he was appealing to her natural inclination for excitement? Or did he merely guess?

"Then that makes it all right."

"Do not pretend you did this just for me, my lord. You are newly arrived to these circles and enjoying the exposure. Although it seems you are not unheard of," she added grudgingly.

He gave her a wink. "Amazing, isn't it?"

"Yet I have not seen my father in several years, and I grow anxious at this delay."

His smile faded. "A delay to visit a ruined castle is permitted because you sanctioned it? A request of mine should not be considered?"

She bit her lip, knowing that she blushed at the truth of his words. "I understand what you're saying, William—"

He leaned closer. "Ah, to hear my name upon your lips."

"My lord—"

"Soon I wish to hear 'William' said upon a sigh of pleasurable satisfaction."

She didn't understand his meaning until she realized that his gaze had dropped to the neckline of her gown, where the upper slopes of her breasts were displayed. She felt a rush of heat and knew she was blushing even there.

"My lord," she began hastily, "I have no wish to treat you unfairly. But this visit could last *days*, whereas this afternoon I asked for only several hours."

"Treat this weekend as a chance to explore unfamiliar countryside safe within sight of your intended."

She frowned at him. "Are you saying that I can do nothing without you?"

"I am responsible for you, dearest Jane, and I can't allow anything to happen to you."

"You've made the duke responsible for me this weekend, my lord. He can see to my welfare while I visit the attractions near his estate."

"*On* his estate," William countered. "And accompanied by me."

As she opened her mouth to protest, a bell rang for dinner. Smiling, she put her hand on William's arm and spoke through gritted teeth. "We have much to settle, my lord."

"So you say," he answered back, then followed the organized procession into dinner.

When the evening was over, Jane felt embarrassed when William insisted on walking her to her door. Did the other guests assume they would now spend the night together?

"I know where the room is," she insisted in a low voice, as the ladies farther down the hall glanced back at them and giggled.

"Of course you do," he said soothingly.

She opened a door and, to her consternation, saw the unfamiliar layout of the room. She quickly closed the door again. She didn't have to look at William to know he was smiling.

The next, identical door was certainly hers. She partially opened it to confirm for herself, then looked up at William.

"Might I have my candle now?"

He loomed over her, the glow of two candles shadowing the lean lines of his face and reflecting in the deep chocolate depths of his eyes. He gave her one candleholder, then leaned past her to push her door wide.

"My lord, what are you doing?" she demanded, glancing frantically around the now-deserted corridor.

"Making sure your room is empty."

Though she would have thought he was playing a joke upon her, his eyes seemed too serious.

"Do you think I harbor a strange man in my room?"

He shrugged. "I'm just keeping you safe, my dear."

Then she felt his hand slide up her back and watched a smile curve his mouth.

"There isn't a maid to help you undress," he murmured. "Shall I—"

"No!" Jane backed through the door. "I'll ring for a maid. Have a good night, my lord."

He caught the door before she could shut it. "William. 'Have a good night, William.' "

"Fine. Of course—William. Have it any way you please, just go away."

As she shut the door, she heard him whisper, "Have it any way I please?"

She turned the lock, heard his laugh and then the sound of footfalls on the carpet as he walked away.

With a groan, Jane pulled the bell cord, lit a few more candles, and then sank onto the chaise at the foot of her bed. Scenes of the evening flashed before her tired eyes. William had been his usual talkative self, but everyone had politely listened. She hadn't thought he was saying anything that anyone should find so important, but for some reason the duke had been interested. And the two of them had had such a long conversation before dinner. She didn't think even William would dare discuss the duke's wardrobe with him.

She wished she could stop her curious nature, but the mystery of William called it to the fore.

After the maid had come and gone, Jane sat at an ornate lady's desk and tried to write in her journal. Surely there was something to tell her father, another tidbit that reflected badly on William. But besides his innovation in securing an invitation from the duke—and somehow she dourly thought that her father would be amused—the only thing Jane could picture in her mind was William's laughing face as he'd played with the children earlier that day. The scene continued to disturb her, because she'd never before wanted a woman's lot in life—until William had made her think of giving him children.

And conceiving them.

She closed her journal with a snap, feeling confused and worried. She should just go to bed.

But even the serenity of sleep was denied her. She woke up several hours later, certain that she'd heard something. When she saw the door to the balcony slightly ajar, she sat up quickly, only to feel a male hand press against her mouth.

Chapter 12

"It's me," William whispered.

Though her heart was beating at an accelerated pace, Jane had not been truly frightened—for who else but William would be so foolish?

He released her, and a moment later she heard a match striking, then saw the soft glow of a candle. He wore trousers and a shirt open at the throat, and he tossed his coat over the chaise as if he'd just removed it.

"What do you think you're doing?" she demanded in a calm, cold voice.

"Visiting you when we can speak more privately." He pulled a chair up near the bed, lounged back and sprawled his legs out before him. "And getting a much better view, I might add."

With a start, she realized the light blankets were pooled at her waist, revealing her nightdress. Calmly, she fluffed her pillows, pulled the covers up to her shoulders, and leaned back. All the while, he watched with an admiring smile, and she wickedly allowed it.

"We'll be disgraced if you're found here," Jane pointed out.

He shrugged. "Then we'll marry sooner rather than later. And as I said earlier, there are several people here more guilty than we are."

He obviously planned to seduce her before their marriage, from the way he was looking at her. Since she found her mind racing back to the last night she'd appeared in her nightclothes alone with him, she had to admit to herself that he was doing a decent job of the seduction. But she wouldn't let it happen.

"And why did you need to speak with me privately, risking your neck on my balcony?"

He grinned. "Concerned about me?"

"Concerned that if you're found unconscious beneath my window, people will think you were climbing back *out.*"

He gave a soft laugh that was warm and far too intimate. "Have no worry, my dear. I am like a cat in the dark."

"So you've had much practice stealing into women's bedrooms?" she asked dryly.

"Honestly, no. But since I was a child, the dark has seemed wonderfully mysterious, and I have spent many a night out exploring. But tonight my only mission is to discuss your plans for tomorrow."

"That is your only mission?" she asked suspiciously. She paused to consider him in the near darkness, where his shirt glistened too whitely. Deep inside her, something new and dangerous stirred to life. "You promise to remain in that chair, and only get up when it is time to walk to the balcony?"

His eyes narrowed. "And if I don't wish to make that promise?"

"Then I will know your true plans for the evening, and you can leave immediately."

He heaved a dramatic sigh. "I promise."

Something came over her, there in the shadowy room with only the one candle flickering at her side. She could see his eyes and teeth glittering as he showed his confidence. She felt like setting him back a pace, like . . . tempting him.

Forcing a yawn, she stretched her arms up and allowed the blankets to fall down to her waist.

His smile faded, and an uneasy silence filled the room. An awareness of the two of them as man and woman glowed inside her. It wasn't right of her to tease him—but she wouldn't stop.

"So you want to know what I have planned for tomorrow," she murmured.

He cleared his throat, and with growing excitement she watched the difficulty with which he raised his gaze back to her face. It wasn't as if he could see anything beneath her nightdress—she was covered up to her neck and down to her wrists.

"Precisely," he answered in a voice that was deeper, huskier, than she was used to.

She shivered and pressed her hand against her stomach. When he leaned forward, she held her breath.

"I can see your nipples tighten right through the fabric."

Her mouth fell open, but she said nothing, did nothing to cover herself. She let him look, and the forbidden thrill of it astonished her.

She ignored his comment and answered his question. "William, I am attending whatever outing the ladies choose to amuse themselves."

"Not hunting."

"No. Is that what the men are doing? And you will be attending?"

"I don't hunt," he said shortly, his gaze still below her face.

"You don't?" This distracted her. "I thought all men enjoyed the hunt."

"I kill for food, not for sport." One corner of his mouth turned up. "It seems rather unfair to use guns to chase animals for no reason."

"I've always thought the same," she said, astonished that they agreed on something.

"But I will fish, as you already know, because at least the fish can decide for themselves whether to take my worm or not."

Will watched her laugh, and the rare sight struck him hard with pleasure and gratification. Her laughter was full and unrestrained, with a throatiness that made him shudder. This night she was brimming with a spontaneity he'd never seen in her before. She was a vision lying in bed, her long black hair in silken darkness about her shoulders and across the pillow. Her eyes sparkled with mischief, and a smile was constantly teasing her lips. Although her nightdress was not as sheer as he would insist it be when they were married, the fabric was soft enough that he could see her pointed breasts, and imagine much more.

Suddenly she pulled the covers aside. "It's hot this evening, isn't it?"

Though his mouth fell open, he could say nothing. She was covered down to her ankles, but her slim feet were an erotic sight.

She smiled. "You were saying something about fishing?"

He cleared his throat again and struggled to remember the warning he'd wanted to give. "I might fish tomorrow, if they ask me to. Please remain with the ladies, and don't wander off alone."

"But what if the ladies aren't doing anything I wish to do?"

She swung her legs over the edge of the bed and stood up. Will's mouth dried as he watched the fabric sway, then drape over her curves. She was so close. If he lifted a hand he would touch her. Then he realized he hadn't promised not to.

He caught her nightdress in his hand and slowly pulled her between his knees though she resisted. "I won't have you wandering off, Jane. Promise me."

He heard her breath come in little gasps, saw the quick rise and fall of her breasts just before his face. His thighs touched hers, then tightened.

"William—" Her voice carried a warning.

"I've not left the chair. Promise me you'll remain with the other women."

"I can't."

"Can't what? Can't kiss me? Can't touch me?"

When she put her hands on his shoulders, he felt her trembling.

"I can't promise that I'll remain with the others." She took his chin in her hand and raised it so their eyes met. "I am often so bored by what women of the *ton* do."

This bothered him more than he cared to admit, and a sudden realization worried him even as it made sense: Jane behaved much like his younger self—a feminine version, of course. There was a restlessness in her, just beneath the surface, a longing for something different.

But that wasn't what he wanted anymore. He wanted a wife, a home, children, all normal in every respect. It had taken him years to learn his lessons of loneliness in the hard school of foreign service.

Yet . . . a normal woman wouldn't be deliberately tempting him like this. Though her boldness fired his blood, he would have to show her that only within their bedroom could she give herself such free rein.

She pushed away from him, and he reluctantly let her go.

"Why do you care what I do here, William?"

"You're under my protection, and I don't want anything to happen to you." And he himself was putting her in danger by agreeing to help Nick Wright.

She walked slowly toward the balcony doors. "You've said this before, yet you have not explained what the danger could be, here at Langley Manor with a household full of people."

It was as if she read his mind. She opened the door and leaned against the frame, staring out. Will wanted to go to her, to see her by starlight. But he'd promised to remain in the damned chair.

"The world is full of danger, Jane, and you are too naïve to see it. There are men here who look at you as—"

"As you do?"

"Perhaps, but those men won't remain bound to a chair because of a woman's promise."

She tilted her head to look at him, and the fall

of her hair across her breasts wrenched a groan from him. With quick steps she was at his side.

"Is something wrong?" she whispered, touching his face again.

He turned and pressed his mouth into her palm, then spoke against her skin. "Even I am hard put to honor my promise."

She pulled her hand back but didn't move away.

"I won't trust another man to ignore the temptation of your beauty."

She suddenly went still, then whispered sadly, "You use words for your own purpose, William. You're good at that."

"You think I'm twisting the truth? Can you not imagine what you look like to me by candle-light, wearing so little, your eyes saying so much? Your laughter tonight was as erotic to me as a kiss. The thought of waiting to touch you until we're married is the purest form of torture."

"You wave about these future vows of mar-riage, but you don't trust me to keep myself oc-cupied while you're gone. You're keeping secrets from me, yet you want everything a woman can give, without the trust that's so much a part of it."

How had his secrets become apparent—and made him so vulnerable? He'd always been able to fool everyone. But not her—not his Jane, with her cool intellect on display, and hot passion beneath the surface.

"If you want me to trust you," she continued, "then tell me why we're here. Saying that we're here to see the estate just doesn't make sense. It's not as if it's for sale. What did you and the duke talk about?"

For the first time Will wanted to tell her everything, to unburden himself, but he worried that the danger would be too much for her. He couldn't know how she'd react—and frankly, he didn't want his wife ever to be a part of his other life, the life he so wanted to leave behind.

"We discussed the people he knew and the people he thought I need to know as a peer," he offered. "We discussed things related to the queen, but again, I can't talk about that."

She whirled away from him toward the bed. "I am patient, William, but this secrecy about the queen is haunting me. What have you done that makes everyone want to reward you?"

He could only lean forward, his hands braced on his knees. "I know you want my trust—you have it as far as I can give it. Give me yours, Jane. Say to my face that you'll be my wife."

But she said nothing, only climbed back into bed and pulled the blankets up to her chin. "Go back to your room, William," she said with evident tiredness. "We'll talk in the morning."

"I might be gone with the men by the time you arise."

"Then we'll talk later."

He hesitated, wanting again to extract promises from her, knowing she wouldn't give them. He sighed. "Am I free to leave the chair?"

"Yes." She rolled onto her side away from him. "Good night."

For another minute, Will watched her, then he walked out onto the balcony and closed the door behind him. After an uneventful journey back to his room, he removed his clothing and got into bed.

And stared at the shadowy ceiling.

It was a familiar ritual since he'd returned to England. Visiting Jane had at least enlivened the dreariness of his insomnia. Perhaps when they were married, and he could make love to her whenever he wished, he'd sleep better.

Killer commenced a sudden furious barking next to the bed. Will leaned over and lifted the dog up. He tossed a pillow to the end of the bed, and with a grumble, Killer turned in circles on it, then curled up and began to snore almost immediately. Will sighed and looked back at the ceiling.

Keeping secrets from Jane was becoming far too difficult. She was asking pointed questions he couldn't answer. Truthfully, he and the duke had mostly spoken of people they knew and the current political climate. But it was obvious the duke knew something of Will's past, because he'd asked questions about the military situation in India and what it was like to live there. When Will had asked him not to speak of his past with others, the duke had already known that secrecy was necessary. He was obviously not only a cousin but also an intimate confidant of the queen. It was imperative that the duke not marry a traitor.

But it wasn't Will's job to tell him the truth about Julia Reed without proof. Yet now that he was on easier terms with Kelthorpe, he could begin to subtly question him.

But what to do about Jane? Will could insist she go fishing with him again, and he could keep an eye on her every moment of the day. But he sensed that that would not go over well.

He did not want to lose what ground he'd already gained with her. Her deliberate temptress act tonight had been a welcome revelation that he wanted to encourage.

So he would trust her to follow his wishes—and trust the duke's security.

When Jane awoke at dawn, she stretched and turned her head to look out the brightening curtains. It had taken her a long time to fall asleep after her wanton behavior with William. Even now she shivered with renewed amazement at how close she'd almost come to falling into his arms and letting him do what he would with her.

She had never before felt power over a man, the ability to make him desire her. It had made her feel exuberant and daring as he'd sat in that chair watching her. She wanted to feel more of these sensations, to give into an excitement she'd never imagined.

Ever since her debut four years before, she had never minced words with a suitor, or only spoken of the weather or the Season. A woman with opinions of her own drove off many a man.

But not William.

And it frightened, yet fascinated, her.

After washing and dressing, she went down to the breakfast parlor and found only men milling around at the sideboard of food, or seated at the long, linen-draped table. When they all stood up immediately upon seeing her, she smiled and nodded, and they all went back to eating and talking.

Except William. He gave her a slow, intimate smile, using his dimples to their full advantage. Even her breathing seemed arrested, and she wished he did not affect her so. He was wearing a waist-length frock coat with small tails, surely for riding, but its practicality could not hide the fact that it made his shoulders seem quite broad, and his hips trim. Above high riding boots, he wore his trousers fashionably snug as usual. She quickly slid her gaze from that area. He walked to her, took her hands and kissed the backs.

"My dearest Jane," he murmured in a soft

voice. "If it helps, I much preferred your previous garment."

Smiling, she shook her head. "And would you have me wear my night clothes before all of your new friends?"

His grin turned wolfish. "Such a sight is for my eyes only. If any man here saw you like that, I would have to kill him."

She deliberately widened her eyes. "I cannot believe a gentleman such as yourself knows anything about dueling."

"Are you questioning my manly skills?" he asked with playful affront.

She hesitated, glancing at his mouth. "You might have *some*."

Jane was appalled with herself—was she actually *flirting* with him, this man she didn't want to marry? Before she could back away and distance herself, the Duke of Kelthorpe joined them. She curtsied, and he nodded.

"Good day, Miss Whittington. Your Lord Chadwick was just wondering if he would see you this morning before we departed. And by the look on his face, I can tell that your presence has cheered his day."

Jane dipped her head and tried not to show her skepticism. She'd sooner believe William only wanted to remind her again not to stray from the manor. He always tried to exert his power over her, and his surprising charm was hard to resist.

"You are too kind, Your Grace," she said.

"Watching the two of you eases my own marriage concerns."

"You're getting married, Your Grace?"

William spoke a bit too quickly, she thought with curiosity. Why should he care?

The duke laughed. "Nothing official to report yet, but the possibility is strengthening. Miss Whittington, have a pleasant morning. Chadwick, I'll see you outside."

Silently, William stood beside her and gazed after the duke. Although William still wore a smile, his eyes seemed . . . distant, preoccupied.

Jane studied him. "I wonder which lucky young lady has caught his attention."

"She's not here this weekend," he answered in an absent fashion, his attention still on the duke.

"You know her?"

William's eyes focused on her. "I'm not certain. The duke only mentioned that the woman he was interested in probably wouldn't be joining us. And if she were here, don't you think they would be together? He didn't favor any lady except his sister last evening."

His smile brightened, and he nodded toward the sideboard crowded with steaming tureens. "Can I fetch you breakfast? It is much too arduous a task for a delicate lady such as yourself."

Her smile was reluctant but inevitable. "You don't know my preferences."

"Then I'll stand here and hold your plate, keeping very close eye on your favorite foods. I'll memorize them, of course, in preparation for tomorrow's breakfast."

She bit her lip to hide her laughter. It was becoming far too easy for him to make her smile. She allowed him to wait on her because it was easier than making a scene. He ate his own breakfast seated next to her, and he kept trying to make her laugh by whispering about certain men in the room and why their garments spoke volumes about them.

When it was time for the hunters to leave, William left the breakfast parlor, then came back a few minutes later with Killer in the crook of his elbow.

"Is that dog going on the hunt?" demanded Lord Dudley, a man whom Jane couldn't help but notice the previous evening, when he'd often drowned out any other conversation at the dinner table. "I don't want him upsetting my dog."

"I'm not hunting today, so neither is Killer," William called as the large group worked its way toward the front door. Then he smiled. "You brought your own hound?"

Lord Dudley's mustache twitched as he talked. "I brought several. They're all rare breeds, specially trained for the various sports." He eyed William slyly. "Not hunting, eh? Don't trust your skills?"

"You need all that much skill to follow your dog to a frightened little fox?"

Jane shared an amused glance with William, feeling a kinship she hadn't thought possible. Killer growled and shook the floppy fur out of his eyes. For once, she almost wanted to defend the little dog.

Lord Dudley eyed William's pet. "What sort of name is Killer for that rat? You need a real dog to hunt."

William drew on his gloves, and Jane followed him through the great hall toward the front door. "As I said before, I'm not hunting, but fishing. Wish me luck."

Lord Dudley rudely shouldered his way past them out the door.

Jane followed the rest of the men across the portico and out onto the graveled front drive, where grooms held the reins of at least a dozen horses. There were hounds baying in the distance, and she squinted to see the huntsmen lead them out into the fields, toward a far stand of trees. The sun felt warm, and the air was heavy with the oddly matched smells of horses and roses.

She watched from the front stairs as William walked to a groom who carried fishing tackle.

Glancing back at her, William said, "Are you sure you wouldn't like to join me, Miss Whittington? Hunting cannot hold a candle to the gentlemanly sport of fishing."

Several men around him snorted and rolled their eyes, but it was mostly good-natured teasing.

"I think not, Lord Chadwick. I have several letters to write. I'll see you at luncheon."

With a shrug, he found a horse and swung up into the saddle. The groom put the fishing tackle into a saddlebag, and William tucked the pole under his left arm and settled Killer there as well. Then with a last wave at her, he guided the horse about and rode off with the other men.

Jane wasn't sure what she'd expected of his horsemanship, for a non-hunting man not born into the nobility. He would at least be adequate in the saddle. Yet she found herself amazed at the effortless way he moved as one with the animal, with a physical masculinity that quite . . . overwhelmed her. The day seemed suddenly too warm, almost tempting her to fan her face.

She was disturbed by these feelings she couldn't name, this confusion that clouded her mind when she thought of William Chadwick. Where was the dislike she'd had for him just a week ago? Now he made her laugh, and she found it wasn't so arduous to be in his company.

Surely the mysteries surrounding him were all that interested her.

Jane went back inside the manor, where only servants moved about, performing their duties. Since it was not even eight o'clock, the other ladies had yet to rise. Feeling restless, yet determined to make the best of the situation, she went into the library, sat down at one of the many small desks scattered about the immense book-lined room, and began a letter to her mother.

To relieve the boredom, she willingly went with the other ladies to picnic with the men at noontime. While eating lobster mousse and salmon soufflés, she listened to the recitation of who jumped what hedge, who fell from his horse where, and which hound cornered the fox. When the bragging was over, William did his best to amuse her, but his restrictions limiting her weekend were beginning to fray her temper. She felt rebellious at the thought of playing card games with the ladies for the afternoon. But at least there was a new distraction when the women returned to the manor.

Lady Harriet, the duke's sister, who had remained behind instead of attending the luncheon, found Jane as the other women were dispersing through the household. She held the arm of someone Jane hadn't seen before. The woman was tall and robust, with hair so blond as to be almost white, and a frank, easy smile that seemed refreshing after being with so many timid, proper young ladies.

"Miss Whittington," Lady Harriet said, "this is Miss Julia Reed, the woman who might bring my brother to the altar."

Chapter 13

Jane shook hands with Miss Reed. "A pleasure to meet you."

Lady Harriet smiled. "Miss Reed, this is Miss Jane Whittington, one of my brother's guests. Her intended is Lord Chadwick. Do you know of him?"

Miss Reed shook her head. "No, but that is not unusual. Before this past year, I'd been gone from England for much of the time."

Lady Harriet gave a sad sigh. "She never even had a true Season until this year!"

"And I was far too old for that," Miss Reed scolded with obvious fondness.

Lady Harriet only waved her hand. "Every girl deserves a Season. Miss Reed's brother was in the military in India, and she spent much of her life there. Can you imagine?"

Jane found herself studying the newcomer with interest. "I find that quite fascinating, Miss Reed. I've always wanted to travel extensively, but never thought I'd be able to manage visiting so remote a country. I would enjoy talking to you about it."

Miss Reed smiled. "I must admit, Miss Whittington, you are the first lady to say such a thing to me. My brother, General Reed, warned me that our unusual lifestyle would not be a favorite topic among ladies, and he was correct."

"Then *I'll* warn you that you'll have to stop my questions when you're tired of them."

Lady Harriet looked bemused. "It is a shame you'll only be with us two nights, Miss Reed. It is far too little time to become well acquainted with Miss Whittington and the rest of our guests."

"It is tempting to stay, but I must leave on family business," Miss Reed said with a sigh.

Jane happily recognized the opportunity for an educating conversation. "Miss Reed, after you've refreshed yourself, would you perhaps like to walk about the grounds with me?"

The woman smiled. "That sounds lovely. Just let me change out of my traveling clothes."

"Please take your time, Miss Reed. I'll be waiting in the library."

* * *

When Will returned to Langley Manor, he changed clothes, dropped Killer into a tired heap on his bed, and then went to find Jane. She wasn't in the library, where several women were reading or writing, nor was she in the drawing room, where women were playing cards. He found Lady Harriet there and waited until she'd played her hand before speaking to her.

"Lady Harriet, have you seen Miss Whittington?"

She glanced from him to the other three ladies, who all tried to hide their smiles. "Lord Chadwick, you are so obviously enamored of your betrothed that it is a wonder you went with the men at all today."

"It wouldn't do for Miss Whittington to think I want to spend all my time with her." He lowered his voice. "Even if it's the truth."

Several of the women sighed and glanced at each other with approval.

Lady Harriet gave him a fond smile, a very wise one for someone of her young years. "Miss Whittington went for a stroll with our newest guest. Perhaps my brother mentioned Miss Reed to you?"

For a moment, Will found himself simply blinking at the girl. "Miss Reed?"

"Miss Julia Reed. She and the duke have an . . . understanding."

Several of the women giggled and leaned together to whisper.

He forced a polite smile, while his heart began to beat at a more rapid pace. He did not quite understand what he was feeling, for he was unused to the sensation, but it must be—panic.

Jane had gone off with Julia Reed, a traitor to England, and a woman who thought nothing of causing the deaths of thousands of people.

As he bowed and took his leave of the ladies, a distant part of him wondered where his cool head had gone. Even under threat of certain death, he'd always felt a calm fatalism: if he was meant to die, it would happen, so why bother worrying?

Julia Reed didn't know Jane and had no reason to harm her—especially not at the home of her future husband. He should not have this strange sensation of panic, this feeling that his throat was too tight to swallow.

But—my God, he'd endangered Jane already.

The grounds of Langley Manor stretched out for dozens of acres. There were glades of rhododendrons, magnolia and camellia, and off in the distance was a pavilion for daytime luncheons and evening dancing. Will discovered a maze, and although he called Jane's name into the shrubbery, he received no answer. At a meadow where several women were playing croquet, he finally heard that Miss Whittington and Miss Reed had been seen walking toward the archery fields behind the orchard.

Archery fields? Will's strides lengthened.

When he rounded the bend of an ornamental pond with a wooded glade at one end, he saw two women far to his right at the end of a field. To his left, round archery targets were set up. He saw Jane's sunny yellow gown and heard a sudden burst of her rare laughter. Feeling foolish, he slowed his pace and approached the field.

Although Jane was not a small woman, Julia Reed was almost half a head taller and of a more solid build. She held the bow with a competency that made her look like a woman who could defend herself. Jane let fly with her own arrow, which hit the lower edge of the target. Julia responded, but Will was not quite close enough to hear what they were saying.

As Julia smiled and brought her bow up to aim, there was a sudden gunshot, and she jerked her bow to the left. Will flung himself to the side and felt a stinging blow across his arm. He tumbled, then rolled to his feet in a crouched position.

"Get down!" he yelled, and the gaping women dropped to their knees. "All the way!" He motioned with his hand until they were on their stomachs.

The shot had come from the right of the archery field, where the meadow sloped down to a brook. Small copses of trees lined the bank, and Will thought he saw movement between the branches. Staying as low to the ground as possible, he ran toward the brook, startling a flock of pheasants. As the crack of another gunshot made Will flinch, Lord Dudley strolled out into the open, shielding his eyes from the sun as he followed the flight of the pheasants. A gun was draped over his arm, its barrel pointing to the ground.

He saw Will and gestured victoriously to the sky. "I got one! Too bad your rat's not here to fetch it, eh?"

Feeling a murderous rage he seldom allowed himself to express, Will ran toward Dudley, who stumbled back.

At the last moment, Will stopped himself from breaking the man's jaw. "Do you know how close you are to the manor?" he shouted. "Someone could have been killed!"

"I was aiming at the sky," Dudley said belligerently, then his eyes widened. "Are you bleeding?"

Surprised, Will looked down at his left arm and found a narrow bloodstain soaking through from his upper arm to his elbow.

"It couldn't have been me!"

"You startled the women, and one of their arrows hit me."

Will turned when he heard the rustle of long skirts trailing across the grass.

"William!" Jane cried, staring wide-eyed at his wound. "Were you shot?"

"It was my arrow. Please forgive me." Miss

Reed's healthy complexion had gone pale—quite a nice touch in her arsenal of disguises.

Will gave her a brief nod.

"It wasn't me," Dudley said smugly.

Will turned on him, and his expression made the man fall back. "Get that gun up to the house. If I find you shooting anywhere near here again, I'll make sure the duke knows about your stupidity."

Dudley stomped past them, and Will thought he heard, "Coward."

He ignored it and reached for Jane's hand. "Are you all right?"

"I'm fine. You're the one who's injured. Come up to the house so we can look at your arm."

"Do forgive me," Julia said again. "Shall I have Kelthorpe send for a physician?"

Will turned and really looked at her for the first time. Though several years older than Jane, she was a healthy, good-looking woman whose startlingly blue eyes were very direct. Did those eyes look cold as glaciers when she betrayed her country?

"There's no need for a physician. It was an accident," he said, though he could not stop the suspicions clouding his thoughts. "You've drawn blood, and we haven't even been properly introduced yet."

She smiled, and the stiffness left her shoulders as she offered her hand as confidently as any man. "I'm Miss Julia Reed."

"And I am Lord Chadwick, Miss Whittington's betrothed."

"Ah yes, Lady Harriet mentioned you," Julia said, turning to glance at Jane, "but we haven't discussed all the details."

Jane blushed. "I've been too busy pestering Julia about her life in India."

Will's smile remained normal only out of habit. They were on a first-name basis already—and talking about India?

He couldn't leave Langley Manor soon enough.

He had to get a message to Nick, telling him what was going on. He was debating making their departure this evening when Jane stepped closer and touched his arm.

"Does this hurt?" she asked, concern causing a furrow in her brow. "We must control the bleeding."

He stopped himself from saying he'd had worse. "I can move the arm just fine. I'm sure it's barely worth your worry."

Julia took Jane's bow. "And here I've been chatting on about your betrothal. Do take your young man back to the house and see him bandaged, Jane. I'll put the equipment away."

Your young man, he thought, knowing he must have at least five years on her. With a bow toward Julia, he led Jane back to Langley Manor. They remained quiet for several minutes, though he saw her frowning occasionally at his arm.

They could have avoided all this if Jane had just listened to him and not wandered the grounds without him. Perhaps his anger was all out of proportion to the incident, but hell, she'd been giggling with one of England's most treacherous enemies!

At the rear of the house, he drew her aside by the elbow and entered a greenhouse. Immediately a humid, musty smell assaulted them. Ferns trailed wetly through his hair as he guided Jane down a row to a less overgrown area. The sun beat down, amplified through the glass.

"William, this is no time to look at flowers," Jane said, trying to pull away from him. "You could bleed to death!"

He turned her about and caught her by the upper arms. "Jane, I distinctly remember telling you that you could not wander off without me."

Her green eyes went wide. "You can't possibly be angry. I stayed on the grounds, and I didn't go anywhere alone. I was perfectly safe."

He wanted to shake her, but she struggled, so he let her go. He felt wildly angry with himself for putting her in danger, then he was overcome by an overpowering need to never let her out of his sight again.

She turned away from him and reached to

gently touch the blossom of an exotic flower—
and then he recognized it as a gloriosa lily native to India. He thought of a garden he'd
visited just outside of Bombay, and how he'd
longed for someone to share in its tropical
beauty. He'd never feel alone again as long as
Jane was with him.

All his confusing emotions crystallized into
one he could understand—his stark need for
her. He came up behind her, let his chest touch
her back. She stiffened but didn't move away.
He put his hands on her narrow waist, leaned
down to press his lips between her neck and
shoulder.

"I can imagine you in the hot climate of India,
where lilies grow in abundance," he said, his
voice a hoarse whisper.

He licked behind her ear, and she shuddered.

"They would cushion you as I push you
down to the earth and follow, covering you—"

"William," she breathed, leaning back against
him. "You mustn't say such things. And how do
you know what India is like?"

He tilted her chin so that she faced him over
her shoulder.

A breath away from her lips, he whispered,
"I'm well read."

And then he kissed her, one hand on her
throat, the other pressing flat against her stomach to hold her against his hips. She tasted like
sunshine and lemonade, the sweetest combina-

tion, and he licked her as if he could steal a precious drop. He tasted the curve of her top lip, the pouting fullness of the lower, then thrust deep inside, pressing her head back so he could reach as deeply as possible.

Jane trembled and groaned, unashamed of vocalizing how William made her feel. The shock of seeing his blood had done something to her, made her realize that a frightening bond was forming between them. She didn't want to see him hurt. She kissed him back with fervor, letting her tongue explore the depths of his mouth like she hadn't done before, all so she wouldn't have to think about what she felt for him. Her hands were restless, and she finally settled them over his fingers where they rested low on her stomach. She could feel the pressure through her petticoats, just above her pubic bone. She was hot and shaky all over, and then he did something else that drove her to distraction.

William slid his hand down her neck and teased along what she had thought was a proper neckline. She would never have guessed that skin could burn with a torment that made her press even closer to him. She tried to turn into his arms, but he held her still, then dipped the tips of his fingers beneath the fabric. She sagged in his embrace and finally broke from their kiss.

"William—no. Please stop."

He licked along the nape of her neck, leaving

a moist path that tingled as he breathed on it. "You didn't like it?"

"Not like—" She gasped, then clutched his hand as he started to move it lower on her stomach. "That hardly matters. We are in a very public place."

As if to prove her words, somewhere in the distance a door opened and closed. William's arms loosened, and with regret she stepped away from him. Lifting her chin, she called on her bravery as she turned to face him. He was watching her with heavy-lidded eyes, and his mouth was wet like hers. She started to wipe her hand across her lips, but he caught her fingers in one hand. Gently, he dabbed her lips with his handkerchief, and she thought her heart would pound out of her chest at so tender a gesture.

He suddenly frowned. "I think there's blood on your gown."

"Blood—" And then she remembered. "I can't believe we've been kissing while you've been bleeding. Come with me this instant."

She caught his hand, pulled him back down the row the way they'd come, pushed open the door and went outside. When they were within sight of the manor windows, she released him.

"Are you coming?" she asked.

"As long as I can watch your hips, I'll follow you anywhere."

She found herself smiling. When they went in the front door, the house seemed quiet, with everyone in their rooms resting or preparing for a late dinner. She asked a passing maid for some cloth William could use for bandages. After assuring the girl that everything was all right, Jane instructed that hot water, as well as bandages, be sent to his room.

She looked up at an amused William. "Lead me to your room," she said briskly after the maid had gone.

He took her arm and leaned down to grin at her. "Now that is what I like to hear."

She shook her head and reluctantly smiled. "You are incorrigible."

"And that's why I'm so perfect to marry."

She turned away, her smile fading as she realized with dismay she didn't immediately disagree. As they walked up a flight of stairs into the bachelors' wing, she imagined herself on a small country estate, forever seeing the same horizon, the same faces. How could she bear the boredom?

But then she thought of the nights lying in his arms, feeling the pleasure she was only just beginning to recognize. How would she feel, never experiencing his touch again?

Chapter 14

In the corridor outside William's room, Jane hesitated and glanced about. She almost hoped someone would appear to stop her, for she knew she wouldn't stop herself.

He opened the door, took her hand, and pulled her inside. She froze, looking around at her first view of a man's room. It was not all that different from hers—darker colors and less decorative scrollwork on the wood furnishings.

Behind her, she heard the door shut.

She made herself look at his bed. It was the place he slept—there was no reason to blush, and she didn't. Then she saw that he was watching her, and she realized he could be misreading her intentions.

Clearing her throat, she drew herself up and coolly said, "Please remove your coat."

His eyes were full of laughter, but he did as she asked. She pushed him onto a chair by the desk, looking at the blood that stained his white shirt. There was a rip through the fabric on his upper left arm.

She touched the area gently and frowned. "The blood has begun to dry your shirt against the wound. I don't wish to rip it off and start the bleeding again. We'll have to wait for the water and bandages."

He folded his hands across his stomach, stretched out those long legs, and then simply watched her. Jane turned away and found a chair beside the balcony doors. She perched on the edge to look outside.

"Miss Reed seems like a decent person," William finally said into the awkward silence.

She glanced at him. "I found her to be quite fascinating."

"Why?"

He was studying her a bit too intently, and she frowned. "Why? I don't understand you. I have made a new acquaintance—must there be another reason?"

"I was just making conversation, Jane." His voice lowered, as did his gaze. "We don't have to talk at all, if you don't wish to. There are . . . other things we could do."

With only those words, he made her remember the fevered humidity of the greenhouse, the way his hips had pressed into hers from behind, the taste of his mouth.

"You're blushing," he murmured.

"And you are behaving in a decidedly ungentlemanly fashion."

"Then talk to me about Miss Reed. Why was she so late to arrive?"

"She did not say," Jane answered. "But she can't stay long because she has family business to attend to. I understand she'll be leaving the day after tomorrow."

"Lady Harriet told me that she spent most of her life in India."

Jane tried to relax back in her chair. "It seems very exciting to me, but Julia insists that society is much the same there as here. The British upper classes keep to themselves, do they not? Such a shame."

"Is that her sentiment or yours?"

"Both, I think. She seems to have great regard for people of all classes. She even had an Indian tutor."

"Did she spend all of her time in India?"

"No, she was in Afghanistan for over a year, with her brother's army," she said, leaning toward him. "I had so many more questions, but she was also trying to improve my use of the bow, and then there was the gunshot."

William tilted his head as if studying her. "It sounds as if you envy her."

"Envy?" She found it hard to meet his gaze. "No. But she has done things in her life that I find fascinating, that I wish I could do."

"Such excitement is not all it seems, my dear. There is much hardship, especially in the places Miss Reed has mentioned. Do not romanticize her life."

"Do you think I'm that foolish?" she asked, allowing her temper to show. "Do you think I imagine the entire world is exactly like my life in England?"

"I did not say that."

"Why are you threatened by the things I might want to do with my life?"

"I am not threatened, Jane, but I am realistic."

"And I am not?" She got to her feet and stalked toward him. "Do you think it so impossible for a woman to travel and find the kind of excitement a man seems to think he's entitled to?"

"And what of your family's wishes—your husband's wishes?"

He, too, stood up, and she wondered if he meant to overwhelm her with the differences in their height and strength.

"I don't have a husband, yet, do I?" she said coldly.

William blinked, his face impassive. There was a sudden soft knock on the door.

"That will be the maid," he said.

"I will stand over here by the fireplace." She walked away from him.

"Hiding?"

His voice held a subtle taunt, and she folded her arms over her chest in defiance. "I am not ashamed of my conduct."

"And I don't wish you to be either. But at least that position will keep you out of the line of sight from the door."

She almost stalked into the center of the room just to disobey him, but she didn't need the servants gossiping about them. He opened the door, took a basin of steaming water and a bundle of linens from someone, then shut the door with his foot.

Jane took the basin before he spilled it, and they both set everything down on a chest of drawers near the washstand. Without saying a word, she pointed to the chair, and he sat back down. After pouring hot water into the basin on the washstand, she dipped the towel in, then pressed it against his wound. He inhaled but said nothing.

"No complaints?" she asked.

"I like the water temperature of my baths hot. How do you like yours?"

"That is none of your concern." She repeatedly dampened his shirt, then gradually pulled the fabric away from his wound. "No worries about the ruination of this fine shirt? I wonder if there is a tailor in the village who can handle such emergencies."

William lifted an eyebrow and smiled, then he began to unbutton his shirt. "I assume you are spoiling for a fight so you won't have to think about how we feel when we're alone together."

Before she could disabuse him of that fantasy, he slid his arm out of his sleeve, keeping himself covered. She wondered why, for he hardly seemed like he worried about her sensibilities. But then he bared just his arm, and anything else she had meant to say went right out of her head. He had the well-developed muscles of a man who obviously led a more physical life than he implied. The shade of his skin was darker than hers, as if he actually spent time in the sun bare-chested. She shocked herself with the sensation of wanting to run her hand down the entire length of his arm.

She licked her lips and swallowed, feeling as parched as a desert explorer. He made some kind of sound, and she found herself looking up into his eyes. She'd expected amusement or open laughter, but he was watching her mouth with an intensity that made her knees feel like jelly.

All that expanse of maleness called to her, and she lifted her hand. She didn't know what she meant to do.

"You can touch me," William said, his voice as low as a growl.

Touch him? The shocking thought caused her to come to her senses—if a bit reluctantly. "Shh."

She lifted his arm to view the wound in better light and tried not to think about the sensation of his warm, smooth skin.

Will refused to sigh his disappointment when she began the business of bandaging him. He could barely keep his breathing under control with her so close to him, her face full of concern, her breath light on his skin. He had to concentrate on keeping his chest covered so she wouldn't ask about the mementos of his various missions. But he'd removed his gloves, and she frowned at the white scar on the back of his hand.

"How did you get that?" she asked.

He didn't hesitate. "A piano lid fell on me—ruined the cuff of a very expensive shirt, I might add. Pianos can be quite dangerous."

She met his eyes doubtfully. "How can pianos be dangerous?"

"I was examining the quality of the instrument, of course, and the velvet that lined the interior. Obviously the piano was defective."

"So you were injured inspecting fabric."

"Essentially, yes." He refused to even blink as they locked gazes.

Then she slapped hot water and soap on the scratch across his biceps and began to rub.

"Hey!" he exclaimed. "Where's that hallmark of femininity called gentleness?"

"Perhaps it's gone somewhere with your other outdated notions about women," Jane said. "Do you wish your wound to fester?"

"It's not going to fester. It barely qualifies as a wound."

"You're whining."

"I am not whining!"

He folded his arms—one bare, one clothed—across his chest and heard the slight catch in her breathing. Good, at least she felt something for him, if only something physical.

She turned away to fuss with the bandages. "Should I ask the housekeeper for some ointment?"

"No, it'll heal just fine by itself, especially after the wonderful bathing job you've done."

Rolling her eyes, she pressed a clean cloth to the cut and began to wind strips of bandages around his arm to hold the cloth in place.

"I'm finished," she said, turning her back and facing the balcony. "You can put on a fresh shirt now."

He almost reached for her, but he thought better of it. He had to remember his mission and discover what Julia had done after the archery incident.

After taking a freshly pressed shirt out of his wardrobe; he slid it on and did up the buttons. "I'm dressed." When she faced him, he asked, "What will you be doing now?" If he had his way, she'd return to her room and stay there safely until dinner.

"I think after today's excitement, I might rest."

What a surprise—she was actually doing something he wanted her to do!

"I understand there'll be dancing tonight," she continued.

"And who told you that?"

"Julia. She enjoys waltzing so much that the duke always obliges her by having musicians ready."

Will wondered how often he was going to hear "Julia says" from now on. "I appreciate your help. Allow me to escort you to your room."

"That is not necessary," she said, moving toward the door.

"But I insist. There are wild gunshots and stray arrows about this place. A young lady needs protection."

She rolled her eyes. "I don't suppose protesting will do any good."

"No. Now do take my arm, and we'll be off."

Jane put her hand on the doorknob, then looked back at him. "Would you see if the hall is empty first?"

He grinned and put her mind at ease by obliging. "If you're nervous about being seen with me, I could boost you up to your balcony."

Shaking her head, she dragged him out into the hall.

Will spent the next few hours watching over Julia—who must have been resting, because she never left her room. He couldn't help wondering why she wasn't in more of a hurry to reach her accomplice in Leeds. Perhaps she really didn't know about the letters incriminating her.

The reality of what he was doing was sobering.

He was supposed to be protecting Jane. It was his fault that she was being led into this treacherous game. But now he was going to have to use her as a source of information on Julia Reed.

Why would Julia choose to confide in Jane, a woman she'd just met? Perhaps it was all an attempt to get to *him*, a known associate of Nick's. Julia had been in Afghanistan; Nick could have mentioned Will's name to her.

But was it worth killing him "accidentally" with a stray arrow? It didn't make any sense. Dudley would have to be under her control to time the gunshot just right.

His thoughts turned to Julia's past. She'd had an Indian tutor. This man or woman could have negatively influenced a young girl's thoughts about her distant home country. But what could have turned her against her brother? Was the general a cruel man, not a good relation to the girl?

Then again, Julia had been intimate with Nick. Perhaps she'd been susceptible to another lover's politics—or to blackmail.

Will had to find out more about her, either through Jane or by talking to Kelthorpe himself.

At dinner that evening, Julia and the duke spent most of the time together, and Will watched suspiciously, trying to tell if she was really in love. But Jane noticed his behavior, so he concentrated his attentions on her.

After dinner, Kelthorpe, accompanied by a radiant Julia, led everyone into the great hall. All the large furniture now lined the walls, and the carpets had been rolled up. Musicians were already playing on a dais in the far corner.

Jane stood at Will's side, her foot tapping to the beat, as they watched the first quadrille. The duke and Julia swept past them, and Will followed their progress with his gaze.

Jane leaned closer. "I spoke to Julia before dinner."

"Yes, I saw."

She eyed him. "Watching over me?"

"I always do."

"I don't appreciate—"

He took her arm and linked it with his. "There is no reason to be offended. If you have not noticed yet, I can't keep my gaze from you for long. I am still so amazed and pleased to be marrying you."

She had no answer to that, and Will's uneasiness rose. "So what did you talk to Miss Reed about?"

"Afghanistan. I know some dreadful things have happened there recently, but the culture is so different from ours that their very way of life fascinates me."

"So you've found a new country to study?"

"Perhaps," she answered.

He could tell she wondered if he was teasing her. "So what did you discover?"

"She told me about the bazaars of Kabul,

where they sold Russian slaves right next to melons and shoes."

"Surely British women cannot attend such things," he said without thinking.

Jane leaned even nearer, and he bent his head to hear. "Several times she dressed as a *boy*."

"I hope this is not giving you ideas," he said, frowning.

"This is England, William, and women are earning new freedoms every day."

He didn't like the way this conversation was going, but he let her talk in hopes of learning something to report to Nick. But all she related was about life in the British encampment built on the plains outside Kabul, and how General Reed—and, consequently, Julia—had been recalled to India several months before the British evacuation that ended in a bloody massacre. How convenient that Julia had escaped all that, something her betrayal had caused.

"She's even heard of my father," Jane added.

Will froze. Was that another way Julia could have traced his name? Colonel Whittington had been his—and Nick's—spymaster for years.

Just before Will was about to distract Jane with a dance, an elderly neighbor of the duke, Mr. Yates, bowed before her and almost fell over. When she took his arm to steady him, he smiled his gratitude, asked her to dance, and led her slowly out onto the floor.

Shortly after that, Will claimed her for the first

waltz and held her just a bit closer than was proper. She met his gaze boldly. As they whirled through the crowd, he tried to impress upon her with his eyes alone that she was his, that there was no use pretending otherwise.

"You are an excellent dancer, Jane," he said softly.

"And you are, too, though it doesn't surprise me."

"No?" Someday he would tell her that he'd only taken lessons in the last few months, that dancing was one of the things he'd forgotten when he left the country.

"You pay strict attention to behaving as a proper nobleman when we're amongst company."

"I do?" He swung her through a tight corner. It was true; "Lord" Chadwick was a man very conscious of all that was proper. But Will was finding out that he himself did not care so much about the rules of the *ton*.

"But with me, you are . . . different," Jane continued.

Their gazes locked together, and her speculative eyes probably saw more than he wanted her to see. He felt that all his talents of deception were becoming useless with her.

"Different?" he asked blandly. "How?"

"You are . . . amusing."

He thought she blushed, but it could just be the excitement of the dance. He was sweeping her across the floor at a pace that made them both slightly breathless. He swung her through a turn and felt the muscles of her back flex. He found it oddly arousing.

"But I strive to be amusing as much as possible," he said. "It makes conversation at these events so much more pleasant."

"But you're not trying so hard when you're with me, which makes it all the more . . . natural."

She wasn't even meeting his gaze now, and he suspected she regretted starting the conversation. Without realizing it, she was basically telling him that she could see through his "Lord" Chadwick persona. *Was* he trying too hard? Perhaps with Jane, he was becoming the man he was meant to be. How could he tell?

She gave a great sigh, and as the last strains of the waltz filled the air, she turned the subject to her previous dance partner, Mr. Yates, who, though doddering with old age now, had been a war hero under Lord Wellington. Will accepted the topic with relief.

Later in the evening, Will made his way to the group of men surrounding the Duke of Kelthorpe. Soon he had the man alone and subtly turned the conversation to Julia Reed.

"She is a fine woman," Kelthorpe said, watching as Julia danced an energetic polka with another guest.

"I understand she recently returned from India."

He nodded. "I met her at a ball thrown in honor of her brother General Reed's military achievements."

"She must be fascinating to converse with, since her life has been so different from ours."

"Yes, she is no simpering miss," Kelthorpe agreed with a laugh. "I find it quite refreshing."

"I understand she won't be able to visit for long."

"She has family business." The duke shook his head. "Damned hard to keep her all to myself when she feels so obligated to her brother."

Will wondered if that was merely her excuse for escaping to conduct her own affairs. It must have galled her that, in order to keep up appearances, she'd been forced to appease the duke by coming to Langley Manor. Ah, the things one had to do to marry nobility.

He kept an eye on Julia for the rest of the evening, but she did nothing suspicious and spoke to no one for an unusually long time—except Jane, of course. Will couldn't see any way to keep them apart.

Jane awoke in the middle of the night and wasn't quite sure why. After a half hour of trying to force her eyes to stay closed, she finally put on her dressing gown and lit a candle. The clock on the mantel said it was three in the morning, only two hours after she'd gone to bed. Warm milk always put her to sleep when thoughts rolled around in her head, so, taking up the candleholder, she went out into the dark corridor in search of the kitchens.

At the end of the hall was a softly glowing lamp, and she followed it to the stairs. Below her the great hall stretched on into the gloom, where her candle couldn't penetrate. With her hand on the banister she descended into the darkness, as if she were entering an earthen cave.

She knew the kitchens were at the end of a long corridor off the great hall. She passed many other drawing rooms and parlors and the library, then saw light spilling out from a door only partially shut. Curious, but not wanting to intrude on the duke or his guests, she peered inside.

William leaned over a billiards table, his profile to her, prepared to strike a ball with his cue. Jane didn't see another person inside. They were alone in the night.

Recklessness almost made her go to him, for he was dressed casually in trousers and an open-necked shirt, his sleeves rolled up above his elbows to reveal muscular forearms. He looked so attractive. Just as she conquered her intense desire to step inside, he struck the balls hard, then looked up and saw her.

Chapter 15

William straightened, resting the long cue on the floor. His slow smile sent a frisson of lightning through Jane that settled deep in the pit of her stomach. Oil lamps cast light into even the darkest corners, illuminating the upholstered benches lining the paneled walls and, on either side of the hearth, the pillars carved with the faces of lovely women.

"Looking for me?" he asked, crossing his arms over his chest and leaning his hip against the billiards table.

She felt ridiculous, her feet bare, her long black hair sliding across her shoulders. Yet she stepped inside, hesitated, then shut the door behind her. "No. I couldn't sleep."

"Me neither, but I'm used to it."

He leaned over to line up another shot, giving her an interesting view of the taut fabric over his backside. She stared in fascination, for she'd never imagined such a sight would be . . . stimulating.

These feelings confused her, for she sensed they were powerful and could make her do things she shouldn't. She remembered how strong his arm had felt, how she'd wanted to caress him instead of bandage him. Something wanton inside her had taken over her thoughts.

She forced herself to remember their conversation. "Why can't you sleep?"

"I don't know. It's been almost a year now."

She walked to the edge of the table, watching him line up the cue and stroke through smoothly, scattering the balls and landing two in the pockets. "A year of not sleeping? Surely you would be ill by now."

He lined up another shot on the far side of the table. As he bent forward, he lifted his head and smiled up at her, his dimples dark shadows etched in his lean face.

"Oh, I eventually sleep, but only for a few hours before dawn. Sometimes I rest before going out in the evening."

"Perhaps that is your problem," she said, walking to the rack and picking up her own cue. "If you stopped that, you might sleep better."

"I've tried—it doesn't work." He paced on the

far side of the table from her, watching.

Her eyes felt heavy-lidded, but not from exhaustion. She felt slow, languid, warm from the late summer heat. Her body wasn't her own anymore; it seemed to be changing into something still coming to life.

William nodded toward the cue in her hand. "Shall we play?"

"I've always wanted to learn, but we never had a table."

He sketched her a bow, as if he were formally dressed instead of showing tantalizing glimpses of tanned skin below his neck. "Then allow me."

She dutifully watched him as he demonstrated the rules, trying to pay attention to his instructions instead of studying the faint line of perspiration down his back, or the way his arm muscles flexed when he shot.

When it was her turn, she rested the cue between her fingers and tried to copy his form. She had to stand on her tiptoes to bend over the table, and he casually walked behind her until she could no longer see him. Her breathing grew shallow, every sense concentrated on him. She felt a wisp of a breeze shimmy through the thin skirt of her nightdress and dressing gown.

"Are you going to show me how I should hold the cue?" she asked, her own voice hoarse.

He put one hand on the edge of the table beside her. "That would be unwise."

"So you're just going to watch me bend over?"

He chuckled deep in his throat. "How do you know I'd do that?"

Jane told herself to stop this foolishness and flee to the safety of her bed. Instead she told the truth, probably because she couldn't see his face. "I was doing the same thing to you."

His other hand came down on the table, with her now trapped between his arms. She felt the brush of him against her clothing, felt her heart skip a beat before increasing to a dizzying speed.

"Aren't you going to shoot?" he murmured behind her ear.

She felt his breath like a caress on her cheek. "But then I'd have to stand up."

With a low growl he nipped at her neck with his teeth, scattering goose bumps up her arms. It was shockingly primitive, yet it sent a strange flood of heat pooling between her thighs. Then he leaned against her, using his hips to press hers into the billiards table. She could feel the long, hard ridge of him between her buttocks. No statue on display at a museum had prepared her for that.

A groan escaped her as he rocked into her, his chest pressing into her back, his hips teaching a new rhythm.

His hands caressed her neck, then moved slowly down her back. Her nightdress began to sag. He caught the fabric and pulled it down her back to the left until she felt his mouth on one bare shoulder. As he left moist kisses there, she pressed her palms hard against the table, trying not to cry out, ignoring the fading voice inside her that warned of danger.

But that voice was finally drowned beneath the excitement of what William was doing to her, how wild and uninhibited and different she became beneath his hands.

He tugged on her clothing again, and she felt her neckline slide over one sensitive breast, leaving it bare against the table. Nothing had ever touched her there except her garments, and she watched in languid astonishment as her nipple tightened and ached.

He caught her shoulders and lifted until she arched back against him, her body held to the length of his by his hand flat against her stomach. He pulled her away from the table, and she felt she'd fall to the floor without his support. When her hair slid back to cover her body, with one hand he gathered it behind her. His breathing was rough and loud in her ear, and as her head lolled against him, she realized he was tall enough to look over her shoulder. In the lamplight, her uncovered breast was muted cream, the dusky nipple hard. She desperately wanted him to touch her, to somehow ease the ache his nearness caused.

Instead he took the billiards cue off the table, and from in front of her, began to slide it slowly up the inside of her leg. When it reached just above her knee, she was panting and restless and trying not to squirm against him, for surely he wasn't supposed to do such a thing. Then she caught her breath as he tilted the upper narrow end toward her chest. She watched in astonishment as he rolled it up and over her breast, and the cool wood on her nipple made her cry out.

The stick clattered to the floor and was replaced by his big, warm hand. He cupped her breast, making her shudder hard against him at how wonderfully right it felt. When he rolled her nipple between his finger and thumb, the shock of it tugged between her legs as if he touched her there.

Will didn't think he'd ever met a woman more responsive than Jane. Her muted cries, her soft gasps were driving him quickly toward an urgent need he might not be able to control. Her breast was the softest skin he'd ever touched, and it filled his hand with a heavy warmth. He stroked his fingers across her nipple, circling, teasing, rewarded by the way she rubbed against him. He cupped her other breast through the cloth of her nightclothes, tempted to pull the rest of the garments aside. There would be nothing stopping all of her clothes from landing in a heap on the floor.

And then she'd be naked. The last threads of his control would be gone, and he'd do anything to be inside her.

But not now, not here.

Keeping one hand on her bare breast, he slid the other down over her soft belly, teasingly circling her navel, tormenting himself as well as her. She'd gone still in his arms, waiting, and he knew she was innocent, that she had no idea what he would do to her. It was an erotic thrill he hadn't thought to feel.

He slid his hand ever more slowly, until he could gently tease her curls through her thin fabric. She swiftly inhaled, then leaned back against his shoulder and looked up at him with wide, desperate eyes. They stared at each other, barely breathing, as he pushed against the silk between her thighs and gently rubbed the most sensitive part of her. He was overwhelmed with the pleasure it gave him just to touch her, to please her.

Her lips parted, her eyes fluttered shut, and he muffled her moan with his mouth. Thrusting his tongue between her lips, he mimicked the act of love. He cupped her with his hand, his hips pushing against her from behind, and drowned in the sensation of her.

He had to stop this before it was too late, he thought, reluctantly dropping his hands. But he couldn't move away from the feel of her body languid against his. If he slept with her now, it would be a seduction, not a mutual decision. And he wanted more for the beginning of his life with Jane than a billiards table against her back.

Much as that would be enjoyable. . . .

"William?"

When she turned to look up at him with questioning, dazed eyes, she swayed, and he caught her arms. He stared down at her naked breast, every chivalrous thought fleeing his mind except his urgent need to make her see how it could be between them. He dropped to his knees and pulled her to him, taking her breast as deeply into his mouth as he could. She gave a smothered scream as he suckled her hard, then gentled and soothed her with his tongue. He traced the tightened aureole, and then the tiny bud at its peak, teasing with a fluttering motion that made her shudder against him. She caught his head and held him to her, her fingers deep in his hair. He clutched the globes of her buttocks, pushing her hard against him until he could feel the soft pressure of her pubis against his stomach.

With a gasp, he released her breast and pressed his face between them both, inhaling the scent of her. "Jane, sweet Jane, I want this to continue, but I don't think you yet realize all that this leads to."

Her breath was coming in gasps, yet she did not release him. "I can't imagine . . . how much more there could be."

He slowly stood up, brushing against the length of her, sifting his hands through her hair when he tilted her head back. By lamplight, her face glowed with classic elegance. "I want to give you pleasure as you've never imagined. This is only the beginning, the way our bodies prepare for consummation. Shall I come up to your room with you?"

He heard the plea in his voice, felt uneasy at his desperation, but he couldn't regret it. Lovemaking would bind her to him in a way she couldn't imagine.

Her hesitation stretched out, until she finally sighed and pushed herself away from him. Turning her back, she covered herself and straightened her clothing.

"I'll leave you to your game," she whispered.

He caught her arm as she turned away. "As if I could continue after I've held you in my arms. Is that your answer to my question, Jane?"

She searched his face. "We can't do this. Thank you for showing the common sense I seem to have lost."

He released her. "Sweet dreams."

Looking confused, she murmured, "Good night," and left the room.

Through the night Jane had cried into her pillow over her conflicting passions, but in the morning she could not forget that William was still injured. Before dawn she knocked on his door, carrying bandages and a basin of hot wa-

ter. He looked stunned to see her, but he let her
in and obligingly bared his arm for her, all without saying a word.

Was he just as unsure as she was? She
couldn't stop thinking about him, couldn't forget the hot impression of his hands on her
body. Even now her skin tingled with awareness, and she ached with a restlessness she
couldn't assuage.

But the wound was healing well, so she tied
on fresh bandages and tried not to notice how
she trembled when she touched him, how her
mind betrayed her with passionate memories.

He said her name softly, but she only smiled
and backed away.

"I'll see you when you're finished dressing,"
she said before escaping.

Jane hurried down to the breakfast parlor and
found that Julia had also joined the men. The
two women came together with a smile and
light conversation about how lovely the day
promised to be, only to find several men vying
for the chance to bring them food. William must
have come down from his bedchamber almost
immediately, because he and the duke crowded
the other men away. Kelthorpe escorted Julia to
the sideboard to assist her, while William led
Jane to a chair.

"I can serve myself," she said, not yet daring
to meet his eyes for fear of riotous blushing.

"Don't forget—I have memorized your favorite selections. I'll return with the perfect meal."

She glanced up, but he'd been waiting for that. Their gazes met and held, and even *his* smile died as they both thought about what had occurred between them in the dark of the night.

How could she want him so, when everything he wanted in a marriage was so opposite of her dreams? Yet she was drawn to him when he entered a room, could not stop kissing him once they started. She had even forgotten to write in her journal every night, as if she no longer wanted her father to put aside this marriage bargain.

Jane forced a smile. "I'll take you up on your offer." When William's eyebrows rose, she quickly added, "Of breakfast!"

He grinned and bent over her hand, pressing a kiss to her fingers. "I'll return in a moment."

She had to be stronger than these . . . these feelings between them. Desiring him did not mean she had to marry him. She had only to remember the role he planned for her—the perfect society wife, like her mother—to make her heart harden against desire and her frightening lack of control.

Jane was thankful when Julia sat down at her table. As they chatted about their plans for the day, Jane discovered that the men were heading off to hunt pheasant for dinner, and that Julia would be going as well.

"Would you like to come too?" Julia added.

"Will there be time to change my clothing?"

"Of course."

"Change your clothing for what?" William asked as he sat down on the other side of Jane.

She glanced at him. "I'm going riding with the hunting party. So is Julia."

He frowned, then shot a strange look at Julia. "Seeing that I'm going, too, I cannot much complain."

"What happened to your insistence that you don't hunt?" Jane asked skeptically.

"Kelthorpe has decided that since we hunt for pheasant, and we'll be eating our catch for dinner, that should overcome my distaste for hunting for mere sport."

From his nearby table, Lord Dudley suddenly leaned toward them, hands spread wide. "You're hunting, Chadwick? I knew you couldn't resist the urge to try your rat against a champion dog."

Jane waited for William to laugh, but instead he only said, "You're pressing your luck, Dudley. Surely you don't want me to prove how important heart is in a dog?"

Lord Dudley shook his head and straightened. "Go ahead and try. Tag along with old Yates—you might need his *expertise*."

The sarcasm was evident to all within hearing range. Jane saw that Mr. Yates, who'd been dozing over his plate, perked up when he heard his name. He gave a bleary grin, and her heart softened with pity as she remembered what a marksman he'd been considered in his day. Now he could barely hold a fork steady to reach his mouth.

William's eyes flashed with a coldness that startled her. "I would consider it an honor to hunt with Mr. Yates."

She looked at William thoughtfully, knowing she could not fault his kindness. More and more she thought she understood her father's motivation in choosing him as her husband. But it still wasn't right for her father not to consult her about her own future.

"Suit yourself," Lord Dudley said, striding out of the breakfast parlor.

Grumbles and dark looks followed in his wake, but he ignored them.

Julia leaned over and whispered to Jane, "Hurry and change! You won't want to miss what might happen between your betrothed and Lord Dudley."

Jane eyed William, trying to imagine him deliberately provoking a fight. He didn't seem the sort—but then he was full of surprises lately.

Chapter 16

Jane rode at Julia's side at the rear of the hunting party. The weather was unseasonably cool for August, reminding her of the approaching autumn. But the sun was out, and as they rode along a ridge on the lip of a hollow and looked out over the green countryside cut with hedgerows, she felt at peace.

Well, as much peace as she could feel with William turning around regularly to check up on her. He had Killer tucked in the crook of his arm, and Jane swore that if she were closer, she would hear the dog growling at her.

"That is an interesting . . . creature your Lord Chadwick has," Julia said in an amused voice. "Not the usual sort of pet for a man."

"He's not your usual man," Jane said dryly.

"Why of course you would say that—you're in love with him."

Jane glanced at Julia. "I'm engaged to him. There's a difference."

Julia's smile was good-natured as she directed her horse with an ease Jane could only envy. "There is something between you, even if you don't wish to give it a name. How did you come to be engaged?"

Jane told the story briefly, knowing it reflected the fate of many of her friends.

"But you just didn't think it would happen to you," Julia said with sympathy.

"And you are so very in love?" Jane immediately regretted her words. "It is none of my business. I do apologize."

"I was being direct with you—it's only right that you question me. No, Kelthorpe and I do not have a love match, but we are . . . interested in each other. It is more than I could have hoped for, considering my negligent dowry."

Jane glanced away, embarrassed for her friend, knowing such things were not normally discussed.

"I think Kelthorpe is closer to love than I am," Julia continued softly. "But he is a good man, and I am certain I will someday feel the same for him." When Jane met her gaze, Julia grinned. "So your father chose Lord Chadwick for you. Are they good friends?"

Jane shrugged, quieting her mount as the first gunshots sounded and the dogs were released to run barking down into the fields to fetch the dead birds.

"Apparently our estates are neighboring in Yorkshire, but I did not know it."

"Could they know each other because of something else?"

"I'm not sure how—my father has spent much of the last twenty years in India, as you know."

"And Lord Chadwick has never traveled there?" Julia said thoughtfully.

"He says he doesn't like to travel."

"But that is not a true answer, is it?"

Jane hesitated, frowning, unsure of what to say. Julia was right—had William ever claimed exactly *where* he'd traveled? He said he knew the flowers of India from a book. But that didn't mean he hadn't traveled.

Kelthorpe called Julia's name, and she excused herself with a smile. Jane noticed that this time when William turned around, his impassive gaze followed Julia instead of her. How strange.

Jane rode toward him and saw with surprise that Lord Dudley was not far away, as if it was truly a contest. She watched his retriever lay another pheasant at his feet, noticing that Killer was nowhere to be seen. Mr. Yates stood nearby, trying to aim a shotgun with hands that trembled uncontrollably. She was well impressed by his courage, and sad that even war heroes had to grow old.

She dismounted, holding her horse's reins as she stood at William's side. A pouch hanging from his shoulders seemed heavy with his catch.

"Where's Killer?" she asked.

Before he answered, the little dog came bounding up, carrying a rather large bird in its mouth. He dropped the carcass at William's feet, earning him a "Good dog!" and a pat on the head. Together they watched as the high grass was being beaten on the far side of the field, startling hundreds of birds into the air.

"Too bad, you missed it again," said a nasty voice.

Both Jane and William turned to see Lord Dudley standing beside them at Mr. Yates's back. The old man lowered his gun as if it were too heavy for him, his face confused and resigned. Jane felt a surge of anger, and when she would have stepped forward to confront the cruel Lord Dudley, William caught her wrist.

"Don't worry," he murmured against her ear.

The brush of his skin startled a shiver out of her. But she waited, wondering what he would do for Mr. Yates.

When another flock soared into the air, all three men aimed, but there were few birds to hit, and they were quickly flying too high. Lord Dudley lowered his gun, but Mr. Yates and William fired.

William gave a cheerful scowl. "I missed—but your aim was incredible, Mr. Yates. I'll send Killer for your bird."

Mr. Yates looked befuddled but happy; Lord Dudley arched a brow with suspicion and walked away. Jane felt an overwhelming tenderness as she gazed at William. He had taken the precise shot not for himself but to make an old man proud again. Confusion at her feelings made her look away, but as they waited for Killer to return, she put a hand on William's arm and squeezed.

He glanced at her, smiling enigmatically, then leaned nearer. "So do I receive a kiss as a reward?"

She failed to withhold a smile. "Haven't you received enough of those lately?"

"I can never have too much of the sweetness of your lips."

She looked into his warm, serious eyes and felt a strange tightening in her chest. She couldn't look away, could barely breathe, and didn't even care that they were standing in the middle of an open field full of people.

Mr. Yates cleared his throat. "I may tremble now and again, but the hearing's just fine. Should I leave you two alone?"

Jane blushed and looked away as William shot a grin at the old man.

"Mr. Yates," he said, "we promise to control ourselves. We're to be married, you know."

Mr. Yates rolled his eyes good-naturedly. "Who doesn't know? You're a sign for eagerness, boy."

Will glanced at Jane, who met his gaze with determination, though her cheeks were red.

"I say!" Dudley suddenly yelled in an angry voice.

With a sigh, Will turned to see what the commotion was about, and he found Dudley's prize retriever lowering herself for Killer to mount her. Laughter broke out all around them, and Will barely stopped himself from cheering Killer on.

Dudley himself was on the far side of the field, and he started running toward them. "Stop that rat! Princess is a champion breeder!"

"Princess?" Will echoed. "What a name for a hunting dog." He walked to the dogs. "Down, Killer."

Dudley swiped Killer off onto his back before the dog could even obey the command. Killer gave a high-pitched yip, then flipped onto his feet and started growling.

"Hey!" Will called.

Jane cried out a warning too late as Lord Dudley threw his arms around William and dragged him to the ground. The men quickly gathered to call out their opinions and their offerings of bets. Jane pushed her way through.

Lord Dudley was a much taller, heavier man than William, who was hardly a fighter. She remembered how clumsy he'd been when Mr. Roderick had drunkenly fought with him at her mother's dinner party. She didn't know if she should try to stop this foolishness or allow William to be beaten in front of all these men he so wanted to impress.

There was a moment of grappling between the two opponents, and then Lord Dudley seemed to flip in the air and land on his back past William's head. He lay dazed as William scrambled to his feet.

"So sorry, Dudley. I was just trying to get you off me. Didn't mean to knock the wind out of you, old boy."

Dudley almost growled as he staggered to his feet. Jane wanted to cry out for someone to take hold of him, but she knew William wouldn't appreciate her interference. She cringed as Dudley charged again, but at the last second William seemed to stumble aside. Dudley landed flat on his face in a patch of mud.

A roar of laughter ensued, but Jane could not join in. She felt as if she were reliving an event all over again. This exact thing had happened with Mr. Roderick. William had made himself look incompetent, yet he'd kept his opponent from landing a blow.

Her doubts mounted as she realized that William's movements were too precise, hardly accidental. He knew just how to make it seem like he wasn't fighting—when he really was, albeit with his own methods.

Suspicion and confusion warred within Jane as she watched William try to help Lord Dudley to his feet. The man pushed William away and stalked through the crowd. He called for Princess, who gave Killer one last, regretful look before dutifully following her master as he rode off toward the manor.

Jane studied William as he accepted hearty congratulations. She realized none of them took him as a threat because he'd shown his supposed incompetence. While most men wanted to display their manliness, he took pains to sometimes appear otherwise. And it hadn't hurt him. He'd made friends among the nobility—including her father—and had landed a wealthy bride. But what true purpose did it all serve? He was hiding much from her, but she didn't know how to make him confess if he refused to.

And why was he so interested in Julia Reed? Not only had Jane caught him watching Julia but he had also once or twice steered their conversations toward her.

Jane told herself that jealousy was not motivating her curiosity. William had behaved in an unusual fashion, and she just wanted the truth. After all, he did not watch Julia with the same intent, smoldering eyes with which he watched Jane.

Yet . . . she tried to distance herself from her

emotions and think logically. *Could* she really be . . . jealous?

William shook the last hand thrust at him, then watched as the men returned to their shooting. For several minutes he basked in the satisfaction of having made Dudley look like a fool. The day was better with the man's absence, and at least he'd taken away his dog, the famous purebred who flinched every time a gun went off.

He glanced at Jane and noticed that she was studying him with an intensity that made him uncomfortable. She'd already been suspicious of his secrets, and he realized that today's behavior probably hadn't helped.

But there was nothing to be done now, and it was time to refocus on his mission. He glanced around for Julia Reed but didn't see her immediately.

Masking a frown, he tramped through the high grass, pretending to admire the marksmanship of Kelthorpe and his guests. He still didn't see Julia. He looked back to where the horses were held by grooms.

She was nowhere to be found.

A cold sweat chilled his back, but he made himself stroll slowly back to Jane. With her hands on her hips, she was frowning down at Killer, who held a bird in his mouth as if he was waiting for her to take it.

Will smiled at her. "So, you're the last brave female remaining? I'm proud."

"Julia is"—she looked about and frowned— "gone, I see."

So Jane didn't know anything about her disappearance. Surely if Julia were simply returning to the manor, she would have said something to her new dear friend.

"She must have gone back already," Will said. "Did you want to return with her? I could escort you, if you'd like." He waited, hoping for her agreement.

Jane sighed. "All right. I've seen as many dead birds as I need to. Are you sure you don't mind leaving?"

"I can return. Killer is already in the lead where bird retrieval is concerned. Such a shame Dudley left before we could do a count." When Jane stared suspiciously at him, he quickly said, "Did you see where Killer went?"

He looked about for the dog, only to find him in the midst of the pack, trying to get another female to notice as he pranced with his fluffy head in the air.

Will sighed. "He's not going to want to stay in the bedroom tonight."

William escorted Jane back to Langley Manor, made sure Julia hadn't returned to the house or the grounds, then went back to the hunt. He dismounted and moved silently through the woods surrounding the field, but nowhere could he find evidence that Julia had passed this way. If she'd simply ridden away across the field, surely he would have seen her. He didn't believe she would have left permanently without a formal farewell to the duke.

So was she off meeting someone who had information that could put them all in danger? He was worried and frustrated and unable to do a thing about it.

When the hunt was over, he and the other men returned to the manor for luncheon. Not surprisingly, Julia was among the ladies as they waited in the drawing room.

As Will escorted Jane into the dining room, he casually asked her where Julia had gone off to. Jane frowned at him, and he knew he'd gone too far. He tried to hint that Kelthorpe had been worried, but he didn't want to fabricate a lie so easily verified. Jane had no answers for him, and all he succeeded in doing was raising her suspicions.

That night, even a private concert by the Royal Italian Opera did not make Will drowsy. After hours of pacing, he had finally fallen asleep when a faint sound out on the balcony startled him into silent wakefulness. At the end of his bed, Killer began a soft growling.

"No, Killer. Sleep."

The dog put his head down, although Will could still see the sheen of his open eyes. Will lay back and kept his breathing deep and even, adding an occasional soft snore, all the while keeping his senses attuned for anything out of the ordinary.

A floorboard creaked near the balcony. Will stayed relaxed and Killer remained still.

He heard the faintest, shallow breathing coming nearer. He gave another snore, then slit his eyelids to peer into the shadowy darkness. A man approached, wearing all black, with a mask across his face. Will forced himself to wait until the intruder loomed over him. The man raised his arm, and a knife glittered in the moonlight.

Will shot up and grabbed his upraised arm. The man's only response was a grunt of surprise. Killer began a furious barking. As they grappled for the weapon, Will thrust his knee into the man's stomach. The air whooshed out of him, and the knife clattered to the floor. Will punched him several times in the face, and the intruder staggered back toward the open balcony door. He fell through it, then scrambled to his feet and vaulted over the edge.

When Will reached the balustrade and leaned over it, his attacker was fleeing into the darkness of the gardens. Killer stuck his head out between the posts of the balustrade, barking an obvious warning not to return. Realizing he was still naked, Will swore and went back inside, firmly closing and locking the door. He'd been a fool to leave it unlocked—as if he could hope that Jane would ever climb his balcony to be with him.

The usual rush of restlessness swept over him after such a near escape, and he paced the room, pausing occasionally to give the dog a congratulatory petting. This was not a random robbery attempt; Julia must have discovered Will's connection to her pursuers. During the hunt, had she gone to meet that man, then given him orders to kill Will?

She couldn't possibly think that Jane was in on the scheme—could she?

He pulled on trousers, a shirt and boots. It was the middle of the night, so he felt relatively confident he could run through the dark corridors unseen. The occasional lamp glimmered, lighting his way to the opposite wing of the house, where the ladies slept. He found Jane's door, paused to listen, then slowly opened it.

Chapter 17

Motionless, Will first searched the shadows with his eyes, seeing that all seemed normal in Jane's room. She was asleep in bed; the balcony doors were closed. Moving cautiously, he checked inside the wardrobe and behind the changing screen. He dropped flat on his stomach to search beneath the bed, but to his relief he found nothing. As he rose onto his knees, he came eye to eye with a disheveled Jane propped on one elbow, watching him.

He smiled. "Good evening."

She frowned. "I know you have trouble sleeping, but this penchant you have for invading my room must cease."

"Forgive me. Our last encounter is still too vivid in my mind."

She hesitated, and he imagined she was blushing.

Softly, she said, "I understand that my . . . behavior might lead you to think that I welcome your seduction."

He leaned his elbows on the bed. "Don't you?"

"No. I've allowed unfamiliar emotions to sway me, and now that I know what to guard against, it will stop."

"So easily?" he said, lowering his voice. He reached out and ran his fingertip up her clothed arm. "Then you are better than I. Now that I've kissed you, touched you—"

He lifted her hand, and though her eyes remained skeptical, she allowed it.

"—licked you—"

When he touched his tongue to the center of her palm, she inhaled swiftly, then pulled back.

"Don't you see?" he whispered. "I can't help myself."

"Then you had best return to your bed." Though her voice sounded shaky, she looked resolute.

He gave a deep sigh and pushed to his feet. "I'll leave you then, and we'll both ache through the night with frustration."

She lay back, pulling the coverlet up to her chin.

"There is just one more thing. We'll take our leave first thing in the morning."

She eyed him curiously but only nodded. "We won't go to church with the other guests?"

"No."

"Very well. I'll be ready."

"No other protests?" he asked, standing over her bed, enjoying the view of her sleep-tossed hair scattered across the pillows. "Aren't you enjoying the duke's guests and many entertainments?"

"I would rather see my father. Now shall I come first thing in the morning to change your bandages?"

"No, I'm healing well." He paused and grinned. "But if you simply must come to my room—"

"Good night, William."

Will remained awake and restless for the final hours of the night, alternately walking the corridors and circling the outside of the manor to keep watch on the balconies. The thought of Jane in danger made his usual confidence feel raw and shaken.

When this was over, he would make it clear to Nick that he was finished. Never again would he put his wife or future children in harm's way. He had done enough for England.

* * *

Just after dawn, Jane sat alone in the breakfast parlor eating. She heard footsteps outside the door and looked up to see William.

He raised an eyebrow. "I am so pleased at how easily you obey me."

"Only because I am in agreement that it's time to resume our journey. Although I'd like to remain until we've had a chance to say good-bye."

"If you mean to Miss Reed and the other ladies, it could be hours until they descend. We'll give Kelthorpe our regrets and be off, so as not to waste the day. You can write them all letters."

She watched him help himself to the breakfast tureens on the sideboard. Today he was moving with a briskness that was unusual for him, as if he was distracted from his normal routine. He seemed so—alert.

A man who could fight while pretending not to.

Within the hour they said their farewells to the Duke of Kelthorpe. Julia had even come down early, and the two women kissed cheeks and promised to write.

Jane found their carriage already out front, loaded with their trunks. She greeted Mr. Barlow, who helped her up inside. Sitting down with a sigh on the padded leather seat, she realized she had appreciated the few days away from the rolling confinement. But she was perfectly happy to be back on the road and heading for Yorkshire—and her father.

The carriage rocked as William swung himself inside and deposited Killer on the opposite bench. She waited for him to begin an inane conversation, or attempt to steal a kiss, but surprisingly he only gave her a brief smile and turned to look out the window. She noticed the carriage was traveling a bit faster than it had before.

As the minutes turned into hours, she tried to read her book when the road was good; otherwise she studied the countryside—and her betrothed. Something was very different about him, and it made her curious and uneasy. His eyes, normally so good-natured and genial, now seemed cold, as if weighty thoughts occupied him. Though he tried to mask the movement, every so often he leaned out and quickly glanced behind the carriage. Did he think someone was following them?

And he had stopped talking.

This was a man who could hold an entire conversation all by himself. Now, except for occasional inquiries about her comfort, or telling her the distance to the next inn in Newark upon Trent, he remained mute, preoccupied.

What was going on?

At dusk they reached the courtyard of the inn, a large, sprawling, shabby affair with galleries on each floor above the courtyard. William stepped outside to speak to Mr. Barlow, then helped her down and insisted on escorting her into a private dining room.

"But William, you know how I enjoy talking to people." Jane stared down at her elbow, where he gripped her almost urgently.

Without answering, he led her through a gloomy hallway off the courtyard, past offices and parlors, following the innkeeper at a pace she almost couldn't keep up with.

When they reached their dining chamber, she watched William look about at the little sitting area, with its sofa and upholstered chair, and the table before the hearth. He nodded to the innkeeper, who beamed and rubbed his hands together, as if anticipating a large reward for good service.

William walked to the door. "Mr. Tupper, could you go over the menu with my intended? She'll want to know what you're serving to-night."

Jane gaped at him. Since when did she care about the particulars of their meals? "William—"

"I've got to go help Barlow with the trunks and the horses, my dear. I'll return in a moment."

Help Mr. Barlow with his coachman's duties? He'd never done that before.

The door closed behind him, Mr. Tupper started talking, and Jane stared about almost wildly.

What was going on?

She had had enough of being kept in the dark. Wearing a fixed smile, she told the innkeeper to serve them the inn's specialty. She walked around him as he stuttered in confusion, then she went back down the hall and out into the courtyard. At least he didn't follow her.

She lifted her hood up, pulled the cloak tighter and looked about her. The night was almost dark now, although there were lanterns hung from pegs on various buildings and poles. Horses were being led past her, weary passengers jostled her, and she had to make way for porters carrying trunks on their shoulders. She asked where carriages would be parked for the night and was directed outside the courtyard, to another yard where the outbuildings were grouped.

She walked through the dark tunnel underneath the first-floor gallery. When she was once again in the open, a cool wind buffeted her, and she gathered her cloak tighter. There were fewer lanterns now, but she followed the noise of horses and stable lads. The stable was a large cavernous building, and off to the right, a line of coaches was parked near a coach house. Men moved to and fro carrying lanterns, and she followed them along the line of coaches until she came to the last one, William's, closest to a field, which stretched away into darkness.

Jane was about to give up, but she took a

chance and walked around the far side of the carriage. By the light of a wildly swinging lantern, two men silently grappled with each other, their feet braced on the ground as they tried to knock each other over. In the shadows, she could not see who it was, but she had an overwhelming feeling that one of them might be William. She hesitated—panicked, frightened, uncertain if she should call for help.

She suddenly heard a low moan and realized the bulky shape on the ground nearest the carriage was a man. She took a cautious step forward, then stopped.

"Hello?" she called softly, glancing back quickly at the combatants. "Do you need help?"

"Miss Whittington?"

It was more a croak than a regular voice, but she recognized it at once.

"Mr. Barlow!" she gasped, going down on her knees in the mud beside him. "Are you all right?"

When she tried to cradle his head, he groaned, and she felt the stickiness of blood.

"Lord Chadwick, he needs—" was all he said before he fainted.

She pulled off her cloak and used it to cushion Mr. Barlow's head. Then she turned and looked at the two fighting men just as one landed a solid punch to the other's jaw.

It was William fighting with a pugilist's grace

and skill, and she stared in shock and even a bit of rising admiration—which she quickly squelched, of course. Killer, abnormally silent for a dog, circled the two men with frantic steps.

The stranger yelled something in a language she'd never heard before—and William replied. Jane sat back on her heels and just gaped at him, feeling as if everything she thought she knew about him was crashing down around her. She didn't know what to do but kneel there beside Mr. Barlow and watch the fight until it was finished.

And it was finished rather quickly. William landed a series of blows to the head and stomach of the stranger that sent the man reeling.

William glanced over at the carriage as if he suddenly knew someone else was watching. "Jane?"

But the distraction was enough for the stranger to seize victory by lunging for a bucket and swinging it in a wild arc.

"William!" she screamed, rising to her feet as if she could help.

He lifted up his arms to ward off the blow, but he still ended up tumbling to his knees as the bucket caught him in the side. The stranger flung the bucket to the ground and ran into the fields. William took off after him. With a sudden wild barking, Killer followed.

"William!"

He ignored her, and she stared openmouthed as the darkness swallowed him up. Mr. Barlow groaned again, and she knelt back down at his side.

"Are you awake? Can you walk if I help you?"

For several minutes, she spoke to the coachman in a soothing voice, trying to ascertain if he was well enough to return to the inn.

"Allow me," said a voice just above her.

She fell back onto her rump before realizing it was William, almost a stranger to her by the light of a single lantern. Killer panted at his side.

"How did you do that?" she demanded angrily. "I didn't even hear you coming! Did that man escape?"

He nodded. "We almost had him. Killer and I trailed him to his horse. Killer bit his thigh as he mounted—"

"Bit his thigh!"

"If you haven't noticed, the dog can jump rather high. But it was all for naught, since the brigand pushed Killer off and escaped." He squatted down beside his dog, ruffled his furry head and hugged him. "The fall must have hurt him. And is that blood on your mouth?" he said to Killer. "Wounded the bad guy, did you? What a good dog."

Killer leaned against his leg in an adoring fashion, and Jane sighed.

She tersely asked William to fetch the lantern

off a hook on the stable wall. He held it over Mr. Barlow, who lifted a hand to rub his head. She pushed his hand aside and looked at the wound above his ear.

"There's a lot of blood," she whispered, feeling rather queasy.

"It's a blow to the head—they always bleed," William answered matter-of-factly.

"Do they?" she said, watching him.

He spared her a puzzled glance, then pulled off his coat and waistcoat and wrapped the latter about Mr. Barlow's head.

"Barlow," William said, "do you think you can make it inside the coach with my help?"

"Perhaps we shouldn't move him?" Jane asked hesitantly.

But Mr. Barlow nodded, and Jane stood up as William lifted beneath his arms and hauled him to his feet. Mr. Barlow was not a small man, but William managed him rather . . . effortlessly. She quickly opened the door to the coach, then watched as William helped their driver inside. Mr. Barlow slumped against the seat with a sigh. With the flick of a match, William lit the interior lantern, then all four lanterns on the outside of the carriage.

"Are we going somewhere?" Jane asked.

"Somewhere safer than this. That bastard'll be back eventually. I'll have the horses brought around, and I'll find some water and bandages for Barlow's tough head."

"Tough head?" she repeated, although she was still dwelling on the fact that the mysterious villain would return. She stared out across the dark fields and wondered if they were being watched.

"This has happened to Barlow before," he said with a grin that gleamed in the low light. "He's probably used to it by now. A coachman lives a dangerous life."

Mr. Barlow gave a snort, as if the two shared a private joke.

"Up inside, Jane."

"But—"

"I'll be right back. Make sure old Barlow's not bleeding to death."

"The innkeeper is preparing our dinner!" she protested.

"We won't have time to wait."

"But—"

William took her by the waist and effortlessly set her inside. She smoothed down her skirts and gaped at him as he put Killer onto the opposite seat. As the door shut behind her, she perched on the edge of Mr. Barlow's seat with apprehension, but he smiled at her, and his eyes twinkled.

"It'll be all right, miss," he said hoarsely. "I'm feelin' better already."

Men and their bravado. But she gave him a tight smile and pressed the waistcoat more forcefully against his head.

When William returned, he gave her a bucket of steaming water and a cloth bundle. As she spread it open to see linens and bandages, she felt the coach rock as the horses were harnessed. The lantern above her head swayed dangerously but didn't spill.

William ducked his head inside the door. "Come on, Killer."

Jane frowned. "Where are you taking him?"

"See how concerned you are—you're smitten with him already."

"Oh, please."

William grinned. "I'm going to have him trail the carriage. He'll let me know if we're being followed."

She didn't bother hiding her skepticism. "I thought you said he was limping."

He picked up his dog in both hands and looked him in the eyes. "Did you hear that, Killer? She doubts your worthiness. Let's prove her wrong, shall we?"

Not a quarter hour later, the carriage swayed as William got into the coachman's box. She heard him call to the horses, then she was tossed back on her seat as the carriage squeaked and began to roll.

"He's never been a good driver," Mr. Barlow murmured.

Jane shushed him and continued to clean and bandage his wound. But inside, her mind was spinning with countless wild thoughts. Worrying about pursuit made her feel very powerless and afraid, something she wasn't used to. Yes, it was a man's world and she always had to deal with that, but . . . this was different. She felt in someone else's control. Her father's and William's manipulations seemed nothing compared to this.

Yet part of her felt more alive than she ever had before. Was it because she'd never felt the thrill of outwitting danger? Or was it that William had seemed to become another person?

Several hours later, the carriage suddenly rolled over bumpy ground, waking the occupants. Jane spilled onto the floor.

"What the bloody hell happened?" Mr. Barlow grumbled, bracing himself to sit up. He groaned and reached a hand to his head.

She had no answers.

The carriage jostled around for at least another quarter hour, then came to an abrupt halt. In the sudden silence, they could hear the neighing of the horses and nothing else but the muted sound of crickets.

She parted the shutters covering the glass windows, but she could see nothing but the faint flare of the outside lanterns. All else was inky blackness. She felt William descend from the box, and a moment later he climbed inside, carrying his exhausted dog. When William took his seat, Killer collapsed in his lap, and even she could see the little thing trembling. The dog's panting shuddered through him, and for once she felt sorry for him.

"Where are we?" she demanded.

"I drove outside the town and far enough away from any farm. The last bit was rough because I entered a little copse of trees for protection."

"Near started my head bleedin' again," Mr. Barlow growled.

William smiled. "I learned coaching from the best."

The driver only harrumphed.

"So we won't be at an inn?" Jane asked.

"We're camping for the night. I want to make sure that whoever that man is, he's unable to find us."

"But what happened? Why did you fight him?"

His smile dimmed. "I assume he was trying to steal any valuables in our trunks. It's a good thing I went out to help Barlow."

"But you never do that," she persisted. "Why did you choose tonight?"

"I guess I had a special feeling," he said brightly.

She told herself she should be happy that there were depths to William she'd never imagined. His "dandy" behavior had all but disappeared, replaced by competence and as-yet-undiscovered knowledge.

But he'd been lying to her, and she had no idea

how major the lies really were. Had he lied about things to get what he wanted—namely, their marriage? How could she believe another word he said? Yet . . . she found him more compelling than any other man she'd ever known. She was starting to care too much about him, and she didn't even know who the real William was.

Chapter 18

Jane watched William lean over Mr. Barlow and touch the bloodstained bandage.

"It's stopped bleeding," he said with satisfaction.

"Then maybe it's time for you to answer some questions," she said.

He glanced at her. "Not now. I have to see to the horses and start a fire."

She gritted her teeth and remained silent, knowing he couldn't keep her that way for long.

Mr. Barlow stirred. "Is a fire wise, my lord?"

William shrugged. "If he'd really been following us—and I don't see how, because Killer would know—he would have seen our lanterns. I had no choice but to use them or risk running into a ditch. The trees are hiding us well enough for a small fire. I'll keep watch—you know I won't be sleeping."

Jane narrowed her eyes. "Then perhaps I can help you stay awake by talking to you."

He met her gaze and seemed to read her intentions. "No, I insist you get your rest. There's plenty of time to talk tomorrow, if Barlow feels up to driving. Now let me see to keeping us warm and fed."

"Fed? Do you plan to hunt in the dark?"

"No, but someone else can. Come on, Killer, let's see what's out there."

Though the dog had seemed exhausted only moments before, he now jumped to his feet, tail wagging wildly. She gritted her teeth as they both went out the door.

For his part, Will considered his escape from the carriage pure luck. He didn't know how he was going to answer all Jane's questions, especially since she would be safer the less she knew, but at least he didn't have to deal with her questions at the moment.

He fell back on his camping skills so easily that he didn't have to think about them. This freed him to ruminate on thoughts of Julia's henchman chasing them. Did she want Will dead, so there would be as few people as possible between her and the accomplice who'd betrayed her?

When Killer brought back a dead rabbit, Will

promptly displayed it to Jane, who, instead of having an attack of ladylike disgust, was quite impressed by the dog's accomplishment. She offered to help Will find firewood, but he wouldn't let her and insisted she stay inside the carriage.

While the rabbit was cooking on a spit over the fire, Will paced and looked up at the stars and tried to collect his scattered thoughts.

Killer's sudden stillness and a suspicious rustle deep in the trees were the first things that alerted him to danger. With a hand signal from Will, the dog quieted at his feet. He silently moved away from the fire toward the carriage so he couldn't be seen. Foolishly, he'd left his guns in storage beneath the carriage benches. But he *was* carrying the knife dropped by the intruder back at Langley Manor. He crouched beside the horses that were munching grass where he'd hobbled them.

An owl hooted softly through the trees. It took him a moment to place the call of the next animal because of its very foreignness to the English countryside: a camel.

Will relaxed and repeated the sound, then went back to the fire and sat on the log he'd rolled up. A few minutes later, an old man dressed in rough country garb shuffled out from the shadows of the trees and into the firelight. He wore a large hat with a wide brim that hid his face, and he was hunched over with the strain of age. He led a horse behind him, although he looked like he couldn't have mounted without assistance.

Will laughed and put out a hand. "Why, Sam, it's good to see you."

Samuel Sherryngton shook his hand and sat down so slowly beside him that Will thought the man's thirty-four-year-old bones really must ache with age. Killer leaned against Sam's ankles and wriggled with delight as he was petted.

"A good evenin' to ye, Will," Sam said, his country voice hoarse and gravelly.

"Fine, fine, just keep showing off." Will shook his head. "I don't know why you felt the need to disguise yourself when there's only me to impress."

"But you're so easy to impress," Sam answered slyly, his voice back to normal. "And then again, we wouldn't want our enemies seeing you meet with the same person."

"I know. So where the hell were you a couple hours ago?"

"You mean the incident by the coach house?"

"We could have used a hand."

"I know," Sam said cheerfully. "But by the time I was close enough to realize what was going on, your attacker was already running away."

"And you couldn't have chased him?"

"You were closer than I was." Sam scratched beneath Killer's chin. "And this little guy is usually a far better tracker than I."

Will could only shake his head. "So how are Nick and Charlotte?"

Sam grinned. "Falling in love."

"Not Nick!"

"Well I didn't say either of them knew it yet. But as for danger, things have been quiet for days since Julia was at Langley Manor. How have things gone?"

Will explained everything that had happened. "What I can't figure out is why Julia bothered to have a man come after me. We don't even know for certain that she's on to Nick, let alone me." Will felt irritable and frustrated with the uncertainty of it all.

"But we have to assume she is."

"If she doesn't know exactly *who* is meeting her old accomplice in Leeds, perhaps she figures she should take care of anyone who might be in on the plot."

Sam stared into the fire, his big hat drooping from his hands. "She doesn't seem to have many men helping her, for no one came near Nick and Charlotte while you were at the manor. Also, Julia doesn't know I'm involved, and I'd prefer to keep it that way."

"Why?"

"Because . . . I've known her since she was in the nursery," he replied, and there was sadness in his voice that he couldn't hide. "She might feel all the more threatened and desperate if she knows about me."

"But you've hardly betrayed her—in fact, the opposite is true!"

"I know." Sam raised bleak eyes to Will. "I wish I knew what happened to her in India. Or maybe it was Afghanistan—I don't know. But my wishes don't matter."

They were silent for several minutes, as both contemplated what could make a woman commit such crimes.

"So what happens next?" Will finally asked.

"Nick wants final proof against her, so he'll follow her to her accomplice in Leeds—"

"If she's even going there," Will interrupted.

Sam shrugged. "Nick wants her to incriminate herself. At this point, he and I will keep following her. I'll let you know if we need you for anything else. Don't go right to Colonel Whittington's estate until we tell you that Julia is in custody."

"I don't want to put the colonel in danger, either. Just finish this quickly. There are only so many estates for sale, and Jane is getting suspicious."

"But you need to be unobtrusive, Will. They've tried to kill you twice now. Hopefully they've lost track of you."

"I'll be careful."

Sam nodded and attempted a smile. "So where is your future bride? I've only seen her from a distance."

Will glanced at the carriage, allowing thoughts

of Jane passionate in his arms to warm him. "I convinced her to stay in the carriage and keep Barlow company while I cook supper. I can't believe she hasn't seen you yet. But then again, you do look like a lost old man sharing the warmth of my fire."

"So she doesn't know what's going on?"

"Not yet. But I think after today, she's going to demand the truth. I'll tell her as little as possible about my past and nothing about the mission itself. The less she knows the better. She likes Julia, and I don't want her putting herself in danger trying to prove we're wrong."

"Very well," Sam said. "I'll go report to Nick everything you've told me. Where will you be tomorrow night, just in case?"

"We're going to tour estates along the border between Nottinghamshire and Lincolnshire. I'll make for the village of Epworth by twilight. There's an old inn called The Crown and the Horse behind the Manor Court House. Think you can find it?"

Sam smiled. "What a cruel question to ask." He got slowly to his feet, as if his knees would barely hold him. With a hand to his back, he hobbled a bit, then leaned against his horse for a few quick breaths.

Will grinned.

Sam winked. "I'll see you soon."

"Don't take this the wrong way, but I hope not."

Then Sam limped slowly off into the night, leading a horse whose head hung as if he'd led a hard life. Even the animal was in disguise.

Very quietly, Jane slid the glass window back in place so as not to disturb Mr. Barlow's sleep. She didn't know to whom William had been speaking, but she knew he wasn't a lost old man. He'd obviously come to see William. But how had he known where they were? Or had William come to this place deliberately?

She'd overheard a word or two between the men: something about a woman with a man named Nick, and then later a mention of her own name.

So now he was talking about her to strangers? Well a stranger to her, anyway, since it was obvious William knew who he was.

Sitting there in the darkness, listening to Mr. Barlow snore, Jane's frustrations and curiosity mounted to an intolerable level. She could not go on trying to solve the riddle of William's character using only subtle clues. It was time he explained himself—no more mysteries or strangers or fights. He was going to tell her everything immediately or she would go on to her father's without him and bring about an end to their association.

She climbed out of the carriage and carefully closed the door behind her so as not to awaken the coachman. She hadn't taken a step before Killer gave a soft bark.

William hushed his pet and glanced over his shoulder at her. "I was wondering when you were coming out. Dinner is served."

She rearranged her skirts and sat down on the log at his side. The rabbit carcass was stretched on a crude wooden spit over the flames, and drops of fat fell and sizzled. William cut off a leg bone and held it out to her.

She stared in dismay at the knife he'd used.

"Don't worry," he said with a wicked grin. "I washed the knife in the stream after I skinned the rabbit."

With resignation, she carefully took the meat in her hand, leaning out away from her skirt to blow on it. He did the same, and they ate their initial helping in silence.

"We should awaken Barlow," he said.

"Not yet. We have things to discuss."

She heard his sigh.

"Who was that man you were just talking to—and don't pretend ignorance," Jane added coldly. "You've been keeping things from me since the beginning of our relationship, and I refuse to accept it anymore. Who was that old man, and why did that other man attack Mr. Barlow? And how did you understand the language he spoke?"

William stared at his sticky fingers for a moment before wiping them with a rag. "All right. I understand that things have gone too far now to keep you in the dark. But I've only been trying to protect you."

"Protect me from what?" she demanded with exasperation.

He hesitated, and she could see from his face that he didn't know where to start.

"Do you know what your father did in the army?"

Her mouth tightened. "You are avoiding my questions again."

"No, this is very pertinent. Answer me."

"He was a soldier with the army of the East India Company. What more do you want me to say?"

"That wasn't all he did. He was a spymaster controlling a team of field agents."

While he continued to study her, she could think of nothing to say as her thoughts whirled in confusion. Could it be true?

"I was under his command, as was the man I was just speaking to."

She had thought nothing more could shock her—but she'd been wrong. "You . . . were in the army," she said slowly, trying to grasp a new picture of William in her mind.

"For thirteen years I've been away from England, first in India, and then in Afghanistan."

"You . . . were a spy." She could barely get the words out. Talkative, irreverent William had lived a life of adventure, of danger and excitement? He couldn't be lying—all she had to do was speak to her father to verify it. But her father had never told her these things either, and she felt sick with the knowledge. "You lied to me," she whispered, then felt tears sting her eyes. "You both lied to me."

"Jane, that is what the government required of us," he said in a low, soothing voice. "Secrets are kept for England's safety, not to play some sort of trick on you. I wouldn't be telling you any of this if you hadn't seen too much today. Even now, I can't answer all of your questions, or I'd be risking the lives of too many people."

"My father—"

"Is a great man, my sweet, and he loves you very much. I have known and worked for him for many years."

She sniffed and tried to compose herself. "So that is why he betrothed me to you. You aren't just a neighbor or a business partner."

"That's true."

Taking a deep breath, she turned to stare directly into his wary eyes, burying her unsettled emotions. Later, she would deal with how all this affected *her*. "So what is going on? Are you still a spy?"

"No. I left that life last year. It wasn't something I'd initially wanted. I'd been an officer, and I was good at it. When the Political department heard about my talent at languages—"

"Languages!" she cried, feeling the heat of embarrassment and anger in her cheeks. "Why did you let me make a fool of myself?"

"But I didn't!" he protested. "I thought you were sweet and earnest and endearing."

"What language did that criminal speak to you in?"

"Persian."

Feeling faint, she whispered, "How many languages do you know?"

"I . . . think I've lost count."

She groaned and put her hot face in her hands. She had a sudden memory of that naughty French book she'd been reading at the estate outside London. Had he known what she'd held in her trembling hands? Had he deliberately made her read aloud? She didn't want to know.

When he touched her head, she reared up and pushed him away. "Even if you couldn't tell me the truth about the kind of life you'd been leading, why was it necessary to hide your proficiency at languages and your skills at so many other things? William, you talked about *fabric*, for heaven's sake!"

"I needed to fit into your world, Jane. You would have asked questions about what I did with such skills, and I didn't want to lie any more than I had to."

"And that monocle? Was even your eyesight a lie?"

"An . . . exaggeration. I thought it made me look the part. The Lord Chadwick character was created to make me seem foolish and gullible."

"Then you accomplished your task."

One side of his mouth curved up in a smile. "Thank you—I think."

Something didn't make sense, but as she studied his averted gaze, she realized that perhaps he wasn't comfortable with his past—and wouldn't choose to answer questions about it. "If your secret life is behind you, what's happening now? Who was that man who attacked you?"

"Actually, that was the second time he attacked me."

"Since you met me?" she asked in stunned surprise.

"Last night he crept in through my balcony door and tried to kill me. That's why we left so quickly this morning. I wanted to outrun him, but it obviously didn't work."

She studied him boldly. "You came into my room immediately after the attack. Did you fear for my safety?"

He returned her gaze. "Yes."

"So you didn't come to try to seduce me again." She hugged her arms over her chest and was surprised to feel hurt.

He reached to cup her face with a tenderness that confused her. "I am overcome by you, Jane. I would spend every moment trying to seduce you if you'd let me. It's just that last night, I was a bit more concerned with keeping you safe."

She wondered what he really felt for her, if he was only doing her father a favor in marrying her. The direction of her thoughts made her too uncomfortable.

"So," she prodded. "This man attacked you twice—the first time in a duke's home, no mean feat. Why?"

"Because I've been asked by another agent to help in a small matter."

"The old man you were just talking to."

"No—and of course he's not really old," William added, grinning. When she didn't respond, his smile faded. "There's another agent who's in charge of this operation. Sam was relaying messages between us."

"I thought you were retired."

"I am. Once this is finished, they're under orders not to ask anything of me again."

"But you won't tell me what it's all about." And she was desperate to know, desperate to understand the danger he was leading her into. Her curiosity burned her, made her restless.

"I can't. It would be even more dangerous for you to know. You can't talk about this with anyone."

"But aren't we bringing this danger to my father's door? Isn't he too old for this?"

"He doesn't know anything about this, Jane,

and I promise we will bring him no harm. It will be finished in a matter of days."

"So I'm just to wait around," she scoffed, "asking no questions, wondering if men with knives or guns could burst in at any moment— how can I even believe any of this? And how did you think you'd keep such a thing from your own wife?" She threw her hands in the air, feeling her emotions, her very thoughts, spiraling out of control. The woods all around them looked menacing, as if her safe England was gone.

"I'll keep you safe—Barlow was a soldier too, so you'll have us both. But Jane—"

He lowered his voice and reached to hold her hand. "—I can offer the only proof I have."

She stared at him. "What proof?" she finally whispered.

To her astonishment, her gaze dropped to his mouth. He smiled and began to unbutton his coat.

"And what do you think you're doing?"

"Be patient." When his coat sagged open, he removed his cravat, then started on the buttons of his shirt.

Chapter 19

Jane felt like another person as William unbuttoned his shirt. She was alone in the woods with a man she'd already proven she couldn't resist.

Even after tonight's revelations, she found herself barely able to breathe, remembering what he'd done to her with his mouth and hands, feeling an even newer excitement because he was not at all the man she'd assumed him to be. Her skin flamed beneath her garments, and a newly familiar ache began deep within her.

But she wouldn't give in to her weakness. She had to think everything through, sort out how she should respond to this new information.

She took a deep breath and said, "I hope you

don't think the sight of your skin is going to somehow distract me from your offer of proof."

"But this is the only proof I have."

When his shirt sagged open, she could see little in the firelit darkness, but her mouth went dry.

"Give me your hand, Jane."

She hesitated, then let him take her hand and bring it toward his chest. Her eyes widened when he pressed her palm against his hot skin.

"How is this proof?" she whispered, though she didn't pull away.

"Use your senses, Jane, and just feel."

He slid her palm slowly to the left, up over the hard muscles of his chest. Her fingertips were alive with the sensation of the forbidden, and she was shocked by the knowledge that his heart raced as fast as hers. When her palm brushed his nipple, he inhaled swiftly, his body tense.

But then in the midst of such smoothness, her fingertips encountered a puckered ridge of scarring. In her mind flashed an image of riven flesh, and the pain that must have accompanied it. This was why he hadn't removed his shirt when she'd bandaged his arm.

Hesitantly, she said, "William?"

"It's from a bullet." His voice rumbled deep in his chest beneath her hand. "I figured you'd know that I couldn't normally get such a thing on a Yorkshire farm. There are other scars, Jane, because my old life was dangerous."

She wondered if there were scars on his soul,

because his voice revealed a bleak honesty that she'd never heard from him before. What had he done as a soldier—as a spy?

He leaned nearer, and his lips gently touched hers, his breath caressed her. Her palm was pressed hard against his chest. Every part of her yearned to kiss him deeply, to take away the pain he must have long ago buried.

But he'd lied to her. He could still be lying.

With a gasp, she pulled away from him. "I can't do this. I have to—I have to think."

"I understand." He slid his shirt closed as a cool wind drifted between them. Quietly, he said, "Would it help to know what I planned to do with myself once this business is done?"

She hugged her arms and said nothing, staring at the fire.

"This past year I'd considered several occupations. It may surprise you to know that I almost went into the profession of the church."

After a moment's silence, she asked, "Why did you choose not to?"

"I've seen too much death. I didn't want to see any more on a regular basis."

She glanced at him, but he was looking into the fire, a reflective tilt to his mouth. Though she was angry with him, it didn't stop her from wondering about the life he'd led.

"You have your father's land," she said. "Was the management of this and your inheritance not enough?"

He shrugged. "It didn't seem like enough to do. I . . . needed something. Using another name, I wrote a travel series in a newspaper." He shot a glance at her. "But I don't imagine you want to hear that."

She arched a brow. "Was it not satisfying to educate people?"

"They said I wasn't very good. I didn't evoke enough feelings." He sighed and then smiled. "I don't seem to do well with feelings."

"I've noticed."

"I tried finance and investments, but—"

"Numbers bore you," she interrupted sardonically.

"Ah yes, you're remembering the infamous gambling encounter with Mr. Roderick." He shook his head. "It wasn't boredom I felt, but . . . restlessness. It wasn't for me."

Softly, she said, "I know exactly what you mean."

They looked at each other, then he reached to take her hand. She pulled away.

"We do have things in common," he murmured.

"Not enough. You're making sure of that."

He rose to his feet and stood staring at her, his hands in his pockets, his shirt hanging open. "Go to sleep in the carriage. The benches aren't too uncomfortable."

"Where will you sleep?" she asked.

"The ground is dry. I have blankets stored beneath the benches. I'll be fine."

William followed her to the carriage, then awakened Mr. Barlow to come eat his dinner. Beneath the benches were stores of blankets and matches and candles—and a rifle. He removed that, as well as the ammunition, before replacing the bench tops. She stared at him, wondering if he expected another attack, but he only shrugged, laid several blankets over his arm, and walked toward the fire with Mr. Barlow.

Jane sat down slowly and pushed the shutters aside to watch the men. Killer moved between them, begging for food. As she wrapped a blanket about herself, she thought of the life the men had led, full of challenge and excitement. And it dawned on her that not only had William misled her about his own character but he'd also experienced the adventures he was now trying to deny her. He'd explored the world but only wanted her to remain in his home, giving him children. It would be like living her mother's life, something she'd swore she'd never do. A helpless anger rose inside her.

Jane had sworn never to let this happen to her—but it was happening. William only masked his true intentions with a pleasant, humorous façade. And she was letting him because of her weakness to his touch.

She would no longer give in to his charm so easily.

With resolve strong inside her, she closed her eyes and tried to sleep. She was finally becoming drowsy when the door opened and cold air invaded the carriage.

"Is something wrong?" she asked, struggling to sit up.

William pressed her back down with one hand, while the other arm cradled his panting dog. "Killer needs some pampering tonight. Do you mind if he sleeps with you?"

She groaned and rolled away from him, gesturing toward the far seat. "If Mr. Barlow isn't sleeping in here, that bench is empty."

"But it's cold."

She felt four paws drop firmly onto her lower legs. "William—"

"He takes up little room."

Killer started growling.

"Don't give me that," William continued, talking to the dog as if it could understand. "She doesn't bite, although I keep asking her to. Stay."

"William—"

"Shh. He'll sleep if you keep quiet."

"I'm not worried about *him* sleeping. I just don't want him sleeping with me!"

"Good night," he said with satisfaction.

She wanted to throw something at him, but all she had was the dog, and that seemed a bit cruel. Especially after the animal had chased a brigand, then run for hours behind the carriage. The door closed, and in the silence, she waited, wondering what the dog would do.

Suddenly Killer scrambled up her body, his paws pressing into her thighs and hips until he found the open area between her stomach and the seat back. He circled once, then curled up against her.

At least he was warm, she thought, resting her head on her arm.

The next morning Will opened the carriage door and saw that Jane was still sound asleep. He'd almost expected to find the dog on the opposite bench—they were both rather stubborn—but he didn't see Killer at first. Silently he climbed up and stood in the doorway, but it took him a moment to discover Killer curled up against her stomach.

Then he noticed that her eyes were open, watching him.

He smiled and said in a husky voice, "Well, Killer, this is just where I want to be, and you got here before me."

She frowned. "I think he needs to go outside."

He reached for the dog, letting the back of his hand slide down Jane's soft stomach. He thought she trembled, but she said nothing. Killer gave an angry growl at being disturbed.

"Yes, Killer, I agree that she's not pleasant in the morning," Will answered.

Jane groaned and gave him a push with her foot—her small, bare foot, covered in the sheerest silk stocking that slid against his thigh. He almost forgot what he was going to say as he found himself stepping back onto the ground.

"Oh, and wear the plainest garments you own, and a bonnet that best hides your face," he called. "There's no point in being more obvious than we need to be."

"Then you'll need to get me my portmanteau."

He sighed. "I have to climb?"

"Too exciting for you?" she shot back.

He was relieved at the return of her spirit. "Touché."

"And you pronounced it right this time."

He stared up at her in confusion, but she closed the door in his face.

After giving her the portmanteau, Will spent several minutes taking the coat of arms off the carriage. He wasn't taking any chances, even though he thought they'd eluded their pursuers. After Jane had emerged wearing a fresh dress, she insisted on changing the bandages for his and Barlow's wounds.

Though he only showed her his bare arm, her face was flushed. Yet her expression showed him nothing of what she was feeling. When he told her he was almost healed and she wouldn't need to bandage him anymore, she said nothing. What had he expected—*Oh please let me touch you, William*?

As Barlow harnessed the horses, Will told himself that today would be better. She would get over her anger and perhaps even be interested in what he'd done in his life. After all, she was not a meek girl to be appalled at the dangerous things he'd had to do. Maybe part of what drew him to Jane was her fearlessness, the many ways she *wasn't* like other women.

But as the day wore on, he realized she was not going to forget his deception. His hope that his revealed identity might appeal to her was dashed. She hadn't liked "Lord" Chadwick, and she was angry and disgusted with Will the Spy. What if there was no other Will to show her?

They visited three estates that day, and she found fault with everything. She'd never expressed an opinion before, but now he realized she was actively against a life with him. She was moving further and further away in spirit, and he didn't know what to do about it.

Jane knew she was being ridiculous, but every home they considered seemed so isolated, so sedate that she felt suffocated the moment she entered the front doors. She had wanted to do so much in her life—visit Italian museums, climb Mont Blanc in Switzerland, walk the seashore at Cannes. She was almost bitter that

William had done more with his life than she could ever imagine.

Yet she couldn't stop watching him, the way he moved, the way he tried to encourage her with his smiles. She wanted to kiss him, to hold him, which only made her more disappointed with herself. He too was floundering, and she knew it was her own behavior that was affecting him. She was appalled to find herself wanting to change just for him.

Was this what happened to women? Did they so easily become enslaved by the need for a man that they'd change themselves just to make him happy?

She knew that no matter what she told herself, she was still drawn to him. When he helped her down from the carriage, and his hands settled on her waist, she wanted to press herself against him, to allow herself to forget all her whirling thoughts and concentrate only on feeling. When she reminded herself about the lies he'd told her, and what else he could be keeping from her, she soon was thinking about his mouth on her breast, his hand between her thighs. This duality in her mind was going to drive her insane.

As the sun settled into the horizon, the road they traveled was lined with more and more stone houses as they approached the small town of Epworth. The Market Square, which was the center of town, was set atop a gently sloping hill, with long rows of two-story brick buildings lined up side by side. A tall gothic tower of a church pointed at the sky, as if leading the way to heaven.

William escorted Jane to a small hotel, The Crown and the Horse, that was surrounded by a weedy courtyard and slanting stables. But the gray stone building looked sturdy enough, and inside a woman had obviously taken care of the furnishings. Although the public rooms were sparsely filled, the furniture shone with polish; the food was plain, but hardy and delicious. She and William were shown to separate rooms, and she was grateful to close the door and not have to face him or her conflicting emotions anymore. Her bedchamber was quaint, with a large four-poster bed, and even a little sitting area. The inn must once have catered to wealthy travelers.

She bathed in a hip tub brought up by the servants. As the water gradually cooled, she lay still, luxuriating in feeling clean. The inn was quiet, but for occasional footsteps, and as Jane drowsed in the water, it took several minutes before a murmuring of conversation penetrated.

William was not alone in his room.

Only a half hour before, Mr. Barlow had said good night, and from the gallery outside her room overlooking the courtyard, she'd seen him head past the stables. Had he returned?

The water was cold, so she dried off and began to dress. She found herself donning a chemise and gown rather than her nightclothes. When leaning her ear against the wall didn't allow her to distinguish their words, she went out onto the gallery, now dark but for the occasional lantern on the outside of the building. After looking about to see if she was being watched, she carefully leaned her head against William's door, but the conversation was muffled.

"What do you mean, 'She's on the move again'?" Will demanded, staring at Sam Sherryngton, who was wearing another ridiculous disguise.

"She left Langley Manor the same day you did, and she's heading north."

"To Leeds?"

"Well, I guess, but she's not moving quickly. She's in Tuxford tonight, being watched over by Nick and Charlotte."

"Charlotte's actively participating now?" Will asked with amusement.

"Not . . . quite. But I think she wants to help. She might even believe we're on the right side. But as for our quarry, I think she's going home first."

"Where's home?"

"Her brother's estate is just outside Misterton, in northern Nottinghamshire."

"How do you know she's going there?"

"Why drive right by, when you can refresh yourself in comfortable surroundings? As for how long she's staying, that I don't know."

"What about her henchmen?"

"We've seen nothing so far, which has us worried. Something is bound to happen soon. If these men know we're nearby, they'll be watching over Julia closely."

"I wish this were over," Will said, pacing toward the hearth and leaning a hand against the marble mantel. "I'm anxious to bring Jane to her father."

"I thought you wanted her all to yourself?"

Will ran a hand down his tired face. "It's not working out as I'd planned—or hoped."

Sam gave him a sympathetic smile, but before he could speak, they both heard a man's voice outside the door, then a woman very close by, answering.

It was Jane, and she was out on the gallery. Will could only imagine what she'd think of their conversation. There was a soft knock, and he gave a heavy sigh. Sam glanced questioningly at him.

"You let her in," Will said, walking to the far side of the room, where he couldn't be seen. "No need to have strangers think she's entering a man's room."

Jane smiled nervously at the servant, wishing he would leave, but knowing he wanted to see her safely inside. The night was dark and brisk for August, and the gallery seemed to sag at the far end. She knocked on the door again, wondering why William wasn't answering when she *knew* he was inside.

The door opened and she looked up—

—into the face of a woman.

Chapter 20

Jane's mouth sagged open, and the possibility of coherent speech fled. Whatever she'd imagined happening, it had not been this. Some unspeakably painful emotion settled like a hard ball in her stomach.

"Jane, my dear," said the woman in a low, husky voice, "do come in."

She had no choice. The servant was watching her, and she herself felt a grim curiosity that had to be appeased. With a patently false smile, she stepped inside, and the woman closed the door behind her.

Jane saw William sitting on the edge of the bed, his arms crossed over his chest, Killer using his thigh as a pillow. William's smile looked . . .

pained. She glared at him, then back at the woman.

"I don't think we've officially met," the woman said, sticking out a rather large hand.

"Don't be cruel." William set the dog aside and walked toward them warily. "Jane, this is Sam Sherryngton."

"Short for Samantha?" she said, turning to stare up at the woman, allowing her hand to be clasped.

But suddenly the woman straightened. A deep breath expanded her shoulders and waist until she seemed quite—mannish.

"Short for Samuel," he said in a suddenly deep voice, lifting his hands to remove a wig.

His hair was a dark, rust-colored brown, plastered to his head with sweat. She gaped as he ran his hands through it.

"That is so much better," he said. "I don't know how you ladies stand so much hair piled on your heads."

Trying to recover her balance, Jane looked him up and down. She could have sworn that she—he was a woman just a moment before, but now it seemed hard to imagine. His face was thin, yes, but he had rather rugged cheekbones—with twin spots of rouge. He'd done something with his eyes that had made the lashes seem fuller. She glanced wide-eyed at William, who grinned.

"Sam was the old man at the campfire last night."

"Oh." She'd already shaken his hand, so she politely said, "How do you do, Mr. Sherryngton?"

Both men started to laugh, but she only frowned at them.

"And what are you doing here, Jane?" William finally asked.

"I heard voices," she admitted. "I am tired of lies, so I decided to listen."

"You mean eavesdrop," he said.

"If you'd like to call it that," she answered coolly. "I prefer to think of it as self-protection."

Sam grinned at William. "I like her, Will. She can be just as fiery as her sister."

William groaned, Sam paled beneath his face paint, and once again Jane found herself gaping like a dead fish.

"I heard you say the name Charlotte," she said hoarsely, "but I had no idea you meant—*my* sister? She's not in London? Who's Nick? And did you say they were nearby?" She knew her voice rose sharply, but she couldn't stop herself.

"Jane, slow down." William tried to put his arm around her.

She pushed him away. "Don't you dare touch me, not after I've caught you in *another* lie!"

Sam looked helplessly between them. "I'm sorry."

Though William remained close, he didn't try to touch her again. "I told you I could not tell you everything for your own protection, Jane, not to mention my oath to the government."

"But are you really talking about my *sister*?"

"Yes. Remember the ball she went to, the reason she couldn't travel with us? She somehow overheard Nick's conversation setting this mission up. She misunderstood and thought he was a traitor. He couldn't just let her tell everyone, so he . . . brought her with him."

"You mean kidnapped."

William shrugged.

"How could they possibly have ended up at the same ball together?"

He looked down, then at the door, avoiding her eyes—which she narrowed with suspicion.

With a sigh, he said, "I made sure she was invited to the ball."

"What?"

"I knew a maid would be easier to handle than your sister. I wanted to spend as much time with you as possible."

"And if you wouldn't have manipulated the situation," she said faintly, "Charlotte would be safe from this—Nick person."

"But she'd be with us, which is hardly any safer."

Jane's thoughts were whirling as she imagined her proper sister, so newly out of mourning, stolen from everything she knew. "Oh my God, I must go to her."

"You can't," William said softly, "not right now."

"Don't you dare say that!"

As she advanced on William, Sam backed quickly out of her way.

"My sister is a gentle, proper woman. She must be terrified. She needs me!"

"Jane," Sam began, but when she glared at him, he amended, "Miss Whittington, I think you are underestimating your sister. She has handled herself—and Nick—quite well. She thought she was protecting her country by trying to escape and turn him in."

"She tried to escape?" Jane said incredulously. "Charlotte?"

"Almost succeeded once or twice. She's been quite a handful to Nick. Frankly, it's been good to see him so nonplussed."

Though he sounded sincere, she knew better than to believe either one of them. "I need to see for myself. You will take me to her."

"I've told you that's impossible," William said.

This time when he tried to touch her, she hit him in the arm with her fist. "That is not acceptable! I will see my sister immediately!"

"Jane—"

Sam stepped between them, his skirt brushing against hers. "Will, I might be able to arrange something, especially if Julia is heading for home. It would be brief, probably tomorrow night. Nick and Charlotte are not so far away. We can pick a meeting place."

Though William looked worried, Jane gave him a smug smile. "Sam can be reasonable. It's a shame you're not. Why does everything hinge on a woman named—" She stumbled to a halt and once again felt like an ignorant fool. She stared at William until he reddened. "Julia Reed? You're following her? Is that why we went to Langley Manor?"

He nodded. Sam groaned and clapped his hands over his face as he realized what he'd revealed.

"Has this entire estate hunt been a lie?" she asked with despair.

"No!" William gripped her upper arms. "I *want* to purchase a new estate. That's why Nick thought I'd be perfect to . . . get myself invited to Kelthorpe's."

"Why are you following Julia?"

The two men looked at each other with grim gazes, and Jane felt almost sick with the building tension.

"What has she done?" she whispered when they didn't immediately speak.

William took her hand, and this time she allowed it. "She betrayed British troop strength in

Afghanistan to the Russians. Thousands of men died because of it."

"I—I can't believe that," she said, feeling light-headed, almost grateful when William put his arm around her. In her mind she saw Julia— graceful, confident, so knowledgeable and well traveled. "Are you certain?"

"We have proof," Sam said in a solemn voice. "We'll take her into custody soon. I shouldn't tell you any more—I shouldn't have spilled even that. Forgive me, Will."

Feeling adrift, Jane sank into a chair and stared at Sam as he turned to the mirror to don his wig. She watched in dull fascination as he literally became a woman again in every mannerism and movement, as if he put on another identity, another body.

As William escorted Sam to the door, she realized that William had been doing the same thing with his foppish dandy imitation. Since she'd known him, he'd been trying to be another person.

After Sam left, William came and squatted down in front of her. When he took her hands between his, he felt so warm, and she knew it was because she'd become icy cold.

"We agreed on a place and time to meet tomorrow night," he said softly. "As long as everything goes smoothly, you'll be able to see your sister for a few minutes."

"Minutes?"

"I can't promise more. We seem to have lost Julia's men, but by bringing us all together, we increase the danger."

"I—" She broke off, surprised to feel tears flood her eyes. "I need to see Charlotte, William."

"I know." He smoothed her skirt down over her knees. "I'm sorry for all of this."

She nodded, too overwhelmed for more words. Julia Reed was a traitor to England.

He seemed to understand. Very gently, he cupped her head and pulled her to lean against his chest. She started to cry, clutching his shirt, knowing she was dampening his garments, but unable to stop. He stroked her hair and murmured words she couldn't hear. Nothing was as it seemed, yet she felt strangely safe within the circle of his arms.

And that frightened her more than any revelation tonight. She pushed away from him, using both hands to wipe her cheeks. He handed her a handkerchief.

"I'll go now," she said, rising to her feet, although she felt wobbly.

"Must you? We could talk." He grimaced. "Not that I can say much."

"No, I'm—I'm tired. I can't think anymore."

"Then don't. Try to sleep and keep confident that we'll be able to see your sister tomorrow."

She stared up into his concerned eyes and

again felt an achy, tender feeling move through her. "But you won't sleep, will you?"

He smiled. "Eventually. And after keeping watch on the camp last night, I feel like I'll sleep before my head touches the pillow."

He was lying. But she nodded and allowed him to check the gallery before he escorted her next door. She tried to smile at him, but it was a lame effort. He cupped her cheek briefly, searching her eyes until she closed her door.

But sleep didn't come easily to her, either. She lay there, staring at the vague shadows thrown on the ceiling by the courtyard lanterns. William was so silent next door that she wondered if he was even there—or maybe he finally was sleeping. She knew he wouldn't leave her unprotected.

Her mind churned along as she replayed every hour she'd spent with Julia. She'd seen Sam and William become different people, and she knew Julia must be capable of the same thing, for never once had Julia betrayed anything out of the ordinary. But why would she do such a thing? Why betray her country—her family? She'd said her dowry was small, so the family must have lost their wealth through the years.

But was it worth treason?

Then her thoughts turned to Charlotte, and she imagined what her sister was going through. What kind of man was Nick to kidnap a woman and hold her against her will? She hadn't told William, but she was determined to take Charlotte away. At least Jane could try to protect her sister.

No matter where her thoughts took her, they always came back to William. Sam had called him "Will" and it had seemed to fit the man, who was apparently not as formal as he'd once tried to appear. *Will* . . .

She considered the way he'd first behaved when she'd met him. Last night, he had claimed he'd needed to fit into her world and hadn't known how else to do it. But . . . surely the man he was would have been just fine.

Unless this excuse was only partly the reason. Will's foppish behavior had kept him distant from people, making him an amusing diversion rather than someone to be taken seriously— someone who could be hurt. He obviously struggled with his identity, for he was looking for an occupation rather than accepting himself for the gentleman he now was. Maybe he was struggling to find not just something to do with his life but who he was.

He'd been a soldier and a spy for thirteen years. It must have been difficult to come back to a life he'd never really experienced. He'd been almost desperate to make her a part of this life, though he hadn't known her.

But the one clear thing she'd overheard was

Will telling Sam that he was anxious to take her back to her father's because nothing had worked out as he'd hoped.

Did that mean Will was giving up on her, on their future marriage?

Jane waited for a feeling of triumph, but it never came, only a rising sense of anxiety.

She didn't want him to leave her.

Heavens above, she couldn't imagine not seeing him anymore. And it wasn't just his kisses, or what his hands could make her feel.

She realized that she didn't want to go back to the life she'd lived. She wanted to be with him, verbally sparring, yet forever wanting his touch. It certainly wasn't the adventure of traveling with him, or even the danger, but he had made her feel . . . alive. Aware, awake to the possibilities of a life with him in it.

Was she falling in love with him?

With a groan, she rolled onto her stomach and buried her head under the pillows. She refused to let herself love him, for regardless of the exciting life he'd led, he wanted to keep them isolated on a remote estate. He was forcing her life onto a path not of her choosing. If she did not marry him, was there anything they could share?

She couldn't sleep, and she knew he was awake, too. They could talk. Perhaps she could figure things out just by making him aware of her problems. She remembered the way he had held her, asking nothing except to comfort her. He was a good man; he would listen.

Without giving herself any more time to think about her decision, Jane slipped out of bed and wrapped her dressing gown over her night-dress. She opened the door, looked both ways, and when she saw no one on the gallery, she hurried to Will's door and knocked.

"Yes?" he said almost immediately from the other side.

"It's me."

The door opened and he stared at her. "Is something wrong?"

She shook her head, then slipped by him to go stand in front of the hearth and the glowing coals. He shut the door and turned to look at her. She could feel his uncertainty, his confusion. She felt them herself.

"Where's Killer?" she asked, knowing it was just a way to delay things.

The dog appeared from behind his feet as Will studied her, then opened the door.

"Find Barlow, Killer. You need a little freedom tonight."

"Won't he—get lost?"

"It will definitely take him awhile to find Barlow. I saw another dog in the yard earlier, and I'm certain it was female, by Killer's reaction. He'll have a good time tonight."

"Oh." She willed herself not to blush.

The dog trotted out onto the gallery, and Will closed the door.

Taking a deep breath, she met his gaze. "You must wonder why I'm here, Will."

As he strolled toward her, he put his hands in his pockets. "Will?" he repeated, a smile lifting one corner of his mouth.

She shrugged, blushed. "I heard Sam use it. It suits you."

He stopped before her, a little too close for comfort, but she didn't say anything. She saw his gaze take in what she was wearing, and suddenly she knew how she must look.

But she didn't care. She allowed herself to explore this feeling of daring.

"Charlotte is very important to me," she began tentatively.

Will blinked. He hadn't known what to expect when he'd seen her in his doorway, wearing so little. He tried to forget her clothing and concentrate on her words. "Of course she is. She's your sister."

"It's not as easy as that. We've never seen things the same way. She is . . . much like my mother, very attuned to her position in society."

"And you've been such a hoyden yourself," he said dryly.

She almost smiled. "But I almost have been— at least according to the rules I grew up with. I never wanted what they had."

"What do you mean?" he asked, wanting to

hold her again because she looked so unsure, so . . . lost.

"A typical marriage, with nothing to do except attend the usual parties and dinners."

He tried not to frown, wondering if she was leading up to something he wouldn't like.

"My mother and Charlotte had that," Jane whispered.

"What do you mean?"

"Charlotte married for the usual reasons: wealth, connections, even affection, at least on her part. But once she was married, I watched everything change. She had no say in her life anymore."

"I wouldn't do that—"

But she put up a hand to stop him, and he saw wonder in her face, as if her words were a new revelation to her.

"Her husband made every decision for her, as if she didn't have a mind or know how to use it. It . . . changed her. I couldn't live like that." She hesitated, then met his gaze with defiance. "You're like him, at least in this matter."

Will wanted to take a step back, but he knew that would be the wrong move. "I won't make every decision for you when we're married."

"But aren't you already?"

He opened his mouth, stunned, but nothing came out.

"Don't you see," she said quickly, "you've decided everything. You and my father decided I should marry. You coerced me into traveling with you. You're telling me how we're going to live, picking out estates, making our wedding plans. I am willing to wager that you have already chosen our honeymoon destination."

He felt himself redden, and she only nodded.

"Have you asked me anything? Have you included me in any of your plans?"

"I've asked for your opinion on every estate we've visited."

"And nothing else," she said.

Now Jane was the one advancing, and he held his ground as she pointed at him.

"I can't live like that," she said fiercely.

He knew it was all true, everything she was accusing him of. He had never thought that in pursuing his dreams, he might be denying her *hers*. He felt a wave of tenderness move swiftly through him, followed by remorse at how selfish he'd been.

He framed her face with his hands. "What do you want, Jane?"

"Not my sister's life," she whispered. "Not my mother's life. My life. I need excitement, Will. I crave adventure. I want to see new places and experience things I've never imagined."

And though part of him looked on in horror, wondering how he could satisfy her wishes, the other part was aroused by her love of adventure. He was relieved that she wouldn't be disgusted by the things he'd had to do in the name of duty. She would take him for what he was.

"Marriage is not what you think," he said hoarsely, sliding one hand down her back and pulling her against him, letting his need for her spark into flames. "There is one way I can make you see that a man and woman can intimately share excitement beyond mere dreams."

He pressed a kiss to her cheek, to the corner of her eye, to the edge of her mouth.

"Let me show you, Jane," he whispered against her lips.

Chapter 21

Will was right, Jane thought wildly, sliding her hands up his back to mold herself even closer to him. She would make her own decisions, regardless of society's conventions. She wanted this—she wanted *him*, and every other decision could wait.

His big hands spread across her back and down to her hips. Without all her many layers of clothing, she could feel him knead her backside. Against her stomach she felt that part of him she'd only seen on statues, so different from her own body, so enticing. She knew little about lovemaking, and she wanted to know it all.

Her head dropped back and he kissed her then, deep explorations of her mouth that made her desperate for his touch. She tasted him, suckled him, and caught his head with her hand so she could push her tongue deep inside him. He groaned against her mouth.

"Stop me now," he murmured, pressing kisses to her chin, her jaw, then down behind her ear. "If you're going to, do it now, don't let me—"

"I won't stop you," she gasped, her hand threaded deep in his thick, brown hair. "Show me, Will, show me everything."

He shuddered in her arms, and she marveled at how her passion was reciprocated. She needed something only he could give, wanted the adventure of intimacy with him more than she'd thought possible. She would have fallen if he hadn't held her so close.

She let herself sink in his arms, arched against him, her head thrown back in exultation. Her dressing gown slid to the floor, then his lips skimmed across the bare hollow of her throat to the thin fabric of her nightdress. As he pressed his face between her breasts, she wrapped her arms about his head, holding him there, desperate for the magic he could work with his mouth. But since she didn't know how she could ask for such a thing, she could only tremble against him.

Between her thighs she was hot and aching and sensitive. When she lifted her leg, she was pressed even more intimately against him. She gasped as he caught her knee and pulled higher. She felt the hard ridge of him against her most private depths, and the urge to push even closer was too much to deny. With a thrust of his hips he rolled against her. She cried out as a shock of awareness and pleasure shivered deep in her stomach.

"Should I do that again?" he asked huskily, raising his head to brush her lips with his.

"Oh please," she murmured.

He watched her face as he ground against her, and she returned the stare with heavy-lidded eyes. His face was etched with an intensity she'd never seen before. He was a hunter after his prey, a savage after the only thing that mattered.

How it exhilarated her! He lifted her into his arms and carried her to the bed, a four-poster large enough for the two of them. When he set her down, she felt a rush of air against her legs and realized he was drawing her nightdress up. She wanted him to see her, wanted to see him. Her skin was alive with sensitivity as she felt the trail of fabric against her buttocks, against her stomach, and over her breasts. She raised her arms, and then clothing obscured her view. When she could see again, she was naked. She tried to release the gown, but he kept her arms trapped in it, forcing her to arch.

He stared at her breasts, and the light of passion in his eyes made her feel like the most beautiful woman in the world. He cupped her cheek softly, then swept his hand down her neck, teasing the edge of her breast, crossing her stomach, along her hip and thigh. Brazenly she wanted to turn into his caress, to make him touch her intimately as he'd done during their game of billiards. That night lived in her dreams, and she wanted it to come alive again and fulfill its promise.

And then her arms were free and she tried to unbutton his shirt. He stopped her.

"Let me," he murmured, pushing her back until she sat on the edge of the bed.

"But—"

"Another time. But right now, if you touch me too much, I won't be able to control myself."

"Control yourself?" she questioned, needing to know everything.

He chuckled. "I want to delay this as long as possible."

"But why?" She stared avidly as his fingers opened each button.

"Because the feelings are so much better the longer you make yourself wait."

His shirt dropped to the floor, and she gasped. "I can't wait much longer."

In front of her face was the broadest, smoothest expanse of skin she'd ever seen. There were muscles she never knew one had, rippling beneath the surface. She saw the bullet wound scar, then the scab on his left arm. White marks like the nick of a knife stood out, and she traced one, only to feel him shudder.

She leaned her head against his chest as he struggled with his trousers. Defiant now, she flicked her tongue against his nipple, as he'd done to her. His groan made her smile with feminine satisfaction.

"Jane—"

She caught the other nipple between her teeth and gently tugged. He shivered, and as the rest of his clothing fell to the floor, she watched in astonishment as his penis fell heavily against her thigh.

She was not ignorant that a man's body was different from hers. But this—she didn't know what he was supposed to do with that. But she wanted to. She tentatively touched the smooth head of it, and it jumped against her hand.

"Jane, no—" His voice was tense, as if he was in pain.

"You don't like to be touched?" she whispered, lifting her head to stare into his face. "I've enjoyed every touch you've given me."

His eyes were closed, his face taut with control. "For a man who has not done this in a long time, just your touch will be enough to start things I won't be able to stop."

"To start what things?"

He opened his eyes and stared at her, his breathing ragged. "Do you not know?"

She shook her head. "There seemed to be no way to acquire the knowledge—not without asking someone."

"Acquire the—" His laughter was another shudder. "Do you want me to tell you—or show you?"

Will gently pushed her, and she fell back on her elbows.

"Which is faster?" she asked breathlessly, watching wide-eyed as he slid his fingers between her knees.

"Are you in a hurry?"

Ever so slowly, he trailed his fingers up her inner thighs. Even though she kept them close together, she shivered and even squirmed, so intense was her feeling of . . . anticipation.

"I think so," she said, her voice faint.

"It only feels that way."

Just before he would have touched the curls at the juncture of her thighs, he pulled away. Everything inside her went tense with disappointment. He only smiled, and repeated the motion, sliding just a fraction higher. He stopped himself again, but this time he put his hands on her hips and slid them up her torso, teasing the undersides of her breasts before gently cupping them. With a moan, she closed her eyes, letting her head drop back with the pleasure of it all. She'd never imagined such a gentle caress could feel so wonderful. He leaned against her, his legs parting her thighs. When her gaze flew to his, he put his hands on her knees and separated them even farther.

She knew she should be embarrassed, but

there was something about the pleasure and awe in his eyes that made her trust him with the secrets of her body. He spread her legs as far as he could, and this time ran his hands down the top of her thighs, letting his thumbs ride her curls. The shock of pleasure was startling, almost painful, and she wanted more.

He suddenly leaned over her, bracing himself with one hand next to her head. She held her breath, her gaze locked with his, as his fingers slid deep between her thighs and parted her.

She inhaled a shocked gasp, arching her body toward him, but he held himself away and watched her. Her hands were restless, and she clutched his shoulders, but he wouldn't lower himself. Again his fingers explored her, and her pleasure reached a new, even more incredible summit when he touched and circled one particular spot.

When he stopped, she heard her own unrecognizable voice cry, "Please!"

He kissed her then, touching her nowhere but on her lips and between her thighs. With her mouth she told him everything, that she wanted more, that she wanted him on the bed with her, that she hoped he was feeling the same things she was. His fingers slid deeper, and she stiffened.

"Right there," he said hoarsely against her mouth. "I'll come inside you there."

His fingers pressed into her, his tongue thrust

into her mouth, and she moaned. "Then do it."

His fingers left her, and before she could express her disappointment, he traced circles on her nipple, and through the pleasure she noticed that his fingers—and now her breast—were wet.

"I—did that?" she asked.

He grinned, then bent and licked her nipple. She convulsed and brought her knees up, feeling his hips between her thighs, his penis nudging her lower stomach.

"You taste good," he murmured and licked her again, a warm rasp of his tongue.

"Oh Will." She covered her face with her hands, not knowing if she should feel mortified or just desperate—or both.

He pressed her breasts together and moved between them, teasing and nipping with his tongue and lips, drawing away until she reached for him in frustration. He finally let his hips rest fully against hers, and his erection was almost as intimate as his fingers had been. She was impatient for it, greedy for all of it.

He suckled her nipple deep in his mouth, and then she felt him probing her. With his big hands, he pulled her hips to the edge.

"Shouldn't you—come up on the bed?"

"Can't wait," he said tightly.

As he bent over her again, she felt him begin to slowly ease inside. It was a large, hot intrusion, and as she opened her eyes and watched his face, it seemed almost painful for him.

"Will—" She broke off when it suddenly became uncomfortable.

He kissed her then, and with a sudden thrust buried himself inside her. A brief stab of pain subsided almost immediately, and she let go her pent-up breath with a sigh. When she opened her eyes, he was watching her.

"All right?" he asked.

She nodded. "Is this . . . it?"

He grinned wickedly, then withdrew from her body and plunged back inside.

She gave a shaky groan. "Oh . . . I see."

And then he was moving against her, mating with her, holding her hips still as he pushed in as deeply as he could. Again he bent over her and kissed her breasts, and every sensation he'd made her feel was spiraling ever higher, reaching for a place she couldn't imagine—straining, wanting.

And then she shattered. There was no other word for the explosion of feeling that tore through her, for the tenderness he made her feel toward him. He shuddered hard against her, groaning, and she realized he felt it too.

He came to rest on top of her, their bodies touching intimately from their heads to their thighs. But he wasn't uncomfortably heavy; in fact, she welcomed the weightiness of him. He pressed his face against her shoulder, his eyes closed, and she let her fingers trace his brow, over his eyelid, down his cheek to his lips.

With a little growl, Will took her finger into his mouth, then opened his warm, brown eyes and looked at her, close enough that she felt his breath, even the pounding of his heart. There was an intimacy now between them that she couldn't imagine sharing with another man. He suckled her finger and flexed himself deep inside her. She gasped at how sensitive and strangely tender she felt.

"Are you sore?" he whispered, releasing her finger to kiss her gently.

Jane shook her head.

"Uncomfortable?"

No again.

"Then would you mind if I climb up beside you, because I'm starting to cramp up."

A giggle escaped her, and she clapped her hand over her mouth. He left her body, and she felt a void of loneliness that she could barely admit to herself.

On his hands and knees Will crawled up, then collapsed on his side, one hand on her stomach, his knee riding hers. He forced himself to keep his touches simple, not knowing if she would welcome another bout of lovemaking. He was more than ready—ready for all of it. He wanted to wake up with her every day like this, and the thought that she had not yet decided whether to marry him sent an unfamiliar jolt of worry through him.

She breathed a deep sigh.

"Jane?"

She lifted her lids and gazed at him with her tropical green eyes. Her face was serious, but there was just enough of a tilt to the corners of her lips to make him think she was not displeased.

"Yes?" she whispered.

"Was it what you thought?"

When she rolled onto her side facing him and snuggled closer, relief eased through him.

"Since I had no idea what to expect, I will admit my only feelings before were curiosity and nervousness."

"And now?"

He couldn't help himself; he moved lower in the bed until before him were the most beautiful breasts he'd ever seen. He leaned into her and let their soft roundness pillow his face. Breathing in her warm, moist scent, letting himself feel surrounded by her—it was like coming home. She stroked through his hair, as if encouraging him to touch her. Even after everything they'd discussed, all the lies he'd been forced to explain a little at a time, she still permitted him this intimacy. She couldn't reject him in the end, not when she could kiss the top of his head with a tenderness that stunned him. He gave a heartfelt sigh and turned to take her nipple into his mouth, biting gently until she gasped.

"And now," Jane said, "it seems I still don't understand. We can do this again?"

"Any time you want," he murmured against her breast.

Suddenly she pushed him onto his back. For a moment, he felt a touch of loneliness as he worried that the past hour was all he'd ever have of her.

"Is it my turn?" she asked.

He frowned, then watched with dawning pleasure as she ran her hand across his chest. "Your turn?" he echoed stupidly.

"You did things to me—now I get to touch you. Is that correct?"

When she rose up on her hands and knees at his side, her breasts swinging gently, his mouth dried to cotton, and he had to swallow to speak.

"We can do anything we want to each other, as long as we always say when something is uncomfortable," he said distractedly.

"Are you uncomfortable lying like this?"

"No."

"Then tell me what pleases you. You seem to know everything about a woman's body."

When she leaned over to kiss him, her breast brushed his arm and he groaned. "Not from too much experience, I assure you." His head was afire with confusion and desire and something so primitive he couldn't name it. No woman had ever asked how she could please him. "Any touch from you is all I'd ask."

She looked down his body and noticed that

he was ready for whatever she would suggest. "Can we do . . . it again?"

"It's making love, my sweet," he said, sliding her long black hair out of her face so he could look into her eyes. "With you it will never be just sex."

And then he realized what his words implied, what neither of them might want to say. She hesitated but said nothing. Then she surprised him by taking his erection into her fist, making him feel like a virgin all over again.

"Must you be on top each time?" she asked, looking away as her blush spread from her face down to her lovely breasts.

Surely she could feel him grow bigger in her hand. "There are many different ways to come together, Jane," he said tightly.

Then he took her knee and lifted it over his body. She braced herself awkwardly, and he watched the sudden knowledge that swept over her face when she found herself seated on his hips, his erection cradled against her.

"Aah," she murmured, arching her back and lifting her hair high before letting it fall.

Such a simple thing, hair, but watching the sleekness of it slide down her back, with several strands swinging forward to curl about her breasts, made him wild with passion for her. He lifted her by the hips but stopped when he saw her quick frown.

"Tell *me* what to do—don't just do it," she admonished.

"Lift yourself up and guide me inside you," he said hoarsely.

He closed his eyes, certain he'd spill his seed at the sight of her gripping him, her tentative efforts to understand how they fit together. When she got it right, and she was burying him slowly inside her, he opened his eyes to see the look of stunned pleasure on her face.

"This feels different," she said, almost to herself. "Do I lift up—"

"Wait! Just wait, or this will end too quickly. Let me pleasure you again."

"But this is pleasurable," she said, wearing the beginnings of a stubborn frown that he was coming to know quite well.

"Just close your eyes and wait," he murmured, reaching up to caress her breasts.

As he touched her, he felt the shudder deep in her womb caressing him. He memorized her expression as passion stole over her. He held the weight of her breasts, rubbed their peaks, and came up on his elbows so he could take their sweetness into his mouth.

With one hand, he reached between her thighs and found the little nub, the source of her pleasure. He stroked her gently, listening to her soft sighs, then her panting moans, feeling the last of his control splinter and break apart. He arched and thrust up inside her, his fingers caressing, his mouth suckling, and felt the shudder of her climax throughout his body. He joined her in oblivion.

When Jane collapsed on top of him, he guided her to the side and pulled the blankets about them both. Her eyes were closed, her body limp and sated.

"I should go," she murmured.

"Sleep here with me." He kissed her gently, then lay down and pulled her against his chest. "We have all the time in the world."

But *he* wasn't tired. He lay, content, and watched her.

Chapter 22

Once or twice during the night, Jane almost came to consciousness, but Will hushed her and stroked her and held her until once more she drifted off.

Yet somehow she knew when he finally fell asleep. The sun had not yet risen when she propped herself up on her elbow to watch him in the gray light before dawn. She didn't know how he functioned with so little rest. Without the vibrancy of his expression, she could see the tired smudges beneath his eyes, the subtle lines that fanned out from the corners. She brushed a curl of hair off his cheek, gently fingered where a dimple would be when he smiled, and studied him.

She had barely thought him handsome when

first they'd met. Now she found staring at him almost painful because of his beauty in her eyes.

She had thought choosing lovemaking outside of marriage would free her from society's conventions. She had thought it would be another grand adventure, the first of many.

But as she watched him peacefully sleeping, she knew that she was no longer free, that she was now bound even more closely to this man she hadn't wanted to marry. What would she do now? What if he had given her a child, the "beautiful baby" her mother had said they'd have together? Logically, this must be how babies were conceived.

She put her head down on his shoulder, feeling confused and uncertain. His skin was warm against her cheek and smelled of him—spicy, exotic, manly. Just the scent was enough to make her loins tighten and ache. She had never felt this way about any man before.

Quietly, she left the warmth of his bed, donned her discarded clothes, then crept to the door.

"Jane?"

She jumped a foot on hearing Will's voice so close to her shoulder. He was beside her, naked.

"How did you do that?" she demanded.

He looked confused. "Do what?"

But she lost the train of her thoughts when her gaze moved slowly down the perfection of his body. Wide sculpted shoulders, narrow hips, the muscular legs of a horseman. Between his thighs, he now looked more like the statues she'd seen. But as she watched, that . . . manly part of him began to grow.

She raised wide eyes and found him grinning at her, his wicked dimples teasing her.

"All you have to do is look at me and I'm ready for you, my sweet."

And then he pushed her against the door, kissing her hard. She forgot her fears and worries and just held on, wishing they never had to leave the room.

He finally nuzzled her neck and whispered, "In a few hours, order a bath sent to your room."

"What?" she murmured dazedly, awash in the sensations of his big body pressing hard against her.

"Order a bath, and after the servants go, leave your door unlocked and get into the tub."

Flustered, embarrassed, she tried to push him away. "I—I don't know what we should do next, what all this means—"

"Don't think. We have all day before we have to meet up with Nick."

He licked a path up her throat, dipped into her ear, and moaned. "Will you do as I ask?"

"Y-yes," she breathed, ready to tear off her clothes if only he would make her feel so alive again.

When the heat of him left her, she sagged against the door. He drew her away, opened it and looked both ways. With a helpful push from him, she found the energy to quickly walk to her own door. For a moment, they looked at each other, and she thought she should refuse his request—but she couldn't, so enthralled was she at the thought of his plans. She went inside and closed her door, then collapsed on the bed, arms flung wide, and relived everything that had just happened. Doubt tried to surface in her mind, warring with the desires of her body, but she pushed the uncertainties away.

Will managed to sleep until he heard the sound of servants lugging a tub into Jane's room. He lay still, dozing, as he listened to the parade of people carrying buckets of hot water. The thought of Jane naked, sunk to her breasts in water, did things to his insides he could barely contemplate.

But he wanted more. He was greedy with it, overcome with the intense need to bind her to him. He wrestled with his conscience, because he knew lovemaking would almost certainly guarantee that she would marry him. Didn't she understand that this passionate attraction between them was more exciting than any adventure he'd ever had?

He didn't know why it was so important to have this one brave, stubborn woman as his wife. He was fascinated with the logical way Jane's mind worked, with the interest with which she faced every challenge. She had long ago ceased to be a convenient wife. Now he couldn't live without her, wanted her body and soul, wanted her to love him.

Did she require his love in return? Did she need to hear it? Her power to hurt him was unlimited now, and he couldn't imagine giving her proof of it.

But he was thinking too much, instead of reveling in her awakening sensuality. He put his ear to the wall between their rooms, thought he heard the slosh of water. He forced himself to wait several more minutes, dressing slowly in simple trousers and shirt, knowing he wouldn't be wearing them long. When he could stand the delay no longer, he left his room, turned her doorknob and was inside.

The first thing that attacked Will's senses was the moist, steamy smell of jasmine. At almost the same moment, his eyes feasted on the sight of Jane in a large tub, her hair piled on her head, a stray curl escaping to cling wetly to her shoulder. She froze when she saw him, one small foot pointed to the ceiling, a washcloth pressed to her calf.

When she started to lower her foot, he hoarsely said, "Stop!"

Unsteadily, he walked across the room to stand above her, looking down into water still clear enough for him to see the wavering image of her body. The dark shadows between her thighs called to him; her breasts broke the surface of the water with each quick breath, sparkling in the candlelight and the muted glow of daylight outside her curtained window.

He took her foot in both hands and pressed his mouth to the delicate, wet arch, then kissed each toe. The sound of his name on her lips made him burn with an arousal fiercer than any he'd imagined.

Jane felt light-headed, feverish, as he gently kissed her foot. When he released it, she lowered it back into the tub, watching in dazed wonder as he stripped the clothes from his body. Naked, aroused, he took the cloth from her numb fingers, rubbed it in soap, and began to wash her.

"Close your eyes," he whispered.

She moaned as she obeyed, letting her senses tingle and come to life as she wondered what he would do next. Every touch of the soapy cloth was a long, slow caress against her limbs. From behind, he lavished attention on her back, massaging any weariness left from their journey. Then his slick, soapy hands slid forward over her shoulders and cupped her breasts, kneading them, playing with them. Her head fell back and rested against his shoulder as she lay in the darkness of sensation, the brilliance of desire. Her nipples ached under his fingertips as he twirled them, rubbed them, soothed them.

When he moved away from her back, she

tensed, but his hands never left her, only slid down around to her bottom and lifted her hips out of the water. She braced her hands on the tub, more than ready to be taken to bed.

"Relax," he said, using one hand to guide her arms until the tub was supporting her back and shoulders.

She hung awkwardly from his grip on her hips, holding her out of the water, one foot balancing her weight in the tub. She couldn't help but open her eyes as he propped the other foot against the edge, then spread her thighs before him. Shocked, she heard the water sluicing off her body, felt the stunned embarrassment of his piercing gaze so close to such an intimate part of her.

"Will—"

"Shhh." He soaped one hand, then slid it down between her thighs.

She gasped, arching involuntarily, then shuddered as he cleaned her, his fingers delving and exploring and caressing. With scoop after scoop of water, he washed the last of the soap away, then met her gaze. To her shock, he put his mouth where his hand had been and kissed her.

"Will!" she cried, stiffening with the onslaught of pleasure.

She couldn't tear her eyes away from the sight of his tongue delving into her then swirling around the swollen bud. Everything inside her tightened and swelled higher and higher, closer to the ecstasy she knew awaited her. Then he suckled her between his lips and she convulsed with her climax, shaking in his grip, overcome with a pleasure so intense she wanted to weep.

Dazed, she could only watch as he lowered her hips back into the water. Then he left her, picking up two buckets that had been placed near the door. He topped each with bathwater until the depth in the tub was down to her waist. Then he stepped in.

She giggled as he sat down and the water rose back up. Only a few drops escaped to the floor. Then she forgot all else as he drew her onto his lap, placed her legs about his hips, then sheathed himself deep inside her.

Against his mouth she moaned her delight, tasted herself on his lips, and trembled at the power of how right and good he made her feel. She caressed his wet skin, felt the flexing of muscles in his hips as he rocked inside her. She played with his nipples and he played with hers, their tongues mimicking the mating of their bodies. She felt his tension and was overwhelmed with the depth of his passion for her.

When he lost himself and shuddered inside her with a groan, she held his head against her shoulder and let herself be at peace with the thought of loving him.

They stayed in bed all day, dozing, loving, talking, and even reading aloud to each other.

They took their meals at the little table in her sitting area, dressed each other as the daylight faded. Since this crazy journey began, this was the most relaxed Jane's body had been—and the most confused her mind had felt, for she now understood the temptation of locking herself away on a lonely estate with only Will for company.

When it was time to leave, she walked out on his arm into the still-warm air of early evening. Mr. Barlow was waiting for them beside the carriage, and Killer wiggled excitedly before launching himself at Will's knees.

Jane blushed, wondering what Mr. Barlow might be thinking, but the older man limped around to open the door for her. He tipped his hat and smiled at her, and she returned it with relief.

As their carriage pulled out of the yard, a lone, longhaired dog stood mournfully beside the building and watched them go. Killer jumped up on Jane's lap and put his paws on the window with a soft whine. Will leaned across them both, saw the other dog, and laughed.

"No wonder he looks so satisfied."

Jane could only smile as she hesitantly ran her hand down the fur on Killer's back. He was very soft, she thought grudgingly. With a little whine, the dog leaned into her hand for more petting. Smiling, Will lifted Killer and put him on the other bench.

The journey took a little over an hour, but they kept the shutters closed, and their attention on each other, and weren't aware of the time passing. When finally the carriage slowed, she righted her clothing and laughed when Will, with a look of discomfort, did the same.

"You're a tease, Jane Whittington," he said as she pushed away, "arousing a man to such heights only to reject him."

"I have hardly rejected you—have I, Killer?" she turned to ask the dog.

Killer curled even tighter into a ball and kept his back to them.

"We're shocking him, I think," Will said.

"Surely he's witnessed other sights. How long has he been with you?"

"Five years—but no, you're the first willing female he's seen in my arms."

"Were there unwilling ones?" she asked sweetly.

"Unwilling to be captured, you might say. But I turned them over to the proper authorities, even though many of them expressed a desire to prove to me that if I promised to let them escape, they would first reward me handsomely."

She cursed her reddening complexion, which so easily gave away her thoughts. "Women tried to—"

"Seduce me?" he offered, grinning. "They tried. But ah, duty bound me."

"And it still does," she said thoughtfully, seeing a new tension in his manner, in the way he peered out at the darkness through the shutters. She thought of him risking his life for his country, thought of all his knowledge, all his strength—and trembled with how much she desired him.

She realized with growing anxiety that she thought about him all the time, anticipated each touch when they were alone. For heaven's sake, she'd trembled foolishly in anticipation of a solitary carriage ride with him. This had to stop. She had to learn to deal with her feelings and still be her own person, with her own life to live. Surely after months in the dull countryside, even lovemaking with Will would lose its potency.

But she couldn't imagine it, and that frightened her more than she cared to admit.

Suddenly they heard Mr. Barlow call, "Hold there!" and they felt the team stop and the carriage rock violently. Several gunshots rang out. Will flung the door open, and over his shoulder she looked out on a nightmarish scene of violence amidst a cold swirl of fog. By lantern light, a brawl of men spilled out of an inn courtyard and onto the road.

Will turned to her, and she caught a flash of unease on his face before his expression hardened into determination. "Stay here."

"But Will—"

"If you follow me, you'll only get us—or yourself—killed. Barlow will keep you safe."

To her horror, he vaulted from the carriage, his legs disappearing in the mist as he ran toward the fight. With a wild bark, Killer followed him.

She heard a crash of metal on metal and realized that there must be swords involved. And Will was unarmed! A sick feeling of terror closed her throat, and she strangled back a scream, as even Mr. Barlow climbed quickly from the coach-box.

"Will!" a man shouted.

From the center of the group, a sword was flung, arcing end over end, reflecting in the lantern light, headed straight for Will. Jane cried out, certain that he would be wounded, but he reached up and caught it with a sure grip born of longtime skill.

And then with a wild cry, he entered the melee.

Chapter 23

Jane clutched the doorframe and watched with wide eyes, trying to understand what was happening. Surely the man who'd called Will's name knew him, so perhaps he was Nick, and another combatant was Sam. That left two men who were strangers.

And where was her sister? Tears filling her eyes, Jane almost jumped from the carriage in her haste to find Charlotte. But Will had told her not to move. She kept her gaze on him so as not to lose him in the near darkness. He wielded a sword like a master, with the skill and power not found in men who only studied the sport to relieve boredom. There were no rules here, no care for injury, only the desperation to live another day.

Will pushed back his opponent, and she saw the flash of his grin, an exultation, a thrill to be alive that she herself had never felt before meeting him.

With Mr. Barlow joining, it was now four to two. With a cry, one dark-clad man fell, vanishing into the low fog, and in the confusion the other escaped, vaulting onto the back of a horse and fleeing even Killer's reach.

She stared at the four men as they breathed heavily or leaned on their swords and rifles, even laughed with each other. She felt sick with fear, angry at their disregard for danger. Where was her sister?

Holding her skirts in her hands, she climbed out of the carriage and ran to the men: Will, Mr. Barlow, Sam, and a stranger. Behind them all, several patrons of the inn peered curiously past the high walls surrounding the courtyard.

Will caught her, flung an arm about her shoulder and said, "Nick Wright, this is Jane Whittington, my future bride. I believe you know her sister, Charlotte."

This made Sam, dressed as a poor farmer this time, stutter with laughter. Jane rounded on Will and pushed him away, angry that he was so cocky while the situation could be so desperate.

She looked up at Nick, and her words died in her throat. He was a big man, taller and broader than Will, with dark hair and eyes so deep and soulless she wondered if any emotion ever showed. *This* man had her sister? Every line of him screamed *domination*. He must be Charlotte's worst nightmare. How could she have devoted two days to her own gratification, forgetting her sister's plight?

Nick gave her a bow that would rival a courtier's. "Miss Whittington, how good to meet you."

He had blood on his face, and his hair was wild, and she was so afraid she wanted to hide.

"Where's Charlotte?" she demanded coldly.

He arched one eyebrow, and in the lantern light his half-shadowed face remained amused.

Will tucked her close beneath his arm, subduing her even though she struggled. "I promised you'll see her, Jane. We need to see to the body first."

Nick glanced at the group of people gathering in the courtyard, then back at Will, and spoke in a low, gravelly voice. "We should probably go our separate ways for tonight. It's too dangerous to stay together any longer, especially since one bastard got away to warn Julia."

"No!" Jane cried, struggling, then looked up at Will. "You promised!"

Sam nudged Nick with his elbow. "Didn't I tell you the sisters were alike?"

While Nick only nodded, Jane tried to remember a lifetime of control. She took a deep breath. "We'll be brief. I just need to make sure she's all right."

After Mr. Barlow discreetly went to calm the horses, some unspoken communication passed between the three men. They'd experienced things together that she could only imagine: danger and intrigue and the possibility of death. She was out of her depth in their world, but they'd forced it on her, and now they owed her.

"Very well," Nick said. "Sam, you and Barlow go explain to the innkeeper about being attacked by thieves. Bury the corpse as discreetly as you can. I'll take Will and Miss Whittington to her sister. We won't be long," he added, giving her a stern warning with his dangerous eyes.

Jane only nodded, and pushed away from Will. This time he let her go, then fell into step behind her as she followed Nick.

There was a sudden impatient bark, quickly silenced, and Nick turned around.

"And what is that?" His voice sounded displeased.

"You remember Killer," Will said, then put his hands on his hips and looked about him into the low, swirling fog. "If I can find him. Ah, there he is." He bent down to scoop up his dog.

Jane thought Nick would laugh at the dog, as most other men did.

"Killer? *The* Killer?" Nick said with amazement. "He survived the shipwreck?"

Will grinned and nodded as Nick ruffled the dog's furry head.

"Shipwreck?" she asked in amazement.

"It was nothing," Will said. "We were almost to Cape Town, so we only floated in the wreckage for two days."

"And Killer survived," Nick repeated, shaking his head. "That dog has the lives of a cat."

He turned to look at Jane, who had so many questions she couldn't think which to ask first.

"Killer was once run over by a barrel aboard ship as he was rescuing a little boy," Nick said. "The dog's broken ribs literally pierced the skin. And still he survived."

Will nodded solemnly. "I had to chew his food for him for a week."

"Chew his food—" she choked out.

Nick laughed. "Has Barlow forgiven Killer for saving his life?"

"You must be joking. That man can hold a grudge."

Jane finally stamped her foot. "Can we please just go to Charlotte now?"

Will handed Killer over to Mr. Barlow, and they followed Nick. They didn't enter the courtyard of the inn but turned into the foggy darkness beyond the road, opposite the way the attacker had fled. Soon, Jane could see nothing. She stumbled as the invisible weeds thickened and the road fell away behind them. Both men seemed to have no problem in the partial moonlight.

It seemed to take forever as they tramped through what she thought was an overgrown field. Her skirts parted the mist. She almost turned her ankle, but Will caught her from behind, then took her arm and walked beside her. They reached a small copse of trees, and she heard the soft whinny of a horse. The outline of a large carriage materialized out of the darkness.

She didn't know what she'd expected, but certainly she hadn't thought of Charlotte alone but for horses. Then she saw the coachman, swathed in dark clothing, watching them silently from above.

Nick put his hand on the door, and she could see the moonlit gleam in his eyes when he turned back to face her. "I just want you to know that for Charlotte's own protection, I had to bind her."

"What!" Jane cried, then bit her lip as she heard the echo of her voice across the field.

"Shh!" Will said into her ear. "I'm certain there is a good explanation."

Nick quickly agreed. "Much as Charlotte understands what we're doing, I knew she would follow me and make even more trouble in her attempt to help."

Shocked and worried for her fragile sister, Jane drew herself up and used her coldest voice. "Let me see her at once."

He opened the door and climbed up inside. As Jane followed, she heard muffled, angry cries, and realized that he had actually *gagged*

Charlotte! Will squeezed in behind her and found a seat at her side, opposite her sister.

"I'll light the lantern," Nick said, and he struck a match.

As light flared up, Jane gaped at her sister, seated in the corner at Nick's side, bound at her feet and wrists, a gag across her mouth. Her normally proper hairstyle was skewed sideways, and several dark curls had tumbled down her shoulder. Charlotte stared fixedly at Nick, surely so frightened out of her mind that she hadn't even noticed that Jane was there too.

Before Jane could soothe her poor, traumatized sister, Nick leaned toward Charlotte and said softly, "I'm going to remove the gag. Let us not have a repeat of past performances."

Charlotte seemed frozen with terror as Nick pulled the gag from between her lips. Then with a surprising swiftness, she turned and sank her teeth into his hand.

"Ow!" Nick said, cursing as he pulled away from her. "I told you not to overreact! You know why—"

"How dare you!" Charlotte cried. "You will never—ever!—do that to me again."

"Charlotte—"

"Untie me this instant!"

There was a command to her voice that a flabbergasted Jane had never imagined possible. She remained silent, watching with wide-eyed fascination as Nick untied Charlotte's ankles and got kicked, then untied her wrists and received a hard point with her finger in the center of his chest. Jane almost didn't recognize this spirited woman as her sister. Had she ever known her at all?

"What happened!" Charlotte demanded, then whirled toward Jane and Will. "And who—" Her mouth suddenly sagged open. "Jane?" she whispered.

With glad cries, the two sisters fell into a tight hug. Jane, who'd never felt close to Charlotte, found herself weeping with relief. Charlotte laughed at her and pulled a handkerchief from her pocket. She handed it over, then said hello to Will as if she were receiving guests in a drawing room instead of being newly unbound by her captor.

Jane wiped tears from her eyes. "Oh, Charlotte, I cannot tell you how I've worried. I had no idea you had been kidnapped!"

"They only tell you what they think you should know," Charlotte said and threw a disgusted look at an amused Nick.

"Are you hurt?" Jane bestowed her own glare at Nick. She could only imagine what such a large, untamed-looking man might do to a helpless woman. "Did he—"

"No, nothing like that," Charlotte said, interrupting her fears. "I was frightened at first, but he never harmed me. I understand that I might have jeopardized everything if he'd have allowed me to escape. But now"—She turned back to Nick and leaned toward him.—"now I can help! And he won't let me."

Nick crossed his arms over his chest, looking uneasy and worried for just a moment, until his face smoothed out into impassivity. Suddenly Jane saw through his posturing and thought he might actually be fond of her sister.

But that didn't matter. She would demand that Will help her take Charlotte away. She wasn't sure how that would be accomplished, but surely a man of Will's resourcefulness could think of something. But he continued to watch the unfolding scene with amused consternation, saying nothing.

"Char, see here," Nick said in a cajoling voice, "I've been trained to deal with such things and you have not."

"But I learn quickly!" she said.

Jane stared in amazement when Charlotte put her hand on the brute's arm. He called her "Char"? He tried to persuade her instead of ordering her about?

He patted her hand awkwardly. "I killed a man tonight, Charlotte. It is not a thing I want you to see."

Charlotte caught her lip between her teeth. "Were you hurt?" she whispered.

And in those words, Jane heard a wealth of information. Charlotte would never leave Nick.

Silently Jane watched Charlotte discover the shallow slice to the back of Nick's hand, then rip her own petticoats to bandage him. All along she kept up a steady, angry patter of words about Nick's inability to take care of himself. When she bent over Nick's hand, Jane saw in his black eyes a fleeting glimpse of tenderness.

Though Jane had never thought herself close to Charlotte, they now shared an adventure that made Charlotte's eyes sparkle with a vibrancy she'd never had before. Was it all Nick's doing? Could she be in love with him, and could such a hard, cold man ever return her feelings?

"We should leave," Will said softly.

Charlotte looked up, her eyes focusing on them again. "But—I thought we could talk."

Jane nodded. "I need to tell her the truth about our family."

Nick moved his bandaged hand off Charlotte's lap. "Make it fast."

Jane took her sister's hand. She felt like she was destroying all her sister's idyllic memories. "Charlotte, it will be difficult to bear, but you must know that Papa lied to us. He was more than just a soldier in the army."

"He was a spy," she answered matter-of-factly.

Jane could only gape. "You knew!" She whirled on Will, whose eyes widened. "Did everyone know but me?"

"Of course not," he said soothingly. "Your

mother still knows nothing." He shot a glance at Nick. "I think."

Charlotte spoke before Nick could, clasping Jane's hands tighter. "I kept it a secret, Jane. I only found out a few days before you left. I was feeling lost and bored, and I decided to explore the attic. I found a box of journals that I'm certain Papa thought he'd lost. So much of his life was there, Jane, and it was fascinating."

"Why didn't you tell me?" Jane asked, trying not to reveal how hurt she felt. She'd gone off with Will in all innocence, when knowledge of her father might have helped . . . somehow.

"Because—because you were focused on this betrothal, and I'll admit, I thought to keep something to myself for awhile." She looked down at their joined hands. "It was wrong of me, Jane, and I was going to tell you the moment you returned. His life was so exciting! He did so many dangerous, brave things—"

"So Charlotte thought she could become a spy like your father," Nick interrupted dryly.

"I did not!"

"Then what do you call hiding in a wardrobe, listening in on conversations that were none of your business, that could have gotten you killed?"

"I was doing my duty for England," she said hotly.

"You're lucky it was me who discovered you."

"Hardly lucky!"

They glared at each other, and Jane stared wide-eyed between them. She tried to imagine her reserved sister deliberately eavesdropping, then being brave enough to face down a man like Nick Wright when she was caught in the act. Jane prayed that when this was all over, she could take the time to get to know Charlotte. She was ashamed that she'd never bothered before.

"Would you like Charlotte to travel with us?" Will asked.

At the same time, Nick and Charlotte said, "No!"

Will only raised an eyebrow in amusement. Somehow he had read Jane's mind, and she softened with love for him. Sooner or later he'd make her a weepy female.

Nick cleared his throat. "For one thing, Charlotte has it in her head that she needs to help me. She'd only cause you concern by trying to escape."

Charlotte gave a smug little smile.

"And the other thing," he continued, ignoring her, "is that the two of you are in just as much danger as we are. So don't worry about Charlotte. I have Sam and my driver aiding me. When this is over, I'll bring her to the colonel, and try to . . . explain everything."

He looked so uncomfortable that Jane couldn't help smiling.

"Now back to the matter at hand," Nick said. "One of the villains escaped, and could be off warning Julia right now. Her estate is not far away. Charlotte and I need to stay ahead of her, and you two need to go off to your wedding."

Jane wanted to protest—they weren't getting married now, simply going to see her father. But her words died unexpressed. She wouldn't give Charlotte any more reason to worry. Reaching across the carriage, Jane hugged her tightly, whispering, "Will you be all right? What if he ties you up again?"

Her sister only hugged her tighter and whispered back, "It will be fine. He doesn't know it yet, but I have everything in hand."

And with that, Jane knew her sister's miserable first marriage had brought out a new strength in her.

Nick spoke to Will. "I'm not sure what Julia is doing at her brother's estate, but I'm certain she'll leave in the morning, headed for Leeds. It will be over soon."

"Take care," Will said, and the two men shook hands. "Send Sam to tell me when it's done."

"If you need me," Nick added, "send a message to the only inn in Misterton. I'm registered as Mr. Black."

Jane allowed herself to be led from the carriage, looking over her shoulder for one last glimpse of Charlotte's reassuring smile. Jane blinked back tears when the door closed. The coachman cracked his whip and guided the dark vehicle away by moonlight. When they were alone in the windy, dark field, Will put his arm around her and led her back the way they'd come.

As they rode back to Epworth, Jane studied Will, whose eyes were closed as he pretended to sleep.

Oh, she knew he was pretending. But what she couldn't understand was why. There was a solemnity about him that was very uncharacteristic. When they'd first gotten into the carriage, he'd seemed distracted, distant. Sleep had been his final excuse not to talk to her.

She let him have his silence, hoping he would work out whatever he needed to. But she wasn't going to ignore his problem. At the inn, he gave quiet instructions to Mr. Barlow, then escorted Jane to her door. He tried to say a simple good night, but she followed him to his room and stood silently by while he put Killer on the bed. The dog rested his head on his paws and watched them.

Will turned to look at her. "Did you want something?" he asked, as if they had not spent almost twenty-four hours in bed together, sharing intimacies that entitled her to more than his puzzling silence.

"I want you to talk," she said simply, dragging him outside by the arm, abandoning the room to his dog. Once she had Will inside her room, she locked the door and looked at him, her hands on her hips. "Tell me what's wrong."

Chapter 24

W ill smiled so naturally that Jane couldn't trust it a bit.

"Nothing is wrong," he said. "I thought perhaps I had exhausted you with my eagerness. After everything that's happened with your sister, you might want time alone."

"Alone?" she scoffed. "You have spent days making sure we are rarely apart. Now that you've gotten beneath my skirts, you think I'll believe that foolish story?"

"It's not a—"

"Will!" she said sternly. At his confusion, she softened. "You want to marry me. Surely that means you can trust me."

His face suddenly darkened, and he turned

away to rest his hand on the mantel over the fire-place. "There are ugly things you don't know, Jane."

"Are they about what's between us?"

"No."

Relief flooded through her. "Your past can't hurt us, Will." She was saying "us," as if they were already married.

"I've put my past so far behind me that to-night, I almost caused your sister harm—caused *you* harm."

She didn't believe him, but she waited patiently.

"Don't you see—I hesitated!" he cried, whirling around to face her. In his eyes was a despondency she'd never imagined seeing.

"*When* did you hesitate?"

"When we opened the carriage door and saw those men attacking Nick and Sam, I shouldn't have thought before jumping into the fray and helping them."

She was genuinely puzzled now. "You were out of that carriage so quickly, I wanted to scream at your foolishness."

"No, no, there was a moment where I tried to overthink the situation."

"When you allowed your concern for me to show?"

It was as if he wasn't listening. "In that heart-beat, lives could have been lost. The entire outlook could have changed. Charlotte—and *you*—could have been killed because I'd lost my edge. I've let the past affect me."

She took a small step toward him, afraid to disturb the pain he was finally showing her. "What happened to you, Will?"

"I've become too cautious for the life of an agent—because the one time I wasn't, I came as close as I've ever come to dying."

She reached his side, treating him like a wild animal that might flee. Gently, she slid her hand into his, felt the tension that stiffened him.

"Tell me," she murmured. "It might help."

He hesitated so long, staring blindly at the wooden floor, that she felt it might be too late to reach him.

Then he heaved a shaky sigh. "A couple of years ago, I was in the Hindu Kush, the mountains of Afghanistan," he said. His eyes became bitter, and his mouth a hard slash in his face. "I thought I was invulnerable, so I foolishly traversed the mountain pass alone. I should have waited for another agent, for Nick or Sam. But I was certain my disguise had been discovered, that I had to leave."

"Disguise?" she echoed, pressing her luck.

"I passed as an Afghani almost effortlessly. Their languages, their customs—I absorbed it all like it was one grand adventure. That's how I gathered information for the Political depart-

ment. I watched the growing relationship between the Russians and the Afghanis, and kept
Britain aware of everything that transpired. We
needed a stable Afghanistan between Russia
and the British colony in India, a buffer of sorts.
If the Russians gained too much control, it could
upset the balance of power in India."

"And the Russians discovered what you were
doing," she prodded.

"They were about to. The Afghanis were the
immediate threat. So I fled toward the border.
My last night in the country, I was attacked
while I slept."

Though her nerves were taut with anxiety for
him, she tried to lighten his mood. "So you
could actually sleep there?"

His gaze lifted, and he seemed to see her,
though his smile was grim. "Strange, but true. I
seldom had a full night's rest there, but when I
could snatch brief hours of sleep, I'd awaken refreshed."

"What happened next?"

"That night was so dark, I could see nothing,"
he said, and she leaned against his shoulder,
watching his face. "I hadn't lit a fire. And in the
darkness, they attacked—five, ten, I didn't
know how many men. I fought blind, I fought
like an animal. I just used my instincts and my
training, without questioning what I did." He
sighed. "I—I don't even know exactly how long
it lasted. It seemed like forever."

"Oh, Will," she murmured, stroking his arm, amazed and awed by the depths to him she had never even glimpsed. And in her superiority, she'd thought herself a good judge of character. "You did what you had to to survive."

He nodded, but again she knew he wasn't in the room with her anymore. His eyes saw distant sights. For the first time she truly realized that there was another side to a life of adventure: a gritty, harsh world that had taken its toll on Will—so much so that he'd become another person so he wouldn't have to think about it.

"Yes, I survived," he said coldly, "but at a terrible cost. I fled in the night for fear others might arrive. When the sun rose, I went back to see the dead and dying. They were just boys, Jane," he said in a soft voice. "My enemies had sent boys after me, as if they were expendable. Not one had more than fifteen years." His voice broke, and then he pulled away from her and straightened. Bitterly he added, "They gifted me with a barony for that. Apparently, that particular tribe's next target was the governor-general of India."

"What happened next?" she asked, trying to help him get past the terrible memories.

He shrugged. "They gave me another assignment, only in India this time. I became 'Lord' Chadwick, undercover in the native army, a British dandy with no idea of danger and no understanding of the Indians themselves. But of course they spoke in their own language in front of me, and I passed on what I heard."

"How long did you do that?" She was beginning to understand what he'd done to escape his memories.

"Almost a year."

"And it was easy for you, wasn't it?"

He glanced at her sharply, as if suddenly remembering she was there. "What do you mean?"

She felt so sorry for him, but he needed to see what he'd been doing. "Are you going to spend the rest of your life playing at being someone else, so that you never truly live?"

He frowned. "It's not like that."

"Maybe when we're married you can go back to being the dandy so no one will ever again demand too much of you."

His face reddened at her sarcasm. "I can see there's not much left to say. I do believe I'll have a drink in the taproom before I retire."

Jane winced when he slammed the door behind him. She clasped her hands together and began to pace. Maybe she had been too forceful with him, too blunt. He was a good man who'd suffered over the things he'd had to do in service to England.

They were alike in so many ways. Both had a need for adventure, though hers had been sparked by absent parents, his by a family *too* pleasant and settled. As a man he'd been able to escape, to do as he'd wished—and discovered the cruelties of the world that she, as a well-bred woman, had never faced. How could she blame him for wanting a safe marriage?

But what did *she* want? She loved him, she knew that much. Could she give up the dreams she'd had for her life? It didn't seem so difficult any longer, but still she felt torn with indecision.

Yet while she fought her inner struggles, Will was down in the taproom facing his demons, unable to seek the solace of sleep. She couldn't leave him like that.

Jane found him alone before the large stone hearth, where he watched the fire with brooding eyes and rested an empty tankard on his knee. The taproom was empty but for the innkeeper drying glasses and a drunk snoring in the corner.

She approached Will from behind and rested her hands on his shoulders. When he didn't even stiffen, she leaned against him, letting his head rest between her breasts. For once she didn't care who watched them.

"I hope you don't take every woman's intimacy so easily," she murmured.

To her relief, he reached up and covered her hand with his. "Oh, drat, you're not the chambermaid."

She tugged his ear with her free hand, then leaned down. "Come to bed," she whispered, then nibbled his earlobe.

He looked up at her, his eyebrows raised with questions she knew he wouldn't ask in public.

"You're thinking too much," she said, putting his tankard on the table and pulling him to his feet. "*I* think too much, which is another thing we have in common. Except I put all of my thoughts in a journal."

"A journal?" He kept her hands gripped in his and studied her. "And what do you write about?"

"My studies, my observations—and lately, you."

"Me?"

"You've rather dominated the last few weeks of my life."

"I can't imagine everything you've written has been complimentary," he said dryly.

She gave him a flirtatious smile. "I admit I was going to use some of it against you when I reached my father."

His look was wary. "And now you've changed your mind?"

"I think so." She slid her arm through his and said softly, "Let me tire you out enough to sleep."

He cupped her face with a gentle caress that touched her deeply.

"An invitation I can't refuse," he murmured.

They walked past the bar and into the gloom of the hall. Before they reached the stairs, a chambermaid approached them, balancing several full goblets on a tray.

"Try the new house wine, milady, milord,"

she said with a smile. "We just brought it up from the cellar. Sure to give you a good night's rest."

Will dropped a couple of shillings on her tray and scooped up two goblets. "Then we'll have to, won't we?" he said, grinning wickedly down at Jane.

She blushed and said nothing.

When they were alone in her room, they stood and stared at each other. She felt suddenly shy, though inside she trembled with the need to be held in his arms, to feel again the pleasure he could give her.

Silently, he handed her a goblet. He saluted her, drained his wine, then firmly set his glass on the small table and began to undress.

Wide-eyed, she sipped her wine and watched him. Before she knew it, the wine was gone, and he was naked, golden-skinned above his waist, lighter below.

She set her empty goblet beside his, then lifted her fingers to the buttons that ran down the bodice of her gown. She took her time, feeling his hot eyes watching her every movement. She laid her dress over the back of a chair, then removed her petticoats one at a time.

"Jane, hurry," he finally said in a hoarse voice.

She glanced up at him from beneath her lashes, smiling, fingering the chemise buttons at her neck.

He groaned and visibly shuddered. "How can you think being a woman is so difficult, when you have such power over me?"

Her smile faded. Was that really the impression she gave? "I have never said I didn't enjoy being a woman."

"Thank God."

"But then again, I have not appreciated the limitations put on me because of my sex."

He took two steps toward her, stopping when she raised a hand. "Jane, if you're not naked soon, I'm going to rip that garment off you."

She only smiled. When the garment was loose at her neck, she slowly pulled it up her body, watched his intake of breath when her thighs and hips were revealed. She slid it over her head and dropped it to the floor. In sudden urgency, she met him in the center of the room, welcomed the crush of his body against her.

He slid his lips across her cheek and buried his face into her hair, murmuring something into her ear.

"What did you say?" she asked breathlessly.

"I called you my dearest one."

"But—"

"In Persian."

She wanted to swoon. "Say something else."

This time his words were harsher, then he translated. "I told you your face is like the moon, with the darkness of your hair the night sky."

"Ooh," she murmured, gasping as he licked her neck. "What language?"

"Russian."

She moaned into his mouth as they kissed, let her hands memorize the hard, smooth planes of his back, welcomed the slide of his palms up her sides to the edges of her breasts. He bent her back over his arm so he could caress their peaks with his mouth.

Whimpering with need, she hung there, safe in his embrace, protected, maybe even loved. His erection was cradled between them, and she instinctively lifted to her toes, wanting to feel his hardness against her softness.

"Jane," he said harshly, giving her another hard kiss, before he released her and pushed her backwards.

Together they fell on the bed. Though she tried to pull him on top of her, he stayed at her side and explored her body. He gave her drugging, deep kisses, even as he parted her thighs and cupped her with his palm. After moving his hand against her until she writhed, he slid his finger deep inside her.

She gasped, amazed at how intense the wondrous pleasure of his touch felt. His fingers mimicked the act of love, his thumb circled her just above, and his tongue swirled across her nipple. She fractured and came apart quickly, quaking, mindless with pleasure. Then his hips were between her thighs, spreading her wide so he could plunge inside.

They moved together as one, lost in the closeness they shared. She was awed by the heat they generated and the power of his flexing muscles, by the way he desperately said her name against her mouth. His passion overwhelmed her, seduced her, and took her to new, intense heights. When she climaxed again, he joined her, and she knew she would always crave his touch.

As Will rolled to her side, he gathered her to him. They said nothing, only shared several gentle kisses until she rested her head next to his on the pillow. She kept her hand on his beating heart, watching as his eyes closed. Her last thought as she drifted off was that he was finally sleeping.

Will was awakened by an intense, pounding headache that rolled through him in waves. He lay still, knowing he wouldn't fall back asleep, yet afraid to open his eyes for fear that would make him feel worse.

The nausea came next, and he swung up to sit on the side of the bed, holding his head in his trembling hands. Through half-slit eyes, he could see broad daylight between the curtain openings. What the hell—

Then he fumbled for the chamber pot and vomited. When the spasms stopped, he remained kneeling for several minutes, his aching head resting on the edge of the bed.

This was no normal sickness.

He staggered to his feet and went to peer through the curtains. The light was like a piercing sword to the brain, but his mind was functioning enough to know that it was midafternoon. He fumbled through his waistcoat for his pocket watch to confirm that it was almost two.

Never in his life had he slept twelve hours—not without deliberate help. His gaze shot to the wine goblets. He picked one up, sniffed it, but smelled nothing unusual. Yet it was the only answer. He didn't think it was poison, or he wouldn't still be standing. But someone had wanted him to sleep a good long time.

Julia Reed?

Had she needed to keep him from helping Nick? His first thought was to check with the innkeeper about the maid who'd given them the wine.

But then he saw Jane.

She lay unnaturally still, and for a moment such a frightening pain seized his chest that he couldn't breathe. He quickly leaned over her, smoothing the hair out of her face. She was warm and breathing, and some of his tension eased.

"Jane?" he said, giving her a small shake. "Jane, wake up."

She didn't move. He shook her harder.

"Jane?" He heard his own desperation and fear, and felt every practical thought leave his mind.

Chapter 25

Will forced himself to calm down. He poured cold water from the ewer into the basin, dipped a cloth in it and rubbed it across her forehead.

"Jane!"

This time a small frown line appeared between her brows. He called her name again, dampened the cloth until it was almost soaked, and pressed it gently across her cheeks and forehead.

Her eyelids fluttered and she moaned. His heart gave a lurch, for it was the sweetest sound he'd ever heard.

"Jane, come back to me," he whispered.

"Will?" His name was but a murmur on her lips.

"I'm here."

"I—my head—"

"If it's pounding as hard as mine, it must be terrible. Open your eyes, my sweet."

When she cracked them open, they were bloodshot, but she looked right at him. "Am I sick?"

"We both are, but I don't think it happened naturally." Anger at their assailant made his head ache even more, but he firmly put aside all his concerns except for Jane.

She gave a weary sigh, and her eyelids fluttered shut. "Maybe if I sleep—"

"No, you must wake up. You have to fight the effects of this drug."

"Drug?" Her voice was growing fainter. "I just want to sleep. . . ."

He sat her up against him, then fluffed her pillows and laid her back, half-sitting, half-reclining. She frowned and tried to push him away, but her strength was like a babe's. She managed a glare.

"Will, I'm fine."

"Then prove it to me by staying awake. I need to go downstairs and question the innkeeper."

He poured a glass of water, made her sip some, then put it on the bedside table. "Every time you think you might fall asleep, drink. Maybe you should get out of bed. Walking, or even sitting at the table will help."

She shook her head. "I'm all right, I'm awake.

If I get out of bed, I'm going to—to—" She blushed.

"Vomit. You can say it. I already did it. I'll empty the chamber pot before I go, and then leave it beside you."

She smiled weakly, but at least she watched while he washed himself and dressed.

He leaned over and kissed her forehead. "Now surely that was a sight to awaken you."

"Hmm." But she smiled and blushed and patted his hand where it rested on her shoulder. "Go. I'll be here when you return."

But as he walked out the door, he took one last look at her and didn't like what he saw. She was very pale, with dark circles beneath her eyes and the look of someone who knew she'd be sick soon. He would hurry back to her.

Will questioned the innkeeper, and the man seemed genuinely worried, especially on hearing that a maid gave them the wine.

"I swear to you, milord, there was only me workin' last night. I don't recognize the girl you describe."

Will kept his anger contained. "Very well. If you see a girl matching the description, let me know immediately."

"I will, I promise," he said, bobbing his shiny bald head repeatedly.

"I need you to find a doctor for me. My betrothed is quite ill."

"Ye don't look so good yerself, milord."

"Thank you," Will said curtly. Somehow he had to get a message to Nick, but he couldn't leave Jane alone. Then he remembered Barlow.

He found his coachman vomiting in the bushes behind the stable. When Barlow saw him, he wiped his mouth, and two red spots appeared on his pale cheeks.

"Forgive me, my lord. I must be getting sick. I overslept and—"

"The same thing happened to Jane and me," Will interrupted. "And it's not a coincidence. Did a maid visit you with a glass of wine?"

"Yes, she did, my lord. She told me it was from you."

"Mine was the new house wine we just *had* to try," Will said with sarcasm. "We were drugged to keep us away from Nick, I think. Clean yourself up, and then come to Jane's room. After you're checked out by the doctor—"

"Lord Chadwick, I assure you—"

"We're both going to be seen by the doctor, and don't bother trying to get out of it. As for Jane—" He broke off, and again something tightened painfully in his chest. He didn't know what his face showed, but Barlow's expression stilled.

"Is Miss Whittington—"

"I think she's fine. She was talking to me before I left, but . . . I don't want to be away too long."

"Then go, my lord. I'll be up in a moment."

"Saddle one of the horses. I'll need you to get a message to Nick."

When Will returned to Jane's room, he found her lying off the edge of the bed, vomiting into the chamber pot. He caught her shoulders and held the hair off her face. When she finally lay back on the bed, he was alarmed by her pallor and the sheen of sweat on her skin.

He rinsed out the cloth and washed her face, but this time she didn't smile.

"Jane?" he said softly.

Her eyelids fluttered but didn't open.

"Jane?" He shook her.

"I'm awake," she murmured.

"How do you feel?"

"Didn't I just embarrass myself by showing you?"

He smiled and tried to relax. "My head is still aching. How about yours?"

She nodded and frowned, and he knew that motion hurt her. Though she protested, he helped her change into a nightdress, knowing that she might be embarrassed to be seen naked in bed, even by a doctor. Then he pulled a chair up, sat down, and reached for her hand.

"So what shall we talk about?" he asked.

"You talk; I'll listen. Tell me about India."

For an hour he described his journeys through Asia, what the landscape looked like, how the people lived. Half the time he thought she was asleep, but whenever he asked her a direct question, she answered.

Finally the doctor arrived. Dr. Plum was a short, round man wearing spectacles, with an air of confidence that Will liked. Will explained the situation, and then the doctor sent him away.

Barlow met him in the corridor, and together they entered Will's room to wait. Killer greeted them joyously. When Barlow offered to take him outside, Will gave him a tired smile.

"I must look a sight for you to offer to watch Killer."

"The dog is not so bad," Barlow said, and Killer happily trotted out the door at his feet.

Will could only pace. It felt like forever until the doctor finally came for them. Dr. Plum looked the two men over briefly, but it was obvious they were on the mend. He was more cautious about Jane's prognosis. She had not been able to keep down the medicine. If the vomiting continued for any length of time, it would not be good for her. He could only promise to return the next morning to check on her.

After paying Dr. Plum and sending Barlow off to find Nick, Will quickly returned to Jane's room. She appeared to be asleep, which the doctor had said could make her stronger.

So he began the longest vigil of his life. For hours he sat at her side, giving her water to sip when she briefly stirred, only to watch her throw it up.

By evening she was no longer talking to him, and by midnight he had stopped trying to awaken her. The doctor had said sleep could help—at least she wasn't vomiting anymore.

Before dawn, every quarter of an hour Will was reduced to making sure she was breathing. She seemed so still, so deathlike in her pallor. When was the doctor going to arrive?

He leaned his elbows on her bed, clutched her cool hand between his, and stared at her face. He tried to imagine a lifetime without her, and his future yawned like a black chasm he couldn't bear to face.

What good were a land and a house without Jane? He didn't want to marry anyone else. He loved her—if he didn't he wouldn't be feeling this pain that closed up his throat and made his eyes blind with tears. He kissed her fingers, pressed his mouth into her palm, and prayed like he never had before. If she died, he had no one but himself to blame.

He heard a quiet knock on the door. Wiping his forearm across his eyes, he went to answer it. Nick stood there, wearing a grin that was wolfish with satisfaction.

"I take it everything went well," Will said tiredly, stepping back for Nick to enter.

Nick came up short when he saw Jane asleep

in the bed. "Is she doing better? Should we step outside to talk?"

"I'd rather stay here," Will answered, taking his customary seat beside Jane. He lifted her hand again and tried not to show that he was feeling for her pulse.

But Nick's somber expression told him he'd seen everything. "She's no better?"

Will shrugged, holding onto a feigned calmness, barely keeping his panic at bay. "She's been unconscious since last night. The doctor said it would help her to sleep."

Nick nodded and began to pace with a restless energy that Will well remembered in him.

"Don't keep me in suspense," Will said mildly. "Did you catch the bitch?"

Nick's dark brows rose. "Unusually harsh for you."

Will glanced at Jane. "I'm not feeling particularly charitable today."

Consciousness came slowly to Jane, and since it hurt too much to move, she didn't. But she could hear well enough, and she allowed herself to just float, content to be feeling the slightest bit better. She listened to the two men talk, knowing that her own decisions still waited, and she didn't want to face them.

"We have Julia in custody," Nick finally said in a grim voice.

Jane was surprised he wasn't more triumphant.

"Did she go to her accomplice, as you thought she would?" Will asked.

"She did—though she claimed to be there on a family errand. She said that the man's mother, her governess, had died. To support her story— which she'd obviously thought out well—she had his mother's possessions. But she also had a pistol strapped to her thigh."

Jane felt sad at such revelations about someone she'd thought a friend.

"Did she turn herself in without a fight?"

"Yes. Claims she's innocent, of course. We showed her the coded letters, and she had nothing more to say, except that she wanted to speak with her brother, General Reed."

"Are you going to arrange it?"

"Maybe. If he even wants to speak to her. Hell, I'll have to go tell the Duke of Kelthorpe the truth, as well."

Jane tried to rally and say that even a villain deserved such a little request, but her eyelids were still too heavy, and sitting up seemed impossible.

"Is Sam guarding her?" Will asked.

"With help from Charlotte."

She heard the softening in his tone and was pleased.

"Trust her already, do you?"

Surely Nick must have shrugged as he said, "She's proven herself. We'll see what happens next."

There was a pause in their conversation, and Jane felt certain that they were looking at her.

Nick said, "So what are you going to do about Jane? Surely you'll make clear to her that she cannot speak about anything that transpired with Julia Reed."

"I have her under control," Will said in an impassive voice.

His words had the same effect as if he'd struck her. *Under control?* What was he implying?

That once again he'd been manipulating her? That he was using sex to make her do as he wished?

God, she could not believe such a thing. Yet— how else to take his words, his meaning? Had she been manipulated again, just as her parents had done when they'd promised her in marriage to him?

But she loved him. She couldn't be so wrong in her judgment, could she? She had grown to trust him, and the merest thought that he was using her for other purposes seemed like a foreign concept.

Distantly, she heard Will see Nick to the door. She didn't listen to what they said, only concentrated on her own pain and what to do next. She couldn't believe her every instinct was wrong about him.

Chapter 26

The room was quiet but for Will's footsteps. Jane imagined him standing over her, wondered if he watched her with annoyance—but no, she didn't believe that. She couldn't be so wrong about him.

She heard the creak of the floorboards, felt the weight of his hands or elbows on the bed, and realized that he was kneeling at her side. He took her hand in both of his, and she felt the warmth of him, the roughness of his palms. But for his gloves, she would have long ago realized he was not a pampered nobleman but a man who had worked hard in his life.

She felt the moist press of a kiss against her knuckles.

"Jane," he whispered.

She heard a wealth of emotion there that he had concealed from Nick, and some deep part of her relaxed with the satisfaction of having been right.

"I've spent the last several weeks letting you see only what I thought you wanted to see," he began in a sad voice. "I only pray it's not too late for you to hear me, for you to understand. I never thought I belonged here in England, even from the time I was a child. I thought my parents were boring and staid, and too content with a life that I thought of as meaningless, just because it was simple and good."

He took a deep breath, and she wanted to grip his hand tighter, to encourage him, but she didn't want to stop this final revelation.

"They're long dead now. When I came back to England, it was as if a part of me was cut off—I had no idea who I was, or what I was once like. There wasn't one soul who knew me before. So I . . . so I stayed like the last character I played. It was easier, I guess, but it was a lie. I knew you didn't like me, but I needed our betrothal. I needed some purpose in my life."

His voice broke, and the lump in her throat tightened.

"I thought if we could be like my parents—happy, settled, far removed from any turmoil—then everything would be all right. But I know I went too far, Jane. I clung to my image of a perfect marriage, forcing you to accept my vision, rather than one we could create together. I was controlling you, but that isn't the case anymore. I love you, Jane, and I can't lose you."

There was a dreadful, awful silence as he pressed his mouth to her hand, and she tried not to cry.

"I love you," he whispered. "I love your bravery, and the cool, intelligent way you think things through. I love your spirit of adventure, something I once had, but lost over the years. My God, I'll do anything—*be* anything to keep you. What kind of man do I need to be?"

As the first tears leaked down her cheeks, she realized that in attempting to have life all her own way, *she'd* been trying to control *him*. He was only a man, trying to find his life's path, just as she was.

Forcing open her eyes made the pain pound in her head again, but as she looked into Will's hopeful, disbelieving eyes, it no longer mattered. Her life would be what she made of it.

"Jane?"

"Will, you don't have to be anyone else," she said, her voice hoarse from sickness. "All I need you to be is my husband."

The warm brown of his eyes swam with tears. "Jane, you've come back to me," he murmured, then pressed his face against her chest and held her.

She stroked her hand through his hair. "I love

you, Will. I fought it too hard, and that was my mistake." She moistened her dry lips. "Maybe we were both so desperate for some idealized version of life that we never thought about the excitement of loving each other, the adventure of having children. You made me see the great joy in just being together."

He raised his head and stared into her eyes. "Then you'll marry me?"

"Yes," she answered quietly, letting all her love show in her eyes. It felt so good not to be conflicted, not to have to pretend anymore.

He gathered her into his arms and sat back against the headboard, holding her safe against his heart. It was a good place to be.

"We'll make our marriage work," he said softly, kissing the top of her head. "And I'll never allow you to be put in danger again. I'm done with that life."

"But the government will know where we are, Will. They'll come to you for help again."

"Not if they have trouble tracking us down." His face smiled down at her with those wonderful dimples flashing.

"And what does your questionable imagination have in mind?"

"The government won't easily find us, because we'll have plenty of travel plans."

"What kind of travel plans?" she asked doubtfully.

"I think we'll start in France."

"France?" She stared up at him, unable to believe what he might be suggesting.

"Well, if you can compromise and marry me, I can compromise and travel occasionally. We could even combine our writing talents on a book about our journeys. The editors said my words lacked emotion—maybe together we could write something spectacular. You have an . . . innocence, a way of seeing things through fresh eyes, something I lost long ago."

"We would be writers," she said softly, feeling as if the last piece of her life slid into place.

"Unless you don't want to . . ."

She weakly swatted him on the arm. "Foolish man."

"Foolish *beloved* man."

She smiled up into his twinkling eyes. "Beloved . . . hmm, yes, that might be appropriate."

He had made a difficult decision—he was giving up the safety of a simple English life for her, to take her places and show her the world. She would never give him cause to regret it.

His expression sobered. "You've made me realize how many things I want to show you, to experience them through your eyes."

"Do you think there are things you can still teach me?" she teased.

His answering grin was wicked.

* * *

Several days later, Mr. Barlow drove the carriage onto the grounds of Ellerton House, Jane's father's estate outside York. She sat within Will's arms, staring out the window at another view of England, so different from the southern part of the country. She'd never grow tired of exploring it, and now she had a very willing partner.

And he was willing in every way, she thought, blushing as she remembered the things they'd done together the past night.

When they reached the ancient, rambling manor house, she could barely contain her excitement. She was about to see her father again after two long years.

He was waiting for them in the paneled library, seated in a wingback chair, a blanket over his legs. He looked paler, gaunter, and *older* than she remembered, but when he smiled, she knew everything would be all right. She left Will's arm and flew to embrace her father.

The old colonel patted her back and greeted Will, but he didn't stand up. She sat back on her heels and looked up questioningly into her father's eyes, then glanced at the blanket across his lap.

He cupped her cheek and smiled at her from beneath his gray mustache. "Jane, my dove, how wonderful to see you looking so happy." He glanced at Will. "I don't suppose you have anything to do with it, do you?"

She heard mostly good intentions in those words, but Will looked pale. Was he thinking about the recent nights, when he hadn't behaved with the utmost propriety?

Will finally smiled. "She is the reason I'm happy, Colonel, and I can't thank you enough for bringing her into my life."

Her father's relief was palpable, but something wasn't right, and she couldn't stop looking at that blanket. She put her hand on his thigh, and when he stiffened, she raised her gaze to his.

"Papa, what's wrong?"

"There's nothing wrong," he said with a joviality that was obviously forced. "It is good to see my daughter again."

"Are you well? Why the blanket?"

This time he hesitated, and she watched as a silent communication passed between the two men. Will tried to hide his sudden sympathy.

"About eight months ago," Colonel Whittington finally said with reluctance, "the army division I was traveling with ran into a bit of trouble with the Sikhs in the Punjab. It was rather exhilarating to find myself fighting for my life again."

Her stomach tightened into agonizing knots as she stared at him. Will walked to her side and put a hand gently on her shoulder.

"In the end, I was wounded in the lower leg—

thought it was nothing, of course, and that I'd had worse. But the surgeons insisted the fool leg come off at the knee—seems the infection couldn't be stopped."

Inside her heart broke for this military man who could no longer serve his country. She knew he didn't want sympathy, that he'd hidden away in the north rather than face people's pity. She'd idolized him and thought of him as larger than life, a man with exciting tales to tell. But he was simply a man too embarrassed by what had happened to come to London. He had his faults and misgivings just like anyone else.

Jane rose to her feet and kissed his cheek. "I'm thankful to those doctors, Papa, because they sent you back to us healthy and recovered."

He blinked and looked up at her, then gave a quick nod. "Right, of course. Not pleasant to deal with, but necessary."

They smiled at each other, and she clasped his hand.

"It is good to see you, Jane. My, what a lovely woman you've become—hasn't she, Will?"

"Yes, *sir*," Will answered.

"And how is my other daughter? I knew she wouldn't want to leave London so soon. And to think I only knew her young man so briefly."

Will and Jane exchanged glances, and she wanted to kick him for betraying that gleam in his eyes.

"Colonel, your daughter did stay in London, but then Nick stumbled upon her."

"Nick?" the colonel said with a frown. "I'm not sure I like the sound of this."

Will briefly told him what had occurred with Julia Reed. Jane kept track of the various dangerous events of the story that Will was leaving out.

In the end, the colonel smoothed his mustache with a finger and looked thoughtful. "Nick and Charlotte," he murmured with interest.

Jane hastily said, "Now Papa, I don't know for certain what is happening. Since she read your journals, I guess she's fancied herself more . . . adventurous than before."

"I confess I left those journals at the town house thinking that *you'd* find them, Jane. You always did seem more interested in things of that nature. But Charlotte . . ." He trailed off and looked thoughtfully into the distance.

Will watched his colonel fondly, glad that the old man might be at peace at last. "Colonel, if you don't mind, Jane and I will be leaving tomorrow for Scotland."

"Scotland?" Colonel Whittington echoed.

"Yes, sir. Gretna Green, to be exact."

She met his gaze and gave him a smile that warmed him in too uncomfortable a way at such a public moment.

"Don't tell me you're not giving my wife a chance to host a lavish wedding?" the colonel asked, although there was amused satisfaction in his voice.

"That would take too long, Papa." Jane put her hand in Will's and looked up at him. "We'll stop at your estate on the way back, won't we? I'd love to see it."

He thought of his parents' home—*his* home— and for the first time did not dread the memories. He looked forward to showing her the places where he'd been happy, and maybe settling there after all, if it was what she wanted.

The dinner bell rang, and a servant came to bring the colonel his crutches. He maneuvered quite well with them, and Will and Jane walked arm in arm behind him.

Will leaned down to whisper in her ear. "I have so much to tell you. Maybe I'll even indulge your love of learning languages—as long as you're naked during the lessons."

Her smile was wicked.

**If you enjoyed *No Ordinary Groom*,
don't miss Nick and Charlotte's story
coming Fall 2004**

Avon Books is sizzling in February, just in time
for Valentine's Day.

GUILTY PLEASURES by Laura Lee Guhrke
An Avon Romantic Treasure

For shy Daphne Wade, one of life's guilty pleasures is watching
Anthony, the Duke of Tremore work on his excavation site. After
all, it's hard not to fall for a man who keeps taking his shirt off.
But when Daphne is transformed into an exquisite beauty, will
Anthony finally realize that the woman of his dreams has been
right there all along?

WANTED: ONE PERFECT MAN by Judi McCoy
An Avon Contemporary Romance

Daniel Murphy loves stargazing, but gazing at sexy Zara is even
more exciting. He senses the immediate chemistry between them,
yet he can't help but think she's just a bit more unusual than most
women. What Daniel doesn't realize is that Zara has come a long,
long way . . . looking for one perfect man.

AN AFFAIR MOST WICKED by Julianne MacLean
An Avon Romance

Clara Wilson has come to London to find a husband, not a rake.
But before she even has a chance to practice her curtsey, she finds
herself in the arms of the scandal-ridden Marquess of Rawdon.
Now with her heart and her future on the line, will Clara dare to
risk it all for a chance at love?

KISS ME AGAIN by Margaret Moore
An Avon Romance

Lady Francesca Epping cannot believe her ears. The man she has
secretly been in love with just declared to his friends that he will
never *ever* marry "mousy Fanny Epping." There was only one thing
left to do—turn on the charm and break the insolent rogue's heart!

Avon Romances—
the best in exceptional authors
and unforgettable novels!